D0035393

RANDOM
HOUSE
LARGE
PRINT

Royal

Also by Danielle Steel
Available from Random House Large Print

The Wedding Dress	Dangerous Games
The Numbers Game	The Mistress
Moral Compass	The Award
Spy	Rushing Waters
Child's Play	Magic
The Dark Side	The Apartment
Lost and Found	Blue
Blessing in Disguise	Country
Silent Night	Prodigal Son
Turning Point	Pegasus
Beauchamp Hall	A Perfect Life
In His Father's Footsteps	Power Play
The Good Fight	Winners
The Cast	First Sight
Accidental Heroes	Until the End of Time
Fall from Grace	Friends Forever
Past Perfect	Hotel Vendome
Fairytale	Happy Birthday
The Right Time	One Day At a Time
The Duchess	A Good Woman
Against All Odds	

DANIELLE STEEL

Royal

A Novel

RANDOM HOUSE
LARGE PRINT

Published in the United States of America by Random House Large Print in association with Delacorte Press, an imprint of Random House, a division of Penguin Random House LLC, New York.

Cover design: Laura Klynstra
Cover photograph: © Richard Jenkins

The Library of Congress has established a Cataloging-in-Publication record for this title.

ISBN: 978-0-593-21334-6

www.penguinrandomhouse.com/large-print-format-books

FIRST LARGE PRINT EDITION

Printed in the United States of America

10 9 8 7 6 5 4 3 2 1

To my beloved children,
Beatie, Trevor, Todd, Nick,
Samantha, Victoria, Vanessa,
Maxx, Zara,

Never give up your dreams,
Be grateful for who you are,
And what you can be,
Don't settle for less than you deserve,

Don't give up!! Dare to be!!
Be True to Yourself!
And always know how very much
I love you!
Bigger than the sky!

All my love,
Mom/d.s.

Royal

Chapter 1

In June of 1943, the systematic bombing of England by the German Luftwaffe, targeting Britain's cities and countryside, had been going on for three years. It had begun on September 7, 1940, with heavy bombing of London, causing massive destruction in the city, at first in the East End, then the West End, Soho, Piccadilly, and eventually every area of London. The suburbs had also been severely damaged. Buckingham Palace was bombed on September 13, six days after the daily raids began. The first bomb landed in the quadrangle, a second crashed through a glass roof, and another demolished the palace chapel. The king and queen were in residence at the time.

Other historic places were rapidly added to the

flight path of the German bombers. The Houses of Parliament, Whitehall, the National Gallery, Marble Arch, various parks, shopping streets, department stores, Leicester, Sloane, and Trafalgar Squares were bombed too. By December of 1940, almost every major monument had been injured in some way, buildings had collapsed, and countless citizens had been injured, rendered homeless, or killed.

The intense bombing raids had continued for eight months, until May of 1941. Then a period called "the lull" set in with daily attacks, but with less intensity than in the earlier months. The damage and deaths had continued. For the past two years, Londoners had done their best to get used to it, spending nights in air raid shelters, helping to dig out their neighbors, volunteering as air raid wardens, and assisting with the removal of millions of tons of debris to make streets passable. Limbs and dead bodies were frequently found in the rubble.

During the first year of the bombing, eighteen other cities were bombed as well, several suburbs, and in the countryside Kent, Sussex, and Essex had suffered grievously. As the years went on, the coastlines had been heavily bombed too. Nowhere appeared to be truly safe. Prime Minister Winston Churchill and King Frederick and Queen Anne did their best to keep up morale and encourage their countrymen to stay strong. England had been brought to its knees, but had not been defeated, and refused to be. It was Hitler's plan to invade the country once it had been severely damaged by the constant bombing raids, but the British government would not allow that to happen. By the summer of 1943, nerves were stretched, and the damage was considerable, but the English people refused to give up.

The Germans were fighting hard on the Russian front as well, which gave the English respite.

The ear-shattering sirens had sounded again that night, as they did almost every night, and the king and queen and their three daughters had taken refuge in the private air raid shelter that had been set up for them in Buckingham Palace, in what had previously been the housekeepers' rooms, reinforced by steel girders, with steel shutters on the high windows. Gilt chairs, a Regency settee, a large mahogany table gave them a place to sit, with axes on the wall, oil lamps, electric torches, and some minor medical supplies. Next door there was a shelter for members of the royal household and staff, which even included a piano. With over a thousand staff members in the palace, they had to use other shelters as well. They waited for the all clear and had been in the shelter close to a thousand times by then. The two elder royal princesses had been sixteen and seventeen when the first air raids had started.

Families had been urged to send their children to the country for safety, but the royal princesses had stayed in London to continue their studies and do war work as soon as they turned eighteen. And when the bombing was too severe, their parents sent the royal princesses to Windsor Castle, for a break. Princess Alexandra drove a lorry now, at twenty, and was a surprisingly competent mechanic, and at nineteen, Princess Victoria was working at a hospital doing minor tasks, which freed up the nurses to tend to the severely injured. Their younger sister, Charlotte, was fourteen when the bombing began, and the king and queen had considered sending her to Windsor, or Balmoral, their castle in Scotland, but their youngest child was small, and had delicate health, and the queen had preferred to keep her at home with them. The princess had suffered from asthma since she was very young, and the queen did not wish to part with her, and preferred to keep her close. Even now, at seventeen, she wasn't allowed to do the war work her sisters were engaged in, or even the things they had done at her age. The constant dust from fallen buildings and the rubble in the streets were hard on her lungs. Her asthma seemed to be growing steadily worse.

The day after the most recent bombing, the king and queen discussed Charlotte's situation again. Although she was Queen Victoria's great-great-granddaughter, a fairly distant connection, Charlotte had inherited her diminutive size from her illustrious ancestor. It was unlikely that Charlotte would ever be on the throne, since she was third in line after her two older sisters. She chafed at the restrictions her family and the royal physician put on her. She was a lively, spirited girl, and a brilliant rider, and wanted to make herself useful in the war effort, despite her size and her asthma, but her parents had continued to refuse.

The dust in the air was particularly thick the next day. The queen gave Charlotte her medicine herself, and that night, she and the king spoke yet again about what to do with their youngest daughter.

"Sending her to the countryside would encourage others to do the same," her father said with a pained voice while the queen shook her head. Many families had sent their children away in the last four years, since war was declared, at the government's insistence. A shocking number of children had been killed in the bombing raids, and parents had been urged to send their children to safer areas. Some concurred, other parents were afraid to let their children go, or couldn't bear the thought of being parted from them. Travel was difficult and frowned on, with heavy gas rationing, and some parents who had sent their children away hadn't seen them for several years since they'd left. Bringing their children home for holidays was strongly discouraged, for fear that the parents wouldn't send them away again. But unquestionably London and the other cities were more dangerous than the rural areas where they were being housed by kind people who had opened their homes to them. Some hosts took in a number of children.

"I don't trust Charlotte to take her medicine if we send her away. You know how she hates it, and she wants to do the same work as her sisters," her mother said sympathetically. Charlotte's oldest sister, Alexandra, who would inherit the throne one day, understood their mother's concerns perfectly, and insisted to Charlotte that she respect the limitations of her health. Her sister Victoria was less compassionate. She had always felt a rivalry with her younger sister, and occasionally accused her of faking the asthma attacks in order to shirk the war work that Charlotte wanted to do desperately, and had been forbidden from doing so far. There were frequent verbal battles between the two girls. Victoria had resented Charlotte since the day she was born, and treated her like an intruder, much to her parents' dismay.

"I don't think she's any better off here. Even

with her medicine, she still has frequent attacks," her father insisted, and his wife knew there was truth to it.

"I don't know who we'd send her to anyway. I don't want her at Balmoral alone, even with a governess. It's too lonely there. And I can't think of anyone of our acquaintance who is taking more children in, although I'm sure there are some we're not aware of. We could let it be known that we have sent our youngest child away, to set the example, but it would be dangerous for her, if people knew precisely where she was," Queen Anne said sensibly.

"That can be handled," the king said quietly, and mentioned it to Charles Williams, his private secretary, the next morning. Charles promised to make discreet inquiries, in case the queen changed her mind, and decided to let the princess go away. He understood the problem completely. She would have to stay with a trusted family that would not reveal her true identity, in some part of England that hadn't been as heavily bombed as the towns close to London.

It was two weeks later when Charles came to the king with the name of a family that had a large manor house in Yorkshire. The couple were older, titled aristocrats, beyond reproach, and the private secretary's own family had recommended them, although he hadn't told his family any details about the situation or who might be sent away, only that the hosts had to be unfailingly trustworthy and discreet.

"It's in a quiet part of Yorkshire, Your Majesty," he said respectfully when they were alone, "and so far, as you know, there are fewer air raids in the rural areas, although there have been some in Yorkshire as well. The couple in question have a very large estate, which the family has owned since the Norman Conquest, and there are several large tenant farms on the estate." He hesitated for a moment, and told a familiar tale. "In all honesty, they have been somewhat in difficulty since the end of the Great War. They're land rich and cash poor, and have struggled to keep the estate intact, without selling off any part of it. I've been told that the house is in poor repair, and even more so since all the young men left for war four years ago. They're running the place with very little help. They're older parents, she's in her sixties, the earl's in his seventies, and their only son is Princess Charlotte's age. He's due to go into the army in the next few months, when he turns eighteen. They took in a young girl from a modest home in London at the beginning of the war, to do their patriotic duty. I believe they would be willing to offer Princess Charlotte safe haven, and perhaps . . ." He hesitated, and the king understood. "Perhaps a gift of a practical nature would help them with the running of the estate."

"Of course," the king said.

"I think she would be safer there," Charles added, "and with papers in another name from the Home Office, absolutely no one except the earl and countess hosting her needs to know her true identity. Would you like me to contact them, sir?"

"I must speak to my wife first," the king said quietly, and his secretary nodded. He knew the queen was loath to send her away, and Princess Charlotte herself would object strenuously. She wanted to remain at Buckingham Palace with her family, and hoped to convince her parents to allow her to do war work the moment she turned eighteen, in a year.

"Perhaps if you let her take one of her horses to Yorkshire with her, it would soften the blow a bit." Princess Charlotte was horse mad and an excellent rider, despite her asthma and her diminutive size. Nothing kept her away from the stables, and she could ride any horse, no matter how spirited.

"It might help," the king said, but he also knew that Charlotte would present every possible argument not to go. She wanted to stay in London, and hoped to do whatever she could as soon as she was allowed, like her sisters. But even sending her away until she turned eighteen in almost a year would relieve her father's mind. Between the constant bombings and his daughter's health, London was just too dangerous for her, or anyone these days. His two older daughters were doing useful work, which justified their being there, but they were not as delicate as Charlotte by any means.

He suggested the plan to the queen that night. She presented almost as many arguments against it as he expected from Charlotte herself. Queen Anne really didn't want to send her daughter away, and perhaps not even be able to see her for the next year, which they both knew was more than likely. They couldn't single her out for special treatment, or people around her might suspect her true identity, which would make the location dangerous for her. She had to be treated like everyone else, and just like the young commoner from London who was already staying there. Also the queen didn't like the fact that her would-be hosts had a son nearly the same age as Charlotte, almost a year older. She thought it inappropriate, and used that as an argument too.

"Don't be silly, my dear." Her husband smiled at her. "I'm sure all he can think of is joining the army in a few months. Boys his age are begging to go to war, not interested in pursuing young girls at the moment. You won't need to worry about that until after the war. Charles Williams says it's an excellent, entirely respectable family, and he's a very nice boy." They also both knew that their daughter was far more interested in her horses than she was in men. It was her next oldest sister, Princess Victoria, who was an accomplished flirt, and her father was eager to get her married as soon as the war was over and the boys came home. She needed a husband to manage her, and children to keep her busy. Victoria had had an eye for men since she'd turned sixteen, and he worried about the men she met now doing war work, but he knew it couldn't be helped. They all had jobs to do, and the queen kept a close eye on her. Princess Alexandra, on the other hand, had never given her parents a moment of concern. She was serious and responsible, and never lost sight of the duties she would inherit one day as monarch. She was a solemn young woman much like her father. It always intrigued him how different his three daughters were.

The following day, after taking a walk beyond the palace gates with her governess, Charlotte had an asthma attack as soon as she came home. She took her medicine without complaint, as it was a fairly severe attack. That night her parents spoke to her of their intention to send her to stay with the Earl and Countess of Ainsleigh in Yorkshire. Their family name was Hemmings. Charlotte looked horrified at the thought. She had pale blond hair, porcelain white skin, and enormous blue eyes which opened wide when she heard her parents' plan for her.

"But why, Papa? Why must I be punished? In a few months, I can do the same work as my sisters. Why must I be banished until then?"

"You're not being 'banished,' Charlotte, and it's more than a few months before you turn eighteen. It's nearly a year. I suggest that you stay in Yorkshire peacefully until your birthday, getting strong, and if your asthma improves in the country, we can talk after your birthday about your coming home to volunteer for the war effort, like your sisters. Your mother, your doctor, and I all agree that the air in London is not good for you, with all these buildings coming down, and heavy dust in the air. You're still young, Charlotte. If there wasn't a war on, you wouldn't be out of the schoolroom yet, not until you turn eighteen. You still have studying to do."

Charlotte set her chin stubbornly, prepared to do battle with them. "Queen Victoria was eighteen when she took the throne and became queen," she used as an argument her father didn't accept.

"True, but she wasn't seventeen, there wasn't a war on, and the Luftwaffe wasn't bombing England. This is a much more complicated situation, and a dangerous one for everyone, particularly for you." Her father knew that she had been fasci-

nated all her life by her great-great-grandmother
Queen Victoria, perhaps because people compared
Charlotte to her because of her size, and because
she had a plucky spirit, and was a brave girl like
Queen Victoria, who had been Queen of England
a century before. Charlotte knew that as third in
line to the throne, she was unlikely to ever become
queen, but she greatly admired her illustrious ancestor, and thought of her as a role model in life.

By the end of the week, the king and queen had
made the decision, despite Charlotte's strenuous
objections. She was only slightly mollified when
they told her she could take her favorite horse with
her. And to emphasize the validity of their plans
for her, a larger scale attack occurred again, targeting the center of the city, which strengthened the
king's resolve to send Charlotte away.

The king asked the Home Office to provide the
papers they needed to protect Charlotte's identity.
The earl and countess knew who she was, and had
promised to tell no one, and with new identity papers
she would be using the name Charlotte White, not
Windsor, which would give her anonymity.

The plan was explained to both of Charlotte's
sisters the night before she left, and Charlotte sat
with them and their parents silently, with tears
in her eyes, trying to be brave. Princess Alexandra

put her arms around her, to comfort her, and Princess Victoria smiled wickedly, delighted to be rid of her younger sister for a year.

"I hope they don't treat you like Cinderella, and have you sweeping out the hearths. They've probably lost their help like everyone else. Will you really be able to keep the secret of who you are?" Victoria said meanly, obviously in doubt.

"She'll have to," her father answered for her. "It wouldn't be safe for her there if everyone knew who she was. We intend to say that she is being sent away to the country, like many children, but we will not reveal where she is. No one will discover her identity, and only the earl and countess and Charlotte will know."

"You'll be back before you know it," her older sister reassured her kindly, and came to her bedroom later that night to bring Charlotte some of her own favorite sweaters to take with her, and several books. She took a little gold bracelet with a gold heart on it off her own arm and put it on her sister's wrist. "I'll miss you terribly," Alexandra said and meant it. She had been protective of her since the day Charlotte was born. Victoria had often been a thorn in their sides, but Charlotte had a happy disposition, and Alexandra was a gentle soul, and stronger than she appeared. She would have to be one day when she was the sovereign, after their father was no longer king. Victoria had a jealous nature, and had often been envious of both her older and younger sister. She resented the easy bond they shared.

Alexandra was as dark as Charlotte was fair. Victoria had red hair, and all three of them had delicate aristocratic features, typical of their bloodline. Both of Charlotte's sisters, and her parents, were considerably taller than she. Like her great-great-grandmother Queen Victoria, Charlotte was barely five feet tall, but perfectly proportioned. She was just very small, and very graceful.

The family gathered the next morning in the queen's private sitting room to say goodbye to Charlotte. Charles Williams, the king's secretary, and her elderly governess Felicity had been assigned to make the trip with her. Both were trustworthy with the secret of the princess's whereabouts for the next ten or eleven months. The earl and countess were expecting them after the four- or five-hour drive from the city. They drove in Charles Williams's personal car so as not to attract attention. He had a simple Austin, and there were tears on Charlotte's cheeks when she got into the backseat. A moment later, they drove away, and rolled circumspectly through the gates of the palace, as Charlotte wondered when she would see her home again. She had a terrible sense of foreboding that she would never be back. But everyone in London felt that way now, living from day to day, with bombs falling all night long and their homes and loved ones disappearing and dying.

"It's just for a year," she whispered to herself, to stay calm, as they drove past newly ruined buildings on their way out of the city. She had her medicine with her, but they kept the windows rolled up so she wouldn't need it, but either from the emotion of leaving her family or the dust outside, her chest felt so tight she could hardly breathe. She closed her eyes as she thought of her parents and sisters, fighting valiantly to make herself stop crying.

Charlotte dozed on and off during the long drive from London to Yorkshire. Felicity, her old governess, had brought a picnic basket with things for them to eat. Military Intelligence had advised Charles Williams that it would be best not to stop at pubs or restaurants along the way in case Her Royal Highness might be recognized, and give people a hint as to where she was going. An announcement was going to be made in a day or two that she had been sent to the country for an extended time, to avoid the London bombings, until her next birthday. Both the Home Office and MI5 were anxious not to give any clues to her whereabouts in Yorkshire. They didn't want that information falling into German hands either, which was another factor they had to consider. The Germans capturing the princess or worse, killing her, would have decimated British morale, and the royal family.

Charlotte ate the watercress and cucumber sandwiches the cook had prepared for her, along with some sliced sausage, which was a rare delicacy now, even on the queen's table. She fell asleep several times, bored with watching the countryside slide by.

Eventually, they reached the rolling hills of Yorkshire. It was a warm sunny day. She looked at the cows and horses and sheep in their pastures, and tried to imagine what her life in Yorkshire would be like. Her horse, Pharaoh, had been sent down with the assistant stable master and one of the stable boys three days before, and when they returned, they reported that the spirited Thoroughbred Charlotte liked to ride had settled well into his new home. He seemed to like the grazing land available to him. There was only one very old man, previously retired, and a fourteen-year-old boy managing the stables at Ainsleigh Hall, the Hemmingses' estate, and the Earl of Ainsleigh's seat. They had reported that there were few horses left in the stables. There was one hunter for the Hemmings boy to ride, and

a few older horses. Neither the earl nor the countess rode anymore. The earl had been master of
the hunt, but all of that ended with the onset of the
war, and the countess had had a bad fall ten years
before, the ancient stable master told them, broken
her leg badly and hadn't ridden since. It reminded
Charlotte of what Charles had told them, that the
Hemmingses were not young. Their son, Henry,
had come to them as a surprise late in life, when the
countess was forty-nine. She was sixty-seven now,
and the earl in his early seventies.

Charles had mentioned that the boy was the
love of their life, and they were dreading when he
would leave and go to war in a few months. He had
joined an infantry regiment, and was waiting to be
called up right after his eighteenth birthday, which
wouldn't be long now. By Christmas, he'd be gone,
and the Hemmingses would be left with their two
young female guests for company.

Charlotte knew almost nothing about the girl
who'd been staying there for two years, only that
she came from the East End of London, and both
her parents had been killed in the bombings right
after she left. She was an orphan now, like so many
other British children. She was the same age as
Charlotte, which would be pleasant for her, if they
got along, and Charlotte couldn't imagine why
they wouldn't.

Charlotte had never gone to a proper school herself, and had been tutored at home. It was tedious at times, particularly once her sisters left the schoolroom, and she had to do her lessons alone, with a French governess who tutored her in French, drawing, and dance. A professor from Eton College taught her history and the basics of mathematics, and another from Cambridge taught her literature, all by British writers and poets. She hoped that she wouldn't have to continue her studies in Yorkshire, although she had promised her father she would read all the books available to her, and a few he had given her about the history of Parliament, to take with her. He wanted all his daughters to be well versed in the process of British government. He said it was their duty as daughters of the king.

Charlotte much preferred riding her horses, and needed no lessons there. She was a bold, skillful rider, and had joined her father numerous times at the royal hunts he'd attended before the war. Her sisters were far less adventuresome. She intended to ride astride in a normal saddle now, like the men, instead of sidesaddle, with no one to stop her or complain about the impropriety of it. She'd been reprimanded every time she'd tried it at Windsor, with her own and her father's horses. She couldn't do it at the royal training centers, but she could occasionally at their country retreat, but whenever her parents found out she was scolded and told to ride sidesaddle like her mother and sisters.

Queen Anne was an avid rider too, but not as much so as her youngest daughter, and the queen was content to ride sedately in their park. The king and queen frequently rode together, while Charlotte rode early in the morning with one of the grooms, so no one could observe her pushing her stallion to his limits and riding like the wind. She planned to do some riding in Yorkshire, and hoped that the earl and countess wouldn't organize schoolroom lessons for her, if they didn't have a teacher for her, which she fervently wished would be the case. She wondered if her young female contemporary liked to ride as much as she did, or even knew how. If not, perhaps she could teach her.

They arrived at Ainsleigh Hall as the Hemmingses were finishing lunch, and the earl and countess and their son, Henry, came out to greet her and introduce themselves. They introduced Charlotte as "Charlotte White." Lucy Walsh, the girl from London, brought up the rear and hung back, too shy to speak to Charlotte at first, when the Hemmingses introduced her. She was content to watch her from a distance. She noticed Charlotte's simple dark blue dress, and the well-cut coat she wore over it. Charlotte was wearing high heels and a small elegant dark blue velvet hat, gloves, and her hair was combed in a loose knot at the nape of her neck. She looked well dressed and very fashionable, as she greeted the Hemmingses and Lucy politely, and she thanked them for letting her stay with them. Their son, Henry, stared at her in fascination, without saying anything. He had never seen a girl quite like her, and hadn't been to London since he was a little boy. His parents preferred their country life, and he wasn't old enough to go into society yet, and would miss his chance now by going into the army. All that went with his rank and title would have to wait until after the war. It was the same for all of his friends. He was struck by how small Charlotte was, which surprised him, having seen her horse in the stables. He was intrigued to think she could ride such a large, lively horse. She looked so dainty and demure, and somewhat shy as they walked into the house. She glanced at Lucy with a smile, and never spoke directly to Henry. Charlotte wasn't accustomed to speaking to boys. The earl appeared to be very jovial, and welcomed her warmly. He looked older than he was, and the countess walked with a slight limp after her riding accident. She had a kind face and snow white hair, and seemed old to Charlotte, compared to her own mother, who was considerably younger. She thought the Hemmingses seemed more like Henry's grandparents than his parents.

"We're delighted to have you with us, Your Royal Highness," the countess whispered to her out of everyone's hearing, as Charles Williams took charge of Charlotte's bags, and a young hall boy from one of the farms carried them upstairs. A meal had been set out in the kitchen for Felicity and Charles to eat before they left. Charlotte said she had eaten on the way, and was hoping for a ride on Pharaoh in the warm weather. Once they settled her into her room, her governess and father's secretary would have nothing left to do there.

"You have a very fine mount," Henry finally said, as he walked into the house beside her, and she thanked him, with her eyes cast down. His parents could see immediately how impeccable her manners were. She was every inch a princess, although they would not be using her title from now on, so as not to alert anyone to who she was. Their son had no idea who she was either, and merely thought her the daughter of some aristocrats his parents knew in London, who wanted their daughter out of harm's way in Yorkshire.

Lucy didn't speak to her at all, as she followed the Hemmingses and Charlotte into the house. Then she disappeared into the kitchen, where she was more comfortable. Henry paid no attention to her, and seemed riveted by the new arrival. She seemed very grown up to him, and he joined her and his parents for tea in the library, and then left to ride over to one of the farms, where he said he was helping repair a fence since there was no one else to do it. He said he worked on the farms a lot now, and enjoyed it, to keep busy.

"We're a bit shorthanded, I'm afraid, in the house as well," the countess said apologetically. "It's never been quite the same since the last war, and I fear that this one will finish off estates like ours. Many of the young people never came back and stayed in the cities last time when the war was over. I fear it will be the same, or worse, when it ends this time. With women needed in the factories, even the young girls have deserted the farms and gone to the cities. Lucy has been a great help to us. We'd be lost without her. We're hoping she'll stay, since she has no one left in London now. Very sad all that. She lost both her parents in the bombing when their apartment building collapsed. It's fortunate that she was here." Charlotte nodded and felt sorry for her without even knowing her. She seemed like a very plain, shy girl. Charlotte hoped they could be friends, since they were the same age.

After they finished tea, the countess took Charlotte up to her bedroom, and for an instant she was shocked.

"I wanted to give you one of our guest rooms, Your Royal Highness," she said in a soft voice, "but we don't want to make anyone aware of your position. Your mother particularly asked me not to, in the letter she sent me, so we gave you the room next to Lucy." It was one of the old servants' rooms on the top floor, with a view of the hills, the forests, and the lake on their estate. The room was just big enough for the bed, a chest, a small desk and a chair, and had been used for one of their maids before the war. There were only two of the women left now. Their rooms were down the hall, and no better than Charlotte's. Since she had never visited any of the maids' rooms in any of her parents' palaces, she had no idea how it compared to theirs. But this was a small, dark, cheerless room with nothing to distinguish it, and nothing on the walls. On the way upstairs she had noticed that the manor was in need of paint, many of the curtains were shredded by the sunlight, and some of the rugs were threadbare in several places. The furniture was handsome, but the house itself was dark and drafty, cool in the summer months, but undoubtedly freezing cold in winter, heated only by the fireplaces in the rooms downstairs. It was not at all the kind of room that Charlotte was used to, and she still looked startled when she came downstairs to say goodbye to Felicity and Charles. They left as soon as they had eaten, to get back to London by that night, before the blackout. They were in a hurry to leave. Charlotte shook hands with both of them, and thanked them for accompanying her. Charles had to stop himself from bowing, and Felicity forgot herself and curtsied to her, but only the countess saw it. No one else was with them.

Charlotte went back upstairs then to unpack her bags. She had to leave some of her clothes in her suitcase, for lack of closet and cupboard space, but she didn't mind. She changed into her riding clothes, and was putting on her hat when Lucy walked into the room, and studied her keenly. Her riding habit was simple, but it was obvious that everything she owned was of the highest quality, perfectly cut, in fine fabrics, and fit Charlotte's tiny form impeccably.

"Are they your parents?" Lucy asked, referring to Felicity and Charles, and Charlotte shook her head, not sure what to say, and how to explain them. She noticed Lucy's East End accent immediately.

"They're friends who offered to drive me here, since they have a car, and my parents don't, and they couldn't leave London." It was all she could think of to say, to explain them, but a closer look would have identified them as employees, which Lucy hadn't noticed. The thought never occurred to her, although she could see that Charlotte must be wellborn, from her manners, her accent, and her clothes. She was very pleasant to Lucy. "Do you ride?" Lucy responded by shaking her head with a look of panic.

"I'm afraid of horses. They look like big frightening beasts to me. What do your parents do?" She wanted to know more about the intriguing newcomer. They spoke with very different accents. Charlotte with the distinct diction of the upper classes, and Lucy's was pure London commoner. They came from two very different worlds.

There was a pause as Charlotte sought rapidly for an answer to Lucy's question about her parents. She hadn't thought of what to say if anyone asked her. "My father works for the government as a civil servant, and my mother is a secretary." It was a long way from the truth, but the best she could come up with. Lucy was a tall dark-haired girl with a plain pale face, and she seemed fascinated by Charlotte, though not particularly warm, and somewhat awkward. Charlotte felt like an intruder on the young woman's turf, which was how Lucy viewed her. Everything had been perfect there till then, and she had Henry's attention for herself, although he didn't speak to her often or at great length. At dinner, he spoke mostly to his parents about the farms, and ignored her.

"That sounds fancy," Lucy commented. "Where do you live?"

"In Putney," Charlotte answered quickly, and Lucy nodded, satisfied with her response. It was a pleasant middle-class neighborhood, and she believed her.

"My father was a cobbler and my mother was a seamstress. She used to help him at the shop sometimes." Lucy's eyes filled with tears as she said it, and Charlotte wanted to reach out to her but didn't dare. "Do you have brothers and sisters? I don't have none. I'm alone now, and I will be when I go back to London after the war."

"I'm so sorry," Charlotte said as Lucy nodded and turned away, as she wiped the tears from her cheeks, and Charlotte adjusted her riding hat, and said she had two sisters, and then picked up her crop and gloves, to go out to the stables. She could hardly wait to see Pharaoh, bringing him here was almost like having a friend from home with her. Charles had told her that her father was paying for his upkeep, so as not to be a burden on the Hemmingses. Her mother had told her that they were paying for her to stay there too. The Hemmingses were grateful to have the assistance, although slightly embarrassed to take it. They had no income from the farms at the moment, since all of what they grew was controlled by the government's Ministry of Food, and they ate whatever was left. Several of the wives on the farms had planted home gardens, and kept chickens and rabbits to eat. And their daughters had joined the Women's Land Army and become Land Girls.

Lucy watched her go as Charlotte ran lightly down the stairs in her impeccable, perfectly shined riding boots. She saw the earl dozing in the small drawing room as she left. The countess had gone upstairs for a nap, and there was no one around, as she left the house and walked the short distance to the stables, circled by beautiful old trees. The gardens along the way were in need of attention and were sadly overgrown. The gardeners had been among the first to leave. One of the grooms was walking what appeared to be a very old horse, which Charlotte assumed was the Thoroughbred that the earl rode, when he still did. The countess had mentioned that he suffered from arthritis and seldom rode anymore.

She strode into the stables, and heard Pharaoh whinny the moment she walked in. He recognized her step and sensed her, and she found his stall easily. He nuzzled up next to her, and she saddled him with the saddle and tack the palace grooms had brought to Yorkshire for her, and then changed her mind. She removed the sidesaddle, and took one of the ordinary men's saddles she found in the tack room, so she could ride astride. She shortened the stirrups to the right height for her. She found a groom to give her a leg up, and a moment later, she was heading down a path toward the lake, passing under splendid tall trees which provided shade along the path. She was warm in her jacket but didn't care, as she reached a field and gave Pharaoh his head. He was as happy as his mistress as they took off at full speed. They galloped for half an hour, rode past the lake, and then doubled back at a slow canter, as she smiled at the scenery around her. It was a beautiful place, and she didn't feel quite so far from home with Pharaoh to ride. As she slowed to a trot on the way back, Henry Hemmings approached on his horse and caught up with her. He looked at her admiringly.

"You're a bruising rider. I saw you galloping in the fields before. He's a splendid animal, fit for a queen," he said smiling at her, and for an instant, she wondered if he knew who she was, but she was sure he didn't.

"He's a good boy. He was a gift from my father," she said.

"I'll race you when you get used to the terrain around here," he offered and she nodded, looking pleased. "Although Winston is no match for him, but we'll try." She laughed and smiled as she looked at him, feeling more comfortable than when she arrived.

"It's lovely here," she complimented him, as he rode the big gray horse, who was a fine specimen, but didn't have the bloodline Pharaoh did, and would have a hard time beating him. She noticed that Henry had warm brown eyes, and a shock of dark hair. His riding clothes were old and worn, and she suspected had been his father's from long ago, since they were of another era. There was nothing fashionable about Henry, but he was open and friendly, and happy to have another young person there, and he couldn't ignore the fact that she was a beautiful girl. He knew that Lucy had a crush on him, but it wasn't reciprocal, so he ignored it and pretended not to know. She was a big, awkward, plain girl, and not very interesting to talk to. Her education in a London school had been brief, and her interests were limited. She had helped out in her father's shop every day and sometimes with her mother's sewing, she had told them, which didn't interest Henry. She hated horses, which were his passion, as they were Charlotte's. He liked Lucy. She was a decent girl, and he could sense that she was lonely and wanted to talk at times, but they had nothing in common. And in contrast, he was dazzled by Charlotte, who seemed like a bright shining star to him. She had a much bigger presence than he had expected judging from her size. And she was a remarkable horsewoman.

They picked up the pace, and cantered the rest of the way back to the stables, jumping over several brooks and some logs along the way. They were evenly matched as riders, and it was fun riding with him. They unsaddled their horses after they dismounted, and Charlotte brushed Pharaoh, and fed him some oats and hay, and then she and Henry walked back to the house together. It was almost time for tea, which was their evening meal. She had stayed out for a long time, and went to change. She met Lucy on the stairs, in a plain blue cotton dress, on her way to the kitchen, to help get tea ready for the family. She didn't mind serving them and thought Charlotte would too.

"You can come to the kitchen to help as soon as you change," Lucy said in a curt voice. She had seen Charlotte and Henry from her window as they rode home, and she worried when she saw them. She still hoped that one day, with time, Henry might reciprocate her feelings for him. In light of that, Charlotte's arrival wasn't a happy development for her. Lucy had spent two years hoping that Henry would become enamored with her, and she could make this her home forever, and she didn't have much longer to woo him, before he went to war. Henry would be leaving in a few months, and now this pretty elfin girl from London had shown up. Charlotte hadn't tried to charm him, but she didn't have to. Everything about her was so enchanting that Lucy was sure Henry would fall in love with her, and Lucy's chances would be dashed forever.

She looked glum as she set the table, and banged a few dishes down on it, angry about something Charlotte couldn't guess at. Charlotte arrived a few minutes later in a navy pleated linen skirt, a white cotton blouse, and flat shoes. There was nothing of the seductress about her. She was all innocence, but she was a very beautiful young girl, which the two ancient kitchen maids had noticed too. One of them did the cooking, which was a challenge because they were so limited by rationing. The full brunt of that hadn't hit Charlotte until now, but it did here. At the palace, their chefs were artful about making up for what they lacked for the queen's table, but here in Yorkshire, it was going to be a slim meal. She wasn't a hearty eater so she didn't mind.

The earl and countess came downstairs to the dining room on time, and the girls sat down with them. They were generous about having Lucy eat with them, and had been since she arrived. It had improved her manners considerably, and she also helped in the kitchen, and served most of the meal. Charlotte tried to help but was embarrassed to realize she had no idea what to do, how to carry the platters in properly, how to set the table, or serve. She was used to everything appearing, with no thought given to how the servants did it, and she knew that here she'd have to learn in order to make herself useful. The countess looked embarrassed when she saw Charlotte carrying in a bowl of thin stew made with pork from the pigs on their farms. She started to tell Charlotte that she didn't need to serve, and the earl gave her a cautioning look. Her Royal Highness would have to be one of the normal people here, pitching in as everyone else did, so no one would suspect her true identity. She was Charlotte White, a commoner now, but nothing about her demeanor made that convincing. She was a princess to the core, and looked it, even in simple clothes. After the meal, she and Lucy carried the plates back to the kitchen. Charlotte looked as though she might drop them but she didn't, much to everyone's relief.

They all retired early and kept country hours, since they woke at dawn. Henry often left to help on the farms before sunrise. He walked Charlotte back to her room that night, and offered to lend her a book about Arabian horses that he had just read, and she thanked him. After he left, she sat down at the small desk in her room to write to her mother. The countess was going to mail her letters for her so no one would see who they were addressed to. With a sigh, Charlotte picked up her pen, wondering what to say to them. She didn't want to shock them by telling them about serving dinner, or worry them, nor tell them about the tiny room that would be hers in the drafty dark manor for the next year. She was anxious to hear from them soon, Alexandra had promised to write too.

"Dear Mama and Papa," she wrote in her elegant penmanship, and began telling them about riding Pharaoh in the beautiful Yorkshire hills. That was something they would understand at least, and she could tell them honestly that she hadn't been troubled by her asthma on the first day there, and didn't need her medicine. She told them about Lucy and said she was very nice. She didn't mention Henry, who had been pleasant to her too, but it didn't seem proper to write about him. She talked about the earl and countess, and their hospitality. It took her an hour to finish the letter, and there were tears in her eyes when she sealed it. Her family, and the palace, and all the problems in London seemed so far away. It was going to be a very long ten or eleven months until she could return. For now, Pharaoh was her only reminder of home in this unfamiliar world. Lucy seemed almost too withdrawn to become a friend, and Henry was a boy, so they wouldn't be close. The earl and countess were kind but seemed so old. She missed her parents and sisters fiercely as she left the letter on her desk and undressed for bed in the tiny room. She had never felt so alone in her life, and the year ahead seemed like an eternity, as she cried herself to sleep that night.

Chapter 2

Charlotte rapidly fell into a routine of leaving the house at dawn every day, and riding Pharaoh through the fields and along paths in the forests for several hours before coming back to the house. There were no morning chores she had to do, and no one objected to her going out riding. Henry saw her leaving the stables one morning, when he was late going to a nearby farm, and asked if he could ride with her. Neither of them could resist the temptation to race each other, and Charlotte always won, because of Pharaoh's extraordinary speed, and her ability to urge him on.

"You shouldn't ride out alone," he chided her gently. "I know you're a very fine rider, and Pharaoh is sure-footed, but if anything ever happens, there would be no one to help you." In part because of her size and the fact that she was a girl, he felt protective of her.

"I don't want to be slowed down by a groom on an old horse," she said, and he laughed.

"Maybe I should ride with you every day." She blushed when he offered, and didn't answer. She could tell that he liked her, but more than anything they liked riding together. Charlotte never flirted with him. She told him about her sisters sometimes, without saying who they were, and he never suspected anything. Charlotte was the companion he would have liked to have had for the last two years, not Lucy. He and Charlotte always found something to talk about, unlike Lucy, with whom he never knew what to say. She was so obviously besotted with him, it embarrassed him, and he felt awkward trying to respond. She was becoming increasingly dour as the friendship between Henry and Charlotte grew. She knew there was no way she could compete with Charlotte's beauty and innocent charm, and within weeks, it was equally obvious to the countess that her son was falling in love with their royal guest. They were becoming inseparable. He now left for the farms later, and came home earlier, changed for dinner, and was always on hand to help Charlotte, even with carrying in the heavy platters for their meals.

He had never offered to help Lucy with the same tasks. Charlotte was learning how to make herself useful in the kitchen. She never tried to shirk from the menial tasks, or even the disagreeable ones, like scrubbing the pots, or washing the kitchen floor, which Henry insisted on doing for her. It caused a deep resentment between the two girls, not on Charlotte's part, but Lucy could see easily what was happening. The only one who seemed unaware of the meaning of his intentions was Charlotte. She seemed oblivious and entirely innocent. He was her riding partner, and her friend, as far as she was concerned, and nothing more.

The countess mentioned it to her husband one night in their room, with a look of concern. "Have you noticed how attentive Henry is to our royal guest?" Their bedroom was the only place she could allude to who Charlotte really was.

"What do you mean?" The earl was surprised.

"He's besotted with her, George. Surely you're aware of it?"

"They're just like pups playing together. It doesn't mean anything," he said blandly.

"Don't be so sure. He's not a child anymore, and she's a very appealing young girl. I think she's as oblivious as you are, but I don't want anything to happen between them. I owe it to her parents to keep her safe, not just from enemy bombs, but from my son as well." She looked genuinely worried and her husband laughed.

"You make Henry sound dangerous," he chided her. "They're just having fun. All he thinks about is joining the army. He's not serious about any girl."

"He could be very dangerous for her, if things get out of hand. We have a responsibility to the king and queen. Don't forget that. She's not just any girl."

"It's impossible to forget, my dear. Everything about her is regal. From the way she walks and the way she holds her head, to the way she speaks, and even her kindness to Lucy. There is an innate modesty and grace to the child. She's a lovely girl, and if something did happen between them one day, I certainly wouldn't object and you'd be foolish if you did. Wouldn't you like to have a daughter-in-law like her?"

"Of course. I'd like nothing better. But if that's ever to be, it has to happen in the right way, after the war. They're both much too young, and I doubt very seriously that Their Majesties would be pleased with a surprise betrothal at this point, based on proximity and nothing more sensible. I think they'd be furious with us if something were to come of this now."

"Wars make people grow up very quickly, and inspire deep feelings. Perhaps this is the right match for both of them," he said, and the countess sighed again.

"It is not the right time, or the right circumstances," she said emphatically. "I've tried warning Henry about that, but he has no wish to hear it, and it would be indelicate and presumptuous of me to talk to Charlotte about it. But her mother isn't here to warn her. I think they're both completely innocent, and falling in love. That could be dangerous for them, and for us, if Their Majesties get upset about it."

"This isn't the dark ages. They're not going to lock us in the Tower, Glorianna. I think you're unnecessarily concerned. They're both innocents, children really, and he won't be here for much longer. He'll be eighteen soon enough and in the army."

"They'll be here long enough for them to get themselves in deep water," she reminded her husband. The earl shook his head, got into bed, and a moment later, he was asleep. The countess lay awake, worrying about Henry and Charlotte for several hours.

She tried to speak of it discreetly to her son a few days later, and he looked shocked. "Mama, do you think I would try to seduce her? I would do no such thing." He was deeply offended by her implication. He was a gentleman, but also a healthy young man.

"I wasn't suggesting that you would. But you're both very young, and love is a powerful force at your age. It could lead you into situations neither of you are prepared for, and must avoid at all costs."

"You do Charlotte a disservice, ma'am," he said haughtily. "She would never do something inappropriate, nor would I." Henry was chilly with his mother for the next few days, and he never mentioned her comments to Charlotte. They were just having fun, and enjoyed riding together. All of his local friends were in the army now, and he was anxious to go too. His plans to go to university had been canceled, and would have to wait until after the war. His only friend whom he considered his equal was Charlotte. He could talk to her about almost anything, which was a first for him with a girl. She was his only close female friend or even friend of any kind now, with the war. She let him ride Pharaoh once, to see what a smooth ride he was, and he was stunned by the power of her horse, and her ability to control him with ease. She made it look effortless. She was an extraordinary horsewoman, which was only one of the many things he liked about her.

Henry's mother continued to keep an eye on them, but there was nothing she could really complain about. She was just uneasy about how close they had become. Charlotte only mentioned him in passing in her letters to her parents, with no particular details. She didn't think it was important, and he was leaving soon. She felt sorry for the Hemmingses about how sad she knew they would be once he was gone. He was their only child, and the light of their lives, just as Charles had said. Her mother and oldest sister had already written to her and given her the latest news from the palace and London. Charlotte pounced on the letter with glee the moment the countess handed it to her. She was starving for news of them. And they said how much they missed her too. When she finished reading her mother's letter, she placed it in a leather box her mother had given her for papers and letters, before she left. The box was her mother's, made of fine brown leather, with the crown embossed on it in gold and her mother's initials in small gold letters inside. It was a reminder of home just seeing it on her desk, and warmed her heart and made her homesick at the same time. To anyone not knowing who had given it to her, the gold crown just looked like a handsome decoration. The queen's own father had given it to her on her eighteenth birthday and it was a smaller version of the daily boxes of official documents Alexandra would receive one day as queen. And now Charlotte could keep her correspondence in it, the letters from her mother and sister. Victoria hadn't written to her yet.

*   *   *

There was a heat wave at the beginning of August, six weeks after Charlotte arrived. She felt at ease on the Hemmingses' estate by then, and in their home. Henry took Charlotte swimming in a stream at the back of the property, near one of the farms, and they cavorted like children, splashing each other, and laughing as they doused each other. Charlotte had thought about inviting Lucy, but she had promised to stay with the countess, to clean up some of the gardens with one of the farm boys. The countess had decided to try and do what she could, and Lucy was willing to help, so Henry and Charlotte went swimming without her, and didn't tell her where they were going so she didn't try to join them. They felt guilty saying it, but agreed that Lucy was dreary company, although she was help-ful to Henry's mother, but no fun for them. And she couldn't swim.

They were sitting on the bank of the stream, their horses tied to a tree, and Henry lay back in the grass, admiring her in her bathing costume.

"You're so beautiful, Charlotte. I think you're the prettiest girl I've ever seen." She blushed and looked away, not sure how to respond. She didn't think of him in that way, just as a boy, and a friend.

"Don't be silly," she brushed off the compliment.

"My sisters are much prettier than I am, especially Victoria. She's a real beauty." Something occurred to him then, an odd coincidence.

"Did your parents name the three of you after the royal princesses?" He had never thought of it before, and the question startled her. She was silent for a moment and then shrugged.

"I imagine they did. I never gave it any thought."

"It can't be an easy life, being royal," he mused. "I would hate it. All those official events they must have to attend. And you have to behave all the time."

"I suppose so," she said vaguely, and then threw a handful of water at him to distract him, which proved to be effective. They got back in the stream again and swam some more. They were both smiling when they got out, and dried off in their bathing suits, and Charlotte noticed him looking down at her. He was very tall, which made her feel even more diminutive next to him, and before she could say anything, he slipped his arms around her, pulled her close to him, and kissed her. He hadn't meant to do it, but couldn't stop himself. A wave of passion for her had just washed over him. At first she was too shocked to react. Then she melted into his arms and kissed him back. When they stopped, she stood staring at him with a serious look in her eyes. She seemed even more beautiful to him.

"Why did you do that?" she asked in barely more than a whisper, and she was stunned at herself for responding so readily. She had never been kissed by a boy before.

"Because I'm in love with you, Charlotte, and I wanted you to know it. I'm going away soon, in a couple of months. I didn't want to leave without your knowing how I feel about you. Maybe we could get engaged before I go," he said hopefully, sounding innocent and childlike, and a ripple of fear and reality ran down her spine.

"I can't do that. My parents have never met you."

"Could we go to London to see them?" he suggested naïvely.

"You know we're not supposed to travel. We can't just go running down to London to see them, and they can't come here. They're too busy. If we ever get engaged, it would have to be after the war." He looked disappointed, but willing to accept it. People were not moving around the country with ease, so she made sense. "Besides, we're too young. We're both just seventeen," she reminded him.

"I'll be eighteen soon, and you'll be eighteen next year."

"That's too young to get engaged. My parents would be upset," she said sensibly. She hesitated for a moment then, and looked at him. He could see that she wanted to say something more, but he had no idea what it was. "Besides, there are things you don't know about me, about my parents, and my family. Maybe things you wouldn't like." He was surprised by that and tried to guess.

"Has your father ever been to prison? Has he murdered someone?" he teased her and she shook her head. "Is he a spy? Or a German?" She hesitated then and nodded.

"Not a spy, but we have German ancestors, quite a lot of them in fact." The British royal house and her family tree had been heavily intertwined with Germans for centuries. Most of the Windsors, including Queen Victoria, were originally Saxe-Coburg-Gothas. There were German Coburgs on every throne and in nearly every royal house in Europe.

"My parents wouldn't like that, about your having German relatives," he admitted. And then he looked at her. "I don't care what skeletons you have in your closet, and I don't care that your father doesn't have a title, if you're worried about that. My parents would prefer it if he did, but they're falling in love with you too. And if we marry, you'll have my title one day." She smiled. It never dawned on him for an instant that she might have a title herself, far more important than his. "None of that makes any difference to me, and it shouldn't to you." He kissed her again then, and in spite of her concerns, she kissed him with abandon, and they were both breathless when they stopped.

"We should get back," Charlotte said modestly. "I promised to help Lucy set the table when she finishes with your mother in the garden." She put her riding clothes over her wet bathing suit and he did the same, and he gave her a leg up onto her powerful stallion. The horses had stood peacefully by, tied to the tree, grazing on the grass. His mare and her stallion were fast friends by now, and always pleased to see each other on their morning rides.

On the way back, Henry looked at her curiously. "Were there other things you wanted to tell me?" he asked her cautiously. He had a feeling that there were, and there were things she wasn't saying that were weighing on her. She shook her head. She didn't feel ready to tell him who her parents were. It was too big a secret to share so soon. He knew her only as Charlotte White, the daughter of a civil servant and a secretary in London. She knew he would be profoundly shocked by the truth. She would have to tell him eventually, but not yet. And his parents knew, even if he didn't.

They left their horses in the stable, and hurried into the house. It was later than they'd thought, and there was suddenly an unspoken intimacy between them that one could sense, now that he had kissed her. Lucy was aware of it when they walked into the kitchen, and Henry's mother when she saw them that night. As time went on, she worried more and more. They were so close and so comfortable with each other. Too much so, in her opinion. And Lucy was mournful and silent all evening. She felt left out by the two of them, as though they had a secret from her.

That night, Charlotte sat at her desk in front of a blank page for a long time, wanting to tell her mother about him, but she hated to do it in a letter, and wasn't sure what to say. That she loved him? That he loved her? That he wanted to ask for her hand one day? Perhaps they could make a pact just between the two of them before he left, and then get engaged after the war. But he had to meet her parents first. She was thinking about it, and still hadn't started the letter to her mother when she heard a soft knock on her door. She tiptoed to it, and opened it a crack, and Henry was standing on the other side, in the moonlight, and smiled at her.

"I wanted to kiss you good night," he whispered. "Can I come in?"

"You shouldn't," she said, her heart pounding with excitement, but opened the door anyway. He walked in quickly on silent feet, and closed it behind him, and an instant later she was in his arms, and they were kissing again. His kissing her that afternoon by the stream had changed everything between them, and his admissions about his hopes for them had opened the floodgates that had been closed until then.

"I love you, Charlotte," he whispered in the dark. Her whole body was shaking when she answered him. She didn't want Lucy to hear him in her room.

"I love you too," she whispered back. "Now you have to go." No matter how much she loved him, she didn't want to do anything foolish, and after several more kisses, reluctantly, he left. She didn't write to her mother that night, but lay down on her bed, thinking about him. She closed her eyes for a minute, her heart full of him, and it was morning when she woke up.

They all went to church in the village that day, and Charlotte earnestly prayed not to do anything with him that she'd regret, and even more earnestly that he'd survive the war, and nothing bad would happen to him. Lucy had gone to church with them, and they all had lunch in the garden afterward, in the part that Lucy and the countess had worked hard to clear the day before, and the countess praised how hard she had worked, which cheered her up a bit. Afterward, Henry and Charlotte took a long, slow walk down to the small lake near the house. There was a larger one they often rode to. They didn't invite Lucy to come and she looked hurt.

"I meant what I said yesterday, you know," he said seriously to Charlotte once they were alone. "I'd like to get engaged before I leave, and I want to marry you one day, after the war. I don't want to get off on the wrong foot with your parents, if you think they'd be angry at your getting engaged to someone they don't know." He had thought about it all night, and in church, and so had she. "Do you think I should write to them, to ask their permission?"

She almost shuddered at the thought. "They'd be **very** angry if we got engaged without their meeting you. And I don't think you should write to them. I know they would say we're too young." It was true. "I want you to meet them. But there won't be any opportunity before you go. We talked about why. They can't come here, and we can't go to London, so we have to wait." She was very firm about it. There was no way they could get engaged now. "They're much too busy at their jobs."

Henry narrowed his eyes then, and smiled at her, as they sat down on the grass. "I think your father must be a spy of some kind. You're very mysterious about him. Does he work for MI5 or MI6?" He was fascinated by military intelligence himself and she laughed and shook her head.

"No," she said simply, "and he's not a spy. I told you he works for the government." But she knew

Henry would have keeled over if she said he was the king, and probably not believe her.

"That doesn't explain anything. He could be a mailman for all I know." She laughed.

"He's **not** a mailman. I can promise you that. He serves his country and the people of Great Britain, and he's very dedicated to his job."

"He sounds like a good person."

"He is," she said solemnly, "and I think he will like you very much. And so will my mama. And Alexandra, my older sister. I can't tell about Victoria. She'll probably hate you because you're my friend. Victoria never approves of anything I do, just to be difficult."

"I want to be more than your friend," he said and kissed her and they lay side by side in the grass and he pressed his body against her, and despite all her resolve, she didn't resist or stop him, as his hand slipped under her dress. No one could see them in the tall grass, but she was afraid that what she was doing was wrong, and knew it was, but it was impossible to resist him. Suddenly, all she wanted was to be with him, and lie in his arms.

They walked back to the house with his arm around her shoulders, and they looked as though they were lost in another world. Fortunately, no one was around when they returned. His parents were taking a nap, and Lucy was in the kitchen, helping to prepare dinner. They had both regained their composure when they sat down for their evening meal with the others.

He knocked on her door again that night, and she let him in, and they lay on her bed and kissed and fondled each other for a long time, and she finally forced herself to stop and whispered to him that he had to leave and was sorry when he did.

His late visits to her room became a nightly occurrence, and they inched closer and closer to the edge of reason day by day. She couldn't stop him anymore and didn't want to, and the inevitable finally happened. The heat wave had persisted, and it was steaming hot in her room, right under the roof. He slowly peeled away the thin cotton dress she was wearing one night and she took off his shirt. The feel of their skin touching ignited like dynamite, and suddenly their clothes were on the floor and they were naked in each other's arms and couldn't stop this time. All they wanted was each other. They did everything they could not to make any noise and their lovemaking was exquisite agony as their bodies joined with all the passion and tenderness they felt for each other. There was no lock on her door, and Charlotte was terrified someone would come in and discover them, but no one did. No one ever came to her room at night except Henry. Lucy was a heavy sleeper and heard nothing from next door.

Henry finally tore himself away from her, and left her just before the sun came up. Before that, they lay in bed awake, after they made love, talking about the future they would share, and all the things they would do together after the war, once they were married. He wanted to take her to Paris for their honeymoon. The birds were already singing, as though celebrating their union. Charlotte knew she was his now forevermore, and whatever would come, she was ready to face it at his side. She could survive anything now, with the added strength of his love. Their youthful passion and desire had overtaken them and they became adults in a single night.

She sat quietly at breakfast the next day, with a dazed look on her face. Henry had already left for the farms, and his mother thought that Charlotte looked strange.

"Are you all right? Are you ill?" Charlotte shook her head, and didn't say a word. All she could think of was what had happened the night before. She had no regrets and only wanted more. The countess was alarmed at how remote she seemed and disconnected from everyone around her. She tried speaking to her husband, who once again laughed at her concerns.

"Even if they fancy themselves in love," he reassured her, "it doesn't mean anything at their age."

"It's different in wartime, George. There's a kind of desperation that sets in when people are no longer sure how long they'll live."

"They'll both live a long time, and fall in love many times after this. This is child's play, my dear. You have no cause for concern." He didn't see the looks in their eyes when they gazed at each other, but his wife did. Charlotte went to bed early that night, and they made love again as soon as they thought everyone was asleep. They were noisier this time than they meant to be. Lucy woke up with a start when she thought she heard a muffled scream. She heard the floorboards creak an hour or so later, opened her door a crack and peered out. She saw Henry tiptoeing to the stairs, with his shirt off, wearing only his pajama bottoms, and guessed instantly what it meant. She closed her door just as softly, with a deep anger burning inside her, and raw hatred for both of them. She felt cheated of all her dreams. Charlotte had stolen them from her. Lucy didn't know what she would do about it, but she knew her time would come one day to get even with them.

As it turned out, retribution came in another form, within weeks. A month later, Charlotte appeared at breakfast looking green. She rushed away from the table within minutes and was violently ill. When the countess came to her bedroom afterward, Charlotte told her that she felt sure she had eaten something spoiled the night before. The countess was worried and sympathetic, and offered to call the doctor, but Charlotte insisted she was fine and it wasn't serious.

Two weeks later, in mid-September, she was just as ill, even more violently than she had been at first. She hadn't been out on Pharaoh in weeks, and despite their innocence, both Charlotte and Henry could guess what had happened. The waistband of her skirt was already tight, and she was so nauseous, she could barely eat. The only time she felt better was in Henry's arms. He spent every night with her now, and didn't want to leave her feeling so ill.

"What are we going to do?" she asked him one night, as tears slid down her cheeks. There was no doubt in their minds. She was six weeks pregnant by their calculations. She must have gotten pregnant immediately. They were both young and healthy, and nature had taken the upper hand once they lost control. Now they would have to ride the wave until the end. Or she would. He was leaving soon.

His birthday was only weeks away, in October, and the army would take him soon after.

"We have to tell my mother," he said, sounding determined. "She'll know what to do. Do you think something is wrong that you're so sick?"

"I don't know. I've never known anyone who had a baby, and my mother never talks about things like that. We should really tell her too. But I don't want to tell her in a letter, and we can't just show up in London and give her this news. It would kill her, and my father too." And they had told her not to call them, the lines weren't secure, and there were always many people listening on the lines at the palace. Everyone would know instantly, and she would be disgraced.

"And they'd hate me forever," he said, worried.

They told his mother the next day. Like two children who had committed an unpardonable crime, they went to her study together after breakfast and told her the truth. She closed her eyes for a minute, trying to stay calm, and gather her wits about her. How was she going to face Queen Anne, or worse the king, with this piece of news? They had entrusted her with their daughter, and her son had gotten her pregnant, at seventeen. There had been no sign of her asthma since she'd arrived, but what she had now was much worse. The countess was desperately trying to think about what was the best thing to do in the circumstances, and how to handle it. They were innocent children in a dangerously adult situation, which could easily become the scandal of the century. And Charlotte couldn't sit down with her parents and discuss it face-to-face. This was wartime, and nothing was simple, let alone for a pregnant seventeen-year-old princess. The countess could guess that her parents would be devastated.

"Do you want to go home?" she asked Charlotte quietly. It would create a scandal ultimately, but she might prefer to deal with this at home, with her own parents, instead of his.

"No, I don't," she said firmly. "They want me to be here. I know they'll be furious at first, but maybe the best thing is to tell them afterward. There is nothing they can do about it then."

"I'm not sure that's fair to them," the countess said sternly, "to confront them with a fait accompli, a love child after the war." The thought of it made her cringe. She wanted to do the right thing, and so did Henry. He was an honorable young man and deeply in love with Charlotte. They were babies having a baby.

"I can't just write to my mother and tell her this, and they don't want me in London, they want me here. There's nothing they can do to stop it now."

There were indeed several options, but in her innocence Charlotte was aware of none of them, and an abortion was far too dangerous for a royal princess entrusted to their care, so the countess didn't suggest it. The countess thought of something else then, which might mitigate the circumstances somewhat when they would finally have to face the king and queen.

"Do you want to get married, or do you plan to have the child out of wedlock?" she asked them, shaking at the thought. "A legitimate baby fathered by the son of an earl might be considerably more palatable to your parents than an illegitimate child after the war."

"Can we get married, Mama?" Henry looked shocked. It hadn't occurred to him since they were both underage. "Do we have to go to Scotland?" It was still where most people went to elope.

"You can get married here, with your father's permission. You're almost eighteen. And we have a document giving us the right to make decisions for Charlotte in the event of an emergency, and I'd say this is. We can give her our consent to marry. I think we should do it quickly. You may have to report for duty very soon after your birthday," which was only weeks away, and then he would be gone, and it would be too late to legitimize the child.

"Will you marry me?" Henry asked her, looking

straight at Charlotte, and she nodded, looking stunned. It hadn't occurred to her either, without her parents' knowledge or consent, but at least the child would be legitimate when she told them what had happened. They wouldn't be pleased, but they would be even less so if faced with what they would consider a bastard child. She knew her mother would be hurt that Charlotte hadn't told her, but she would forgive them if they had done the right thing, and Henry was respectable. They would all avoid disgrace if they married immediately, and it was Henry and Charlotte's fondest wish anyway for the future. The future had just speeded up at a rapid rate in the form of a baby.

"Yes, I will marry you," Charlotte said clearly, suddenly sounding very grown up, even though she looked like a child.

"I'll speak to your father," Glorianna Hemmings said to her son. "I imagine there will be hell to pay with your parents eventually because I let this happen," she said to Charlotte, "but I pray they will forgive me. I agree with Charlotte," she said to her son, "we can't write them about this kind of thing in a letter. It's too complicated to call her parents, and they asked us not to. And if you marry, you'll have done the right thing. It's the best we can do in this situation, since you've both been so foolish. I was afraid of something like this happening. Your father didn't believe me," she said to Henry, and he nodded, embarrassed at the mess they had made. Neither of them had expected this to happen, nor knew how to avoid it. They had thrown caution to the winds, and somehow thought they'd get away with it. They realized now that Charlotte must have gotten pregnant immediately, possibly the first time they made love. His mother wasn't pleased but she felt sorry for them both.

George Hemmings agreed to give his permission for both of them to marry by special license, but he insisted that the marriage be kept secret. If it somehow got out that Princess Charlotte Windsor had gotten married in haste, it would expose the reason for it, and the scandal for sure. And he didn't want the king and queen hearing it as a rumor or idle gossip that would spread like wildfire, and even wind up in the press. He was adamant that their marriage, and eventually the baby, must be kept secret until after they met with the king and queen, which wasn't possible now and wouldn't be for some time. He was calm and sensible about it. And he wasn't entirely sorry, as he told his wife. Charlotte was an excellent match for his son, to say the least. His wife scolded him for it. They all agreed that both the marriage and the pregnancy had to remain a secret between the four of them. Under no circumstances did they want Charlotte's parents to find out about it before they had a face-to-face meeting with the Hemmingses, who intended to beg their forgiveness for the foolishness of their son. And until then, no one was to know that anything was afoot. Henry's father impressed that on both of them, and both young people agreed, with deep remorse for the situation they had created and gratitude for his parents' help.

They met with the vicar the following afternoon, and he agreed to marry them by special license since Henry would be leaving so soon to join the army. He thought it very touching and romantic. The Hemmingses did not tell him about the pregnancy, or who Charlotte really was. Their special license said only that her name was Charlotte Elizabeth White, which was on her identity papers provided by the Home Office.

The ceremony was conducted in secrecy and privacy at the church, with Henry's parents standing beside them. Charlotte wore a simple white wool dress that she had brought with her, and carried a bouquet of white flowers from the countess's garden. Henry looked tall and handsome and suddenly more mature in the role of groom. Then they all went home and had dinner together. Nothing more was said about the marriage. And Lucy knew nothing about their secret wedding, although she knew that Henry spent his nights with Charlotte, but she said nothing to either of them and kept the information to herself for future use.

Lucy had started eating dinner in the kitchen with the two elderly servants a while back, and barely spoke to Charlotte anymore. Her eyes burned with the fury of a scorned woman anytime she saw Henry, and he paid no attention to her. He had bigger things on his mind. And he had no patience with Lucy's fantasies about him, and her petty jealousies of Charlotte. Charlotte was his wife now. It changed everything in his eyes. He was her protector, and had vowed to be forever. His parents were relieved that they had done the right thing for the child Charlotte was carrying, even if it meant facing the ire of Their Majesties at some point once they knew. Hopefully they would forgive them, although it seemed inevitable that they would be angry at first, with their daughter getting pregnant at seventeen and rushing into a hasty marriage, no matter how respectable the Hemmingses were.

The one thing Henry didn't understand was why it was impossible to call them.

"You don't tell people something like this on the phone," his father said and refused to explain it further, much to Charlotte's relief. Henry still had no idea who she was.

Henry and Charlotte retired early on their

wedding day, and she slept in his room discreetly that night with his parents' permission. They had to do something to acknowledge their wedding night. Charlotte was still feeling ill, but she looked happy as she sat next to him on the bed, and he smiled at her. She had tiptoed down the stairs after Lucy went to bed and she felt sure she was asleep.

"So, my darling, we are now secretly married, and are having a secret baby. Do you think your parents will forgive us?"

"Eventually, though it won't be easy at first." She knew her father's temper but also his spirit of forgiveness. And they loved her, and would ultimately accept him and the baby. They had no other choice.

"I don't know why it has to remain such a dark secret. We're married now, our child will be respectable," Henry said, looking pleased.

"It has to remain secret because my parents don't know about it yet." His parents understood it better than he did. "It's a matter of being respectful of them, we don't want a rumor to get back to them before we can see them in person and can tell them ourselves, about the baby and our marriage."

"Why would it become a rumor? It's not so remarkable really. Charlotte White married Henry Hemmings, son of the Earl of Ainsleigh. I should think they'd be pleased. The daughter of a civil servant will be a countess one day." He acted as though it was a gift he had given her. But she had a far more important title of her own.

"Not exactly. It's not quite as simple as that," Charlotte said quietly, looking at her husband, who was half man and half boy. She felt like a woman now. She had grown up overnight, faced with the surprise pregnancy, and it meant a great deal to her that she was now his wife. She took their marriage very seriously, no matter how it had started.

"Why isn't it that simple? Are they anti-monarchists?" Henry was surprised, thinking about his father's title.

"On the contrary." She smiled at him. "It's about who my parents are."

"A civil servant and a secretary. You still haven't told me what branch of the government your father works for," he said casually, as he leaned over and kissed her.

"Your mother and father know who my parents are," Charlotte said mysteriously.

"Then why can't I know too?" He looked petulant. He hated secrets that didn't include him. And she could think of no way to break it to him other than just tell him. It was time that he knew who they were, and who she was, even if they didn't know about him.

She took a breath and said it simply and directly. "My father is the King of England, King Frederick, my mother is the queen consort, Queen Anne." There was dead silence in Henry's bedroom after she said it and he stared at her, and then started to laugh.

"Very funny. All right. Now tell me the truth. Are they communists or spies?" He couldn't stop laughing at the joke she was playing on him, but she looked oddly serious.

"That is the truth," she said in a quiet voice.

"And that means you are Her Royal Highness Princess Charlotte Windsor." As he said it, he stopped and stared at her again. "Oh my God, you're not . . . are you?" She nodded. "Charlotte, why didn't you tell me? Your sisters, Alexandra, Victoria, and you. I should have known. Oh my God. How could you not say anything before this? Your father will have me hanged for getting you pregnant." He looked genuinely terrified at the thought.

"No, he won't. He's a very kind man. They'll be upset at first because of how it happened, and that I didn't tell them. But we're married now, and the baby will be legitimate. That will be very important to them," and it was to her too, and to Henry and his parents.

"Charlotte! You're a royal princess? I never even guessed. I thought your father was a spy or some-thing. Does anyone else know here?" He looked bowled over by her news. He had thought her sisters' names were a coincidence. The truth seemed enormous to him now.

"Only your parents know, and now you," Charlotte said. "It doesn't change anything, but it complicates things a bit. No one is supposed to know I'm here, which is why I'm using a different name, at the request of the cabinet and the prime minister, to ensure my safety."

"And you live in Buckingham Palace?" Henry was still staring at her in disbelief, as it all came clear to him.

"Yes, until I came here," Charlotte said quietly.

"Am I supposed to call you 'Your Royal Highness' now?" He looked nervous and she laughed.

"Hopefully not." She smiled at him. He sat looking into the distance for a moment, trying to absorb what she had just told him. It all felt so unreal, especially when he fell asleep that night with his arms around her, and realized again that his new parents-in-law, whom he'd never met, and knew nothing of his existence, were the King and Queen of England, and his wife was their daughter.

"Good night, Your Royal Highness," he whispered to her as they fell asleep. She laughed and cuddled closer to him. It was even more shocking to realize that the baby they would have would be fourth in line to the throne. In his wildest dreams,

Henry had never imagined anything like this happening to him. He was married to a royal princess, and he was only seventeen. It sounded like a fairytale to him. But all that mattered to both of them was how much they loved each other, for better or worse, and Charlotte was now his wife.

Chapter 3

Two weeks after Charlotte and Henry's clandestine wedding in the little village church, they celebrated Henry's eighteenth birthday at dinner. Lucy sat at dinner with them that night, and drank a little too much of the wine the earl had opened for the occasion. Because of the war, it was a bittersweet event.

Charlotte was sleeping in her own room again, after their wedding night in Henry's room. Henry was spending every night upstairs with her. They tried to be as quiet as possible, so Lucy didn't hear them, but she was well aware that Henry was in the room next door with Charlotte, and more than once she peeked into the hall in time to see Henry head down the stairs before everyone else got up. Lucy fully understood what was going on, or thought she did. She was sure that Henry and Charlotte were having an affair, and she had guessed that Charlotte was pregnant because she threw up consistently. They had admitted nothing to anyone, and Lucy was biding her time to see what they would do. She had no idea that Henry's parents were aware of it, or that the two young people had gotten married. And she had no suspicions at all about Charlotte's royal birth. She thought she was just a fancy London girl, possibly with rich parents, judging by her accent and clothes. It had occurred to her immediately that the information about their affair, and possibly an illegitimate baby, might prove useful to her one day. She had to think of her future and what she would do when the war was over. She had nowhere to go. Maybe they would pay her to keep quiet. And she wondered if Charlotte would give the baby away and have it adopted in secret when it was time for her to go home. Lucy thought she wasn't likely to keep it at seventeen. Lucy wasn't normally a conniving girl, but alone in the world now, she had to think of herself. And Henry's loving Charlotte instead of her still stung. She would have liked to be the one in his arms every night. And she thought she might have been if Charlotte had never come.

* * *

Charlotte had given up her morning rides on Pharaoh ever since she realized she was pregnant. She missed riding him, and meeting Henry along the way.

A week after his birthday, Henry received the notice he'd been expecting for months. He had to report for training in five days, at Catterick Camp in North Yorkshire, the largest training camp of the British Army. He'd already had a physical exam in Leeds, with an A1 designation. His training would last six weeks, and at the beginning of December, he would ship out, and he had no idea where. It was suddenly very real, and Henry and Charlotte spent every night wide awake, making love and talking until nearly dawn. His going to war terrified them both, especially now that they were married and had a baby on the way. The whole house was subdued, with the prospect of Henry leaving for the army. His mother looked panicked, and his father seemed to have aged overnight.

Charlotte's letters to her parents and sisters were brief during Henry's last days at home. She explained that the Hemmingses' son was reporting for duty, as had been expected, and that they were all upset to see him go. Her mother wrote back sympathetically and wished him well. It was the first time Charlotte had mentioned him in any detail and Alexandra commented to their mother that Charlotte sounded sad about his leaving too.

"You don't suppose Charlotte is in love with him, do you?" Victoria commented to them when they got her most recent letter, which sounded extremely serious. The queen brushed it off as an absurd idea.

"Of course not. He's just a child, and so is your sister. If she was in love with him, she'd have mentioned it before. She's barely said two words about him until now. I do feel sorry for his mother, though. It must be very hard to see your only child go to war. They sound like lovely people from the correspondence I've had from his mother. Charles said they're older, and the countess has suggested her husband is in poor health. I do hope Charlotte isn't a burden to them. Maybe she'll cheer them up once their boy is away."

"He may be barely more than a boy, but that's who's fighting this war, Mother," Victoria said tartly, but she decided that her mother was right. Charlotte had hardly ever mentioned him, and she certainly would have if he mattered to her, which made a romance seem unlikely, and Victoria always thought her younger sister childish and overprotected by their mother because of her asthma, which had apparently improved in Yorkshire, or so she said in her letters. Victoria had enjoyed the last four months without her younger sister afoot, although she was starting to miss her, not acutely, but she admitted to Alexandra that she missed arguing with her, which seemed perverse.

The Hemmingses took Henry to the station on the appointed day with the train warrant the army had sent him. Charlotte and Lucy came too, to see him off. Lucy looked longingly at him, and dared to kiss his cheek when she said goodbye to him, and then Henry took Charlotte in his arms and kissed her in front of everyone, as though they had nothing to hide, which made Lucy furious, although she didn't show it. She would have liked him to kiss her that way, but he never had. She silently blamed Charlotte for stealing her rightful place in his affections. She had caught him by sleeping with him and being a whore.

"Take care of yourself," he whispered to Charlotte. He was hoping to come home on a brief leave before he shipped out, but he had no idea if they'd allow him to or if there would be time. This might be the last he saw of them for a very long while. He kissed his mother's cheek, shook hands with his father, wished Lucy well and kissed

Charlotte again, and then boarded the train, and stood waving from the compartment. He opened the window so he could lean out and see them until they disappeared from sight.

They were a somber, silent group when they went back to the house, each of them lost in their own thoughts about him. Lucy went into the kitchen as she did every night, with tears in her eyes now, thinking of Henry, and Charlotte went to lie down. All she wanted to do was think about him and keep the image of him in her mind.

His parents retired to their room, and the countess looked red-eyed when they came down to dinner a few minutes late. The earl was subdued and barely talked. Life at Ainsleigh Hall was going to be very different without Henry. The vitality seemed to have slipped out of the place. Everyone went to bed right after dinner that night.

For Lucy, it was a relief not to see Henry hovering over Charlotte, or know that he was next door in her arms at night. She could cherish her fantasies again, now that he was gone, and hoped he missed her. She and Charlotte hardly spoke to each other anymore, just to chat. The rivalry between them, for Henry's affections, had been too strong. Lucy had never been in that race, no matter how hard she tried, but she chose not to see it that way. She still believed that Henry would have fallen in love with her eventually if Charlotte hadn't come along. As she saw it, Charlotte had stolen her dreams from her.

For the next six weeks, their days were spent waiting for letters from him, which were brief and to the point. He said the training was arduous and he was exhausted every night, but he was well and hoped they were too. He wrote to Charlotte separately and told her how much he loved her, and how happy he was to be her husband. She put his letters in a drawer tied with a ribbon, and his parents shared the letters they'd had from him. They were proud to have a son serving the country. At the end of his training, he was allowed to come home for two days, before he shipped out. He still had no idea where he was going, and couldn't have told them anyway.

Henry looked tall and handsome in his uniform when he came home on leave. His hair was short, and had been shaved at the beginning of his training, he had trimmed down, his shoulders looked broader, and every moment he spent with them was precious. He managed to share himself equally with his parents and his wife, and even spent a few minutes chatting with Lucy, and asked her to take care of Charlotte, which stung. Henry had no idea that Lucy still cherished romantic fantasies about him. She hid them well.

They shared an early Christmas with him, and his mother gave him a few things he could take with him. Then forty hours after he'd arrived, he was gone. Charlotte stood freezing on the platform in frigid weather, watching him go. His eyes never left hers as the train pulled out, and she watched him until he was only a tiny speck in uniform, and then she got in the car and went home with his parents. Charlotte was four months pregnant by then, and it was starting to show, but it didn't really matter since no one knew who she was, and she hardly ever left Ainsleigh Hall. All they could do now was wait for his letters and pray that he was alive and well. Charlotte never mentioned the pregnancy to Lucy and the others, but they could see it now.

Christmas was quiet and dismal without him a few weeks after he left. Charlotte had three letters from him in January, and she guessed that he was somewhere in Italy or North Africa, but he couldn't say, and there were several lines blacked out by the censors when he said too much. The days seemed interminable without him, and Charlotte was homesick for her family now too. Yorkshire suddenly seemed a long way from home. And as her pregnancy became more pronounced, she missed her mother and sisters, although they knew nothing of what was happening to her. Only Henry spoke of their baby in his letters, and then in the beginning of February, his letters stopped. His father suggested that his division was probably on the move from one location to another and reassured his wife and Charlotte that the letters would start again soon. They believed him for several weeks, and then the dreaded telegram came, informing them that Henry had died a hero's death, in battle with the enemy. They regretted that it was impossible to bring his body home. He had died and his body had been lost at Peter Beach in the Battle of Anzio. The War Office extended their sincere sympathy to his parents. His father was inconsolable, and took to his bed immediately. Charlotte felt sick when she read the telegram again and again, and it sank in that her baby would have no father. She was bereft. She reported his death to her parents, and they wrote a personal letter of condolence to the earl and countess.

The earl's health deteriorated from the moment Henry died. He'd had a bad cough for weeks, which rapidly turned into pneumonia, and three weeks after they learned of his son's death, George Hemmings died too. They were all in shock, with one death on the heels of the other. It left the earl's widow and Henry's to console each other. Glorianna Hemmings had lost a husband and a son, and Charlotte her husband and the father of her unborn child. She was less than two months from her due date when her father-in-law died at the end of March, and a widow at seventeen when Henry died in February. Lucy heard her sobbing in her bed at night, and Charlotte looked ravaged. She wrote to her parents of the countess's grief and how sad they all were, but it never occurred to them and she never said that she was grieving for Henry too, and that he had been her husband and the father of her unborn baby. It infuriated Lucy that the countess was aware of the baby and didn't seem to mind. She was even pleased about it.

"You'll be going home in a few months, after you have the baby, when you turn eighteen," her mother-in-law said sadly one night. She couldn't imagine life without Charlotte now. They sat together by the fire every evening, while she told her stories of Henry's childhood. Glorianna had a distant look in her eye most of the time now, remembering the two men she had lost. Waiting for Henry's child to be born was the only ray of sunshine in their lives. And alone in her room, Lucy cried for Henry too. It was a time of loss and sorrow for them all. The countess moved Charlotte to a bedroom close to her own as the due date approached.

The weather warmed slightly in late April, just

before Charlotte's due date in May. Buds began to appear in the countess's garden. She and Lucy had worked hard to clear away the weeds, and plant some flowers, which were the first sign of spring. Charlotte put them in vases on the table when they had dinner, trying to cheer them all up. All she could think about now was Henry and their fatherless child. He had been much too young to die. It seemed so pointless. She read his letters to her every night.

The Germans had increased their air raids since January, and the bombing of London was severe again. Charlotte wondered if her parents would still let her come home even after her eighteenth birthday, since the bombing was worse again. For once, although she missed her parents, she was glad not to be in London, so her baby could be born in the peaceful Yorkshire countryside, without bombs falling every night among air raid sirens. And in their letters, her parents and sisters sounded busy and anxious about the war. They were relieved that she was safe. But at her end, Charlotte was sad not to be able to share the progress of her pregnancy with her mother and sisters, although her mother-in-law was very kind. She missed her own mother terribly and clung to Henry's as the only mother at hand.

It was the second week of May when the pains

finally began. She had written to her mother the night before, and wished she could tell her about the baby, but knew she couldn't until she saw her, hopefully sometime in the next few months, and then she would tell her everything that had happened, about marrying Henry and how much she loved him. She was a widow now, and all she wanted was to see their baby and for it to arrive safely.

The countess sent for the doctor as soon as Charlotte told her that the contractions had started. He arrived quickly, and had been concerned for the past several weeks that the baby had grown too large for her tiny body. There was a hospital nearby, and he hoped she wouldn't need a cesarean section, which was a complicated operation for both mother and child, and one or both frequently didn't survive it. He had shared his fears with the countess, but said nothing to Charlotte, not wanting to frighten her. Her belly was huge in the final weeks of her confinement. She looked so uncomfortable that at the last Lucy wasn't even jealous of her, to be having Henry's child. Until then, it had irked her constantly.

The pains were already powerful when the doctor got there after labor began. Glorianna was sure she'd come through it. She was healthy and young. The doctor sat by Charlotte's bedside from morning to nightfall, and her mother-in-law stayed with her. It was an arduous birth, and after sixteen hours of hard labor, there had been no progress. The baby appeared to be too large to come down the birth canal, and the countess and the doctor exchanged a worried look. It was midnight by then, and Charlotte was too far gone to move her to the hospital, even by ambulance. Glorianna applied damp cloths to her brow, while the doctor tried to maneuver the baby down. The maids and Lucy could hear Charlotte's screams throughout the house, and the doctor looked at the countess in dismay twenty-four hours after labor began.

"Charlotte, you have to try harder," her mother-in-law told her with a sense of urgency now. Charlotte was getting weaker and she couldn't push anymore. "The baby is big, and you have to push it out. Think of Henry, and how much he loved you. You have to do this for Henry. You have to push the baby out." Charlotte renewed her efforts, and the physician attempted to turn the baby to ease its passage, which only made Charlotte scream louder. She was doing the best she could, but getting nowhere. Lucy had peered several times into the bedroom where Charlotte was laboring and disappeared just as quickly at the sounds of her agony. It seemed so much worse than she'd expected and it frightened her.

Charlotte renewed her efforts then, and used

every ounce of her remaining strength to move the baby down, and slowly, it began to emerge, and the doctor gave a shout of victory when he saw the baby's head, which made Charlotte try that much harder as she clenched her mother-in-law's hand and they cheered her on. It took another two hours of agonizing pushing, while Charlotte hung between consciousness and oblivion and felt as though she was drowning, as her baby finally came into the world with the cord tangled tightly around her, which was what had been holding her back. The doctor cut the cord and freed her, and he held her up, cleared her airway with a suction bulb, and the baby gave a hearty cry. Charlotte smiled weakly when she saw her. It was a girl, a very big baby. It was difficult to imagine that a child that size had emerged from such a tiny person, and when they weighed her, she weighed just over nine pounds. Charlotte had slipped into merciful unconsciousness by then, just after the baby was born, and he had given her drops for the pain which allowed him to repair the tears the baby had caused before Charlotte woke up again. She was bleeding heavily, which he assured the countess was to be expected after such a difficult birth, with a baby that large, and he said the bleeding would soon stop.

"What are you going to call her?" her mother-in-law asked her with a gentle smile as she kissed

Charlotte's cheek when she awoke. She had been so brave. A nurse the doctor had brought with him was holding the baby, who had been cleaned and swaddled by then, and was staring at them with wide-open blue eyes, while Charlotte gazed at her with unbridled love, wishing Henry could see her. Seeing her baby now made all the agony worthwhile.

"Anne Louise, after my mother, and one of my great-great-aunts. One of my German relatives," Charlotte said, in barely more than a whisper. The doctor was observing her closely, relieved that both mother and child had survived, which he had begun to doubt in the last few hours of the delivery. Charlotte was very weak now, and spoke in a whisper as she glanced at her daughter. "She's so beautiful, isn't she?" She drifted off to sleep again then from the drops the doctor had given her. He left an hour later, after checking her pulse several times. It was thready and weak, but it didn't surprise him after all she'd been through. He told the countess to let her sleep, and said he would be back to check on her in a few hours, and the nurse would check on her from time to time. She took the baby to the room they had set up as a nursery, next to the bedroom Charlotte was occupying, down the hall from her mother-in-law. The countess went to her room to rest too. It had been a frightening night, and like the doctor, the countess had feared that neither Charlotte nor the baby would survive, but was grateful that they had.

The countess lay down on her bed without getting undressed, and fell asleep instantly. She woke up two hours later, and decided to check on Charlotte, to make sure that she was doing well, and not in pain. She opened the door to her room, careful not to waken her, wishing that Henry were alive to see his daughter, and as soon as she entered the room, she saw that Charlotte was ghostly pale, even more than she had been during the birth. Her lips were blue, she was peacefully asleep, but ghostly white, and as Glorianna approached her bed, she could see no sign of Charlotte's breathing. She reached for her wrist to find a pulse and could find none and saw no sign of movement at all. She pulled back the bed covers instinctively, and saw that Charlotte was lying in a pool of blood. She had bled to death after the delivery, while the nurse was with the baby. Her skin was already cold to the touch. She was dead at seventeen, from a childbirth that her parents knew nothing about. Her mother-in-law's heart was pounding as she looked at her. What was she going to tell them? Their precious child was dead. She had died giving birth to a baby they didn't know existed. She called the doctor with trembling hands, and he returned immediately. She had told no one what had happened, and couldn't believe it herself. First Henry, then her husband, and now this, poor Charlotte, and the poor little girl with no mother now, orphaned at birth.

The doctor confirmed that Charlotte had died of a severe hemorrhage from trauma during the delivery. It couldn't have been predicted, although she'd still been bleeding when he left, which he said was to be expected. And he said hemorrhages like that happened very quickly. It had struck Charlotte even before the nurse could return to the room to check her again. All Glorianna could think of now was how to protect Charlotte's memory, and Henry's, and to spare her parents further grief, until they knew about the baby later.

She looked pointedly at the doctor with an idea. "Would it be possible to list the cause of death on the certificate as pneumonia or influenza, perhaps with the complication of asthma, which she suffered from before? Her parents don't know about the baby," she said in a whisper. "I will tell them about her later of course. But for now, this seems like the least painful course for them, without adding the shock of a child to the death of their daughter." The doctor hesitated only for a moment and then nodded. What difference did it make now? The poor girl was dead, and he assumed the baby had been illegitimate if her own parents didn't know about it. Perhaps it was why she had come to Yorkshire, to conceal an illegitimate birth. The countess wanted to protect them from the truth, and the girl's reputation. And why cause her parents further grief to have lost their daughter to a child born out of wedlock? It never dawned on him that Charlotte might have been married, and the countess didn't say it, since the marriage was a secret too because of who Charlotte was. And despite being a princess, she was just a child herself and now she was dead. Yet another tragedy after too many recently.

"Of course, your ladyship, whatever I can do to help in the circumstances. This is most unfortunate." He looked deeply troubled about it too, and wished he hadn't left, but she'd appeared to be doing well enough when he did. And she might have died even with a cesarean with such a large baby.

"Her parents will be heartbroken." Glorianna knew only too well how they would feel, having lost her son too.

"At least they'll have the infant to console them, once you tell them—if they're willing to accept her," the doctor said kindly. It was clear to him now that the baby was illegitimate, and the countess said nothing to correct him. It didn't matter what he thought, only that the press didn't get hold of the story before she could tell the king and queen face-to-face about the baby, and that Charlotte and Henry had been married. Other than the vicar, she was the only one who knew now. And the vicar knew nothing of Charlotte's true identity. Only Glorianna did. To everyone else, she was Charlotte White. The doctor had guessed that the baby's father was the countess's son, and now the baby was an orphan, with both its parents dead.

"I want to wait until I see Charlotte's parents, to explain the entire matter to them. For now, all they need to know is that they've lost their daughter. They don't need to know the true reason why immediately. It won't change anything." She spoke with the authority of her rank, trying to make the best of a terrible situation.

"Of course, your ladyship, whatever you think best." He had a death certificate in his medical bag, and filled it out listing pneumonia with complications from asthma as the cause of death, as she had suggested. He promised to register it at the county record office, and called the funeral home for her. He wanted to do all he could to help.

Looking dignified and grief-stricken, the countess told Lucy, the housekeeper, and the maids of Charlotte's death. Lucy looked shocked as tears filled her eyes, and the maids burst into tears and went back to the kitchen, and Lucy joined them. None of them had expected Charlotte to die. She was so young and healthy, despite her size.

The funeral parlor came to get Charlotte an hour later, and Glorianna kissed Charlotte before they took her away. Lucy stood in the hall crying with the maids, as they carried Charlotte out on a stretcher, covered with a black cloth. The countess stood in the library alone afterward and poured herself a glass of brandy with shaking hands, before she dialed the number she had for emergencies at Buckingham Palace, and asked for the queen's secretary. A man came on the line after she said her name. She hadn't thought to call Charles Williams, whom she had met when he'd brought Charlotte to them. It seemed more appropriate to call the queen's secretary in this instance, than the king's. She had corresponded with Charlotte's mother but never her father. She explained that it had all happened very quickly. Charlotte had caught a bad cold, which set off her asthma. It had turned to pneumonia within a day, she had been seen by the doctor, and before they had a chance to call the palace, she had a massive asthma attack and succumbed. The countess sounded distraught herself, and offered her deep condolences to the king and queen, and Charlotte's sisters. She offered to bury her in their small cemetery on the estate for the time being, until the royal family had a chance to bring her home for burial, most likely after the war.

The secretary thanked her, and promised to call her after he discussed it with the family, and would inform her of their wishes. Charlotte had died just weeks before her eighteenth birthday. No one had expected this. Other than her asthma, she was a vital, healthy young woman. And Glorianna had fully expected her to withstand the rigors of childbirth, not bleed to death.

She mentioned to the queen's secretary as a detail at the end of the conversation that they would pack all her belongings to return to the palace, and were willing to stable her horse until they came for him with everything else. The secretary thanked her and they hung up. He had a grim task to face, breaking the news to the royal family that Princess Charlotte was dead.

The only consolation for Glorianna was that she knew that Charlotte's reputation, and Henry's, were safe. There would be no scandal about the baby, a rushed marriage, two young people who had been in love and foolish. She would tell Charlotte's parents the whole story when she saw them, but it wasn't a story she wished to tell them in a letter or on the phone. Once they knew it all, she would show them the baby, and respect whatever they wished to do about her, let them take her or care for her herself. But for now, the baby was safe in Yorkshire, with her, until the royal family was ready to acknowledge her existence and welcome her.

The countess went to see her a few minutes later in the makeshift nursery. She sat holding her as she slept peacefully. A wet nurse had already been arranged from one of the farms. The housekeeper had taken care of it. As she held her, the countess mourned the infant's mother, who had brought sunshine to their lives for a year, and had loved her son. And thanks to Charlotte, part of Henry would remain. She was grateful for that. She couldn't believe that Charlotte was gone now too, and she knew that, like Henry, Her Royal Highness Princess Charlotte would live on forever in this child, who was her flesh and blood too. The countess felt a powerful bond with the helpless infant, Princess Anne Louise, named by her mother before she died. Glorianna hoped that fate would be kinder to her in the future than it had been so far, with no parents now to love her. She had come into the world in sorrow, not in joy.

Chapter 4

For weeks after her birth, they all hovered around the nursery, to make sure that the infant Anne Louise would survive the rigors of her birth, and her mother's death. The doctor came to see her every day. He found a nurse for them who would stay, and despite the loss of her mother, she was a thriving, healthy, normal baby, with a hearty appetite and a lusty cry. She was the only ray of sunshine in the somber house.

The royal family had been grief-stricken by the news of Charlotte's death. And the doctor had obligingly done as the countess had suggested in listing the cause of death as pneumonia and asthma. They knew nothing about a clandestine marriage, death following childbirth, nor about the surviving child.

The royal family had gratefully accepted temporary burial on the Ainsleigh estate, with the intention of moving Charlotte's remains immediately after the war, rather than bringing her back for burial now, while London continued to be bombed. They preferred to leave her belongings and horse in Yorkshire too, until they came for her, which the countess said was fine. The secretary said that the thought of burying her in the midst of the ongoing air attacks was more than they could bear.

Both of Charlotte's sisters were as heartbroken as their parents. Princess Victoria suffered even more than her older sister, remembering all the times that she had tormented her, belittled her, and argued with her.

A formal announcement by the palace was made on the radio and in the press that the king and queen's youngest child, Her Royal Highness Princess Charlotte, while staying in the country to avoid the bombing, had succumbed to pneumonia and died shortly before her eighteenth birthday. It said that the royal family was in deep mourning. Everyone at Ainsleigh Hall heard the broadcast, and none of them made the connection with Charlotte White, who had died shortly after childbirth at Ainsleigh on the same day.

"Strange, isn't it?" Lucy had commented to the housekeeper after the broadcast, as they all sat in the kitchen. "She died the same day our Charlotte did, though from a different cause." Everything seemed to be about death these days, in the war, in the cities, and at Ainsleigh. Lucy was spending all her time in the nursery, and loved holding the baby. She was a last link to Henry. She would sit and hold her for hours. She was there when little Anne gave her first smile, and was more adept at calming her than anyone in the house, when she cried for hours sometimes. The nurse said it was wind, but the countess always wondered if she was keening for her mother. Lucy was sorry that Charlotte had died, but she loved the baby.

The funeral for Charlotte in their cemetery had been simple and brief. The countess, Lucy, the housekeeper, and the maids attended. The vicar who had married her and Henry said the funeral service and was genuinely sad over the death of someone so young, and such a lovely person who had brought happiness to all. No one knew exactly what had happened or why, but they knew that there were mysterious circumstances surrounding the baby's birth. No one except the countess and the vicar knew that Henry and Charlotte had gotten married, although they had all guessed easily who the baby's father was. And now the poor child had only her grandmother, since both her parents were dead. The countess shared the baby's history and royal lineage with no one. Charlotte's parents deserved to hear it first, and what they chose to tell after that was up to them. Her birth was respectable, but her conception had been less so, with parents who were so young and unmarried at first.

The countess was particularly glad now that she had encouraged them to get married. There would have been no chance of the royal family ever accepting or acknowledging the child if she had been illegitimate. For now, she was the countess's secret, but at least she was legitimate.

The countess was anxious for the bombing in London to end, so she could go to London with Anne Louise, show her to the queen, and tell her the whole story. It was hard to imagine that she would reject an innocent infant, who was the last link she had to her youngest child, who had died at such an early age. She had sent them a copy of the death certificate, and had received a handwritten letter from the queen, saying how heartbroken they all were, and thanking the countess for her kindness to Charlotte, despite her own grief for her husband and son. They had all suffered too many losses. But it cheered Glorianna a little knowing that the baby would console them all in the end, if the Windsors were willing to accept her, and she felt sure they would. She wasn't the first Windsor, or royal, to be born with unusual circumstances surrounding her birth.

The mood of the public was bleak again. The bombs dropping all over England were distracting and depressing them all with constant deaths and ravaged cities. It was as bad now, or worse, than at the beginning of the war. The Luftwaffe's attacks were relentless, as Hitler continued to hammer Britain with all the force he had.

Yorkshire was still one of the safer spots in England, although that could change at any time. And they had had their share of bombings too, though less severe ones than London.

The nurse had to leave them in September, when her mother got sick in Manchester, after their home was bombed and she had a stroke. Anne Louise was four months old, and Lucy was quick to volunteer to take care of her. The countess was impressed by how loving and efficient she was for one so young. Lucy adored the baby, and every time she held her, she thought of Henry, her one true love. He had been indifferent to her in his lifetime, but now she could lavish all her love for him on his child. She was tireless in what she did for the baby, and never let her out of her sight. Wherever Lucy went, the baby went too, and the countess was grateful to her. Lucy slept in the nursery with her at night.

The countess hadn't been well since Charlotte died. She had had too many shocks in a short time. Three deaths in the space of four months. Everyone she loved had died, except for her granddaughter, who was the only bright spot in her life.

The countess had been melancholy for months, and when winter set in, despite her injured leg from her previous accident, she began riding again for the first time in years. She said it gave her time to think, and in truth, she no longer cared about the dangers. Sometimes she went for long walks on the grounds, and stopped in the cemetery on the way back, to tend to her husband's grave or Charlotte's. They had put up a marker for Henry, although his remains weren't there and had never been sent home. George's parents were there as well, and ancestors for several generations. It brought her comfort to visit them. She seemed particularly pensive one afternoon when she came home, stopped in at the nursery, and saw the baby fast asleep in Lucy's arms. Both Lucy and the baby looked entirely at ease with each other. She left the nursery without disturbing them, and was grateful again that Lucy had made herself so useful. There was a reason now to let her stay after the war, which was a relief for Lucy and the countess. She could be Anne Louise's nurse, unless the queen wanted other arrangements, and decided to bring her home to the palace, once she knew about her. The countess was anxious for that time. The fate of the child was a heavy burden for her alone, and was meant to be shared. She was eager to do so with them, if they were willing and welcomed the baby.

A few days before Christmas, one of the maids went to wake her ladyship, as she always did, and bring her her breakfast. She threw back the curtains on a bleak December day. There was snow on the ground, and most of the house was bitter cold. The maid made a comment about it, as she turned to smile at her employer, and saw her lying peaceful and gray in her bed. She had died during the night of a heart attack that killed her in her sleep. The past year had been too much for her. The vicar and funeral home were called, and after some consternation, the housekeeper called Peter Babcock, the Hemmingses' attorney in York. She remembered his name from when the earl was alive. It was a dilemma knowing what to do next, since no one knew of any living relatives, but they assumed that the attorney would know who was the heir to the

Ainsleigh estate. Henry had been when he was alive, but he was their only child. Neither the earl nor the countess had siblings, so presumably it would fall into the hands of distant cousins now, as often happened with old estates. They often passed on to relatives they'd never even met.

The attorney came to see who was staying at the house, and found two maids and a housekeeper, and a young girl from London living there, and an infant he assumed was her child. No one had told him otherwise. They weren't sure what to say, since Charlotte was dead, and no one had ever confirmed to them for certain who the father was, although they could guess, but they weren't sure and it had never been openly said.

So the attorney attributed the infant to Lucy. No one told him that the baby was the countess's grandchild, since she had taken none of them into her confidence. They had no idea who would take responsibility for the child now. It appeared no one would. The whispers were that Charlotte's family knew nothing about the baby, or didn't approve, since none of them showed up when the baby was born, or even when she died.

There were two men in the stables, one old, and one barely more than a boy. The tenant farms were well occupied. The countess had enough money left to pay their wages for quite some time. She'd been running the estate on a pittance, without extravagance. Once the lawyer knew that all was in good order, he agreed to pay the wages from the estate account, until the lawful heir could be found, which could take time.

It took the attorney two months to locate a distant cousin, by running ads in the York and London papers. He finally received a letter responding to one of his ads. It was from a third cousin of the earl, who had moved to Ireland during the war, since it was neutral. He seemed most surprised to learn that he had inherited the estate. He hadn't seen the earl since he was a boy, and the heir was even older, had never married, and had no children. He wrote that he wasn't eager to return to England while the war was on, but said that he would come to inspect the property as soon as the war ended, or earlier if possible. In the meantime, he authorized the Hemmingses' attorney to continue paying the meager wages to the staff who remained. He said he was sorry to hear that the entire family had died. He seemed unsure about keeping the estate, and said he might put it up for sale, once he'd seen it. He had purchased a large estate in Ireland, a castle, and intended to stay there after the war. He had no real use for Ainsleigh, particularly once he was told it was in need of repairs and required a larger staff to maintain it properly.

It was another three months before the war in Europe ended in May, much to everyone's relief. It had been an agonizing five years and eight months, with such crushing loss of life in England and all over Europe, as well as in the Pacific. Europe in particular was battle-scarred after the bombings on both sides. Anne Louise turned a year old a week after Germany surrendered.

It was June, a month after the surrender, when Lord Alfred Ainsleigh arrived from Ireland to meet with the lawyer from York and inspect the estate. The heir was quite elderly, and was discouraged to see the condition of disrepair of the manor house itself, and to note how much work and expense it would take to modernize it, add central heating, redo the plumbing and electricity, which were old and rudimentary at best. The park was sadly run-down, the gardens in need of replanting, although the grounds were beautiful, and the tenant farms would spring back to life quickly when the men returned from the war. But he said he had neither the energy, nor the youth required to bring the Ainsleigh estate back to what it had been before the Great War. There were thirty years of deferred maintenance repairs to do, due to lack of funds, and he thought the most sensible solution was to sell the property, at the best price he could get. He had no desire to live in England, he and the attorney discussed it at length, settled on a price that seemed reasonable to them, and put it on the market, with realtors in London and York. It was Lord Ainsleigh's hope that an American would buy it, or someone with enough money to restore it to what it had once been. It was a long way from that now. He went back to Ireland after that, and Peter Babcock, the attorney, promised to keep him informed.

Lord Ainsleigh's visit and decision to sell had caused a stir among the remaining staff at Ainsleigh Hall. All of them were worried about what a new owner would mean for them.

"I guess that's it for us," one of the two maids said in her heavy Yorkshire accent, looking glum. She had worked there all her life, and been faithful to the earl and countess for the forty years of their marriage, and all of their son's life. "The new owner will probably sack us all," she said grimly, "and put young ones in our jobs," she predicted. "They'll be lucky if they can still find anyone willing to be in service. I don't think any of the girls are going to be in a rush to give up their factory jobs with better conditions and better pay than we have here. They'd rather live in the cities now than in the country."

Her colleague responded hopefully. "They're

going to need someone to clean the place. We might as well stay, and see who buys this place." The housekeeper agreed and said she was staying until they fired her. She loved the house, and had grown up on one of the farms. "What about you?" she asked, turning to Lucy. She wasn't an employee, but she wasn't family either, and she would need a place to go too, now that the earl and countess were dead and the place was being sold. She had no living relatives anywhere now, with her parents dead. She had a small amount that had come to her when her parents died, after her parents' apartment building was bombed, and their insurance paid her something. She couldn't live on the money forever, but it would last her for a while. Her dream was to return to London and find her way. She liked the idea of working on an estate like this one, maybe in Sussex or Kent. Yorkshire was a little too remote for her. She had just turned nineteen, and had been there for four years. It was the only home she had now. The big question for her was about Anne Louise. They were both orphans now. Annie, as Lucy called her, was thirteen months old. Lucy loved her like her own, and had cared for her entirely ever since the nurse left when Anne Louise was four months old.

"I want to go back to London," she said quietly, and they nodded. It made sense to them. It was where she was from, even if she had no family left there now. There would be better jobs there, and the surrounding countryside, than in Yorkshire. Others would be going back to their original cities once they got out of the army, or returned from the places where they had taken refuge from the bombs being showered on the cities for the past five years. A new era of renewal and reconstruction was about to dawn, and Lucy was energetic and young. "I thought I'd take Annie with me," she said, to see what they'd say, if they'd object or be shocked, or say she needed someone's permission. But the countess was gone, and an elderly distant cousin was the heir. He didn't want the place, and none of them could imagine him accepting a baby, whose parents and grandparents were dead, and whose parents hadn't even been married, as far as they knew. She was an orphan, and presumably a love child, or a bastard, even if the countess had protected her. And illegitimate, she couldn't inherit the estate one day. There was no member of the family to take her now, and if they spoke up to the new Lord Ainsleigh, they were all sure the baby would wind up in an orphanage. They all agreed that she was better off with Lucy, who loved her and took such good care of her, than among the thousands of orphans all over England, who would be struggling for a place to live and on public benefits. Whatever happened, Lucy would take care of her, and it was obvious how much she loved her. She didn't care that she was illegitimate.

"That sounds like a good idea to me," the house-keeper said to Lucy in a matter-of-fact tone. "She'll be safe and loved with you. She has no one else, and you're the best mother she'll ever have." Lucy smiled at her praise, and the other two women agreed. Lucy was the obvious choice to take the child. She had cared for her almost since her birth, and was the only mother the child had ever known. Putting her in a public orphanage, or giving her to an old man in Ireland who didn't want her, seemed wrong to all of them. And even if they had all guessed that Henry was her father, he wasn't there to take responsibility for her. And she had no claim on the estate as heir, so Lucy acting as her mother seemed like the answer to a prayer for both of them. Lucy needed a family and Annie a mother.

"When are you thinking of leaving?" one of the two maids asked her.

"Soon," Lucy said. She had her savings to tide her over, and she was going to look for a job where they would allow her to bring a child, perhaps as a nanny, or a nursery maid, or a housemaid on a large estate. She knew the kind of work that would be required of her, and she planned to say she was a war widow with a child when she applied for jobs. There would be plenty of them on the market now, widowed women with children, and no one was going to ask her for a marriage certificate or Anne Louise's birth certificate. She could always say her papers had been lost in the bombing.

"I'll give you a character if you like," the housekeeper offered, and Lucy was delighted. It was all she needed to get a good job. With that in hand, she could take her pick of whatever was available. She had read in **The Lady** magazine about an agency in London that helped men and women find domestic jobs, and planned to go there.

That night, after everyone went to bed, Lucy went upstairs to the large guest room Charlotte had occupied in the last weeks of her life, before Anne Louise was born. Her things had been moved down from the attic room next to Lucy's to the large guest bedroom, and Lucy knew that all her papers would be there. She wanted to take them with her, not to show to anyone, but in case she ever needed them. She had never known much about Charlotte's history. She had always been vague about it whenever Lucy asked her, and Lucy had always sensed that there was a secret there somewhere, just as there was surrounding Anne Louise's birth. A mystery of some kind.

When she got to the room, she had an eerie feeling, knowing that it was where Charlotte had died over a year before, the night of Annie's birth. The room hadn't been used since. The shades and curtains were drawn. She sat down at the desk, opened the drawers, and was relieved to find they weren't locked. This was easier than she had thought it would be. The drawers were all full, and there was a large brown leather box on her desk. It had a crown embossed on it in gold. Before she examined its contents, Lucy went through each of the desk drawers. Two of them were filled with stacks of letters tied with thin blue ribbons. She removed the ribbons, and opened the letters, and saw the crown on the stationery. They were all signed "Mama," the initials engraved at the top of the page were "AR," and handwritten in the upper right-hand corner, under the date, in a neat elegant hand were the words "Buckingham Palace." A few said "Sandringham," some "Windsor," and several others said "Balmoral." Lucy frowned as she read the locations and wondered if it was a code of some kind. And then she read several of the letters, and suddenly her heart gave a jolt. "AR" could mean Anne Regina, Queen Anne, the crown was the crown of the Royal House of Windsor, and they had been written from all of the palaces that the current royal family used most often. But that wasn't possible. How could it be? Charlotte had said that her father was a civil servant, and her mother was a secretary. Had she been lying? Or was her mother a secretary to the queen? It seemed unlikely she'd use so much of the queen's stationery for letters to her daughter, unless she was the queen.

She began to read the letters more carefully and nowhere did Charlotte's mother, the woman who had signed herself "Mama" in the letters to Charlotte, nowhere did she mention Henry, or the fact that Charlotte was expecting a baby. She obviously didn't know. Charlotte had clearly kept the baby a secret from her mother, presumably because Anne Louise was illegitimate and she didn't want to tell her mother of her disgrace. But the countess knew about the baby and had kept the secret for her.

Lucy vaguely remembered then hearing that the youngest royal princess had been sent to the country to escape the bombing in London. Maybe she had come here. But Charlotte's last name was "White," not "Windsor." There was no doubt in Lucy's mind that the letters signed "Mama" were from the queen, written from Buckingham Palace, and all the palaces where they lived. The envelopes showed that they were addressed to the countess, but the letters were to Charlotte.

She read the letters right to the last ones, and

several from her sisters. She looked for mentions of a baby coming, and there were none. Lucy tied the letters up again, then found the packet of letters that Henry had written her shortly before he died, telling her how much he loved her, and mentioning the baby that was about to be born and how pleased he was. It made Lucy's heart ache to read them, remembering how she had hoped that one day he would love her. But now she had Annie, and he was gone. There were several photographs of him in the desk, and one of him with Charlotte that his mother must have taken, in a small heart-shaped silver frame.

After Lucy finished reading the letters, she carefully opened the leather box with the crown embossed in gold on it. There was a key in the lock, but the box was open, and Lucy was astounded by what she found. Their marriage certificate, for the marriage by special license that they had kept secret as well. So Anne Louise wasn't illegitimate after all, which came as a shock to Lucy. Everyone assumed she was. The queen apparently didn't know about her, but Henry and Charlotte had gotten married before he left, not long before. Glorianna Hemmings had signed it as a witness, so she knew, and so had the earl, but they had waited to tell the queen, and must not have gotten around to it by the time Charlotte died, hours after the baby's birth, because the queen's letters never mentioned the marriage or the child. Perhaps they'd been waiting until Henry returned from the war to face the royal family with the news of a marriage and a baby conceived out of wedlock at seventeen. For whatever reason, the queen appeared to be entirely unaware of Anne Louise's existence, or Charlotte's hasty marriage, after she was pregnant, and before he left. So they had legitimized the child, but kept her a secret. And most shocking of all, Charlotte had been a royal princess. The king and queen's youngest child. Lucy was sure of it now. Things had obviously taken an unexpected turn when she came to Yorkshire and she and Henry fell in love. She had kept that a secret from her family as well. He was never mentioned in a single one of the queen's letters, until after his death when she said how sorry she felt for his mother, but she appeared to have no idea that Charlotte was mourning him as well.

Her travel papers were in the leather box, in the name of "Charlotte White." There was nothing in the box to identify her as "Charlotte Windsor," or as a royal princess, except the letters from the queen signed "Mama," sent from Buckingham Palace and their other homes. There were letters in the letter box too, from Charlotte's mother and both her sisters and a few signed "Papa." The box was too full to contain all the letters. The rest were in the desk drawers. And when she took all the papers out to read them, she saw that there were initials inside the box at the bottom. They weren't Charlotte's initials, they began with "A," presumably the queen's. Charlotte had kept a multitude of secrets until her sudden death, and in the end, had taken them to her grave. The countess had known the whole story, but hadn't told the queen either, since she didn't seem to know. Perhaps she was afraid of the king's and queen's reactions to their seventeen-year-old daughter getting pregnant by the Hemmingses' son, and married in secret without her parents' permission, to prevent her child from being born illegitimate. Some of the mysteries remained unsolved and would be forever, but Lucy could guess. Charlotte was almost surely the youngest princess who had been sent away from London to escape the bombs, and the same one who had died, supposedly of "pneumonia," on the same day that Charlotte White had died in Yorkshire, shortly after childbirth at seventeen. It wasn't a coincidence. Lucy was certain now that she was the same girl.

There was also a copy of Anne Louise's birth certificate, with her father's last name, and the death certificate of Charlotte White, apparently put there by the countess, with "pneumonia" listed as the cause of death, not hemorrhaging after childbirth. It was all there. And when she peered into the box for a last look, she saw a narrow gold chain bracelet with a heart dangling from it and put it on her wrist. She felt like a thief taking it, but she'd never had anything as pretty and couldn't resist. She would give it to Annie one day. She remembered Charlotte wearing it and had noticed it when she arrived.

As Lucy sat back in the chair at Charlotte's desk, contemplating the piles of papers in front of her, she realized that she had everything she needed to blackmail the Royal House of Windsor, if she wished to do so. It was a powerful feeling that she knew about a secret marriage, a baby conceived out of wedlock by their seventeen-year-old daughter, and the child that had resulted from it, and she knew the real cause of Charlotte's death, and she was sure that the royal family were aware of none of those things. Lucy knew everything they didn't. How much would they pay for the information, and to keep her quiet, and not create a scandal involving their dead daughter? But she had gotten married, and the baby had been born legitimate.

But she didn't want money, she wanted Annie, the baby that she loved, and they didn't know existed. They would never miss her, and if Lucy gave her up now, she knew it would break her heart.

Remaining silent now would mean depriving Annie of life as a royal princess, but whatever she did now, Annie's mother was still dead. She could give her up to a life of palaces and royal blood, but Lucy firmly believed she could give her a mother's love as none of the royals would. And if things had been different and Henry had loved her, Annie would have been their child, not Charlotte's. This was a way of keeping Henry close to her forever, but more important, she could lavish love on his child. Annie would never know that she was the granddaughter of a king and queen, and if she took Annie's birth certificate with her, no one would ever know. They would never know that there was a child, when they came to get Charlotte's belongings and remains, and Annie would never know of the life she had missed. Only the earl and countess and Henry and Charlotte had known the truth of who Annie was, by birth, and now Lucy had discovered the secret. She stared at the birth certificate long and hard, and her hands shook as she decided what to do. She knew she had no choice. All she wanted in the world was within her reach. She could let the servants at Ainsleigh continue to believe that Annie was an orphaned love child with no relatives except the very remote cousin who had inherited the estate and wouldn't want her either.

The royal family knew nothing about Annie's

existence, and never would. There was no one left alive to tell them, and no one in the world knew that the baby's mother had been a royal princess, third in line for the throne. If Lucy took Annie with her, no one would ever suspect that she wasn't Lucy's child. The king and queen would never come looking for a baby they didn't know anything about, the servants at Ainsleigh didn't know of her royal connections or who her mother really was, and there was no one to stop Lucy now. Whatever she could have gotten for selling Charlotte's secrets to them, the baby she loved as her own was worth far more to her.

With sudden determination, she decided to keep the letters and documents, the marriage certificate and Annie's birth certificate, and carefully put them all in the royal leather box. She took one of the blue ribbons off the letters from the queen to her daughter, locked the box with the key, slipped the key on the ribbon, and put it around her neck, where no one would take it from her.

In the box, she had everything she needed to guarantee that Annie would be hers forever. All trace of her bloodline had been removed, thanks to Charlotte keeping all her secrets to herself. Everyone who had known the whole story was now dead. The only remaining evidence was the infant herself, and Lucy intended to bring her up as her own, her very own royal princess. Her Royal Highness Anne Louise Windsor. Lucy would always know that the little girl she loved was royal. Her very own princess, whom even the king and queen knew nothing about. Their youngest child was dead, but her baby daughter was Lucy's now, to love forever, and no one would ever take her away. Lucy couldn't bear the idea of another loss if she gave the baby up. For her sake, and Annie's, Lucy was certain she was doing the right thing, and told herself she was. A mother's love was more important than riches and royal lineage. She would love Annie to her dying day as they never could. To Lucy, it justified everything. She realized that she could have destroyed the contents of the box, but the papers seemed too important to do that. She wanted to keep them in the box.

With an iron will, and no hesitation, she picked up the locked leather box, containing all the letters and papers. The desk was empty. Lucy carefully turned off the lights in what had been Charlotte's final bedroom, and all her secrets belonged to Lucy now, along with her child. There was an element of revenge, since Charlotte had stolen Henry from her. But she forgave her for that now. She had Henry's daughter, which meant more to her than Annie being a princess. Annie was Henry's final legacy to her. The child that should have been theirs. Annie was her baby now, and always would be. No one could take Annie from her. Once back in her room, she put the locked leather box in her suitcase, and touched the key around her neck. She had Charlotte's gold bracelet with the heart on her wrist. Annie was asleep in the crib in Lucy's room, where she had slept for months now, and from that moment on, Annie, the little princess no one knew about and never would, was hers.

Chapter 5

Two days after Lucy had packed all of Charlotte's papers into the leather box and slid it into her suitcase, she announced that she was leaving. She said she was ready to go back to London. She bought a gold-plated wedding band in a jewelry store in York, slipped it on her finger in her new role as war widow, and the next day, she packed up Annie's things, said goodbye to the staff at Ainsleigh Hall, with a character from the house-keeper, and took Annie with her on the train to London. Her heart was pounding when she left, afraid someone would try to stop her. But no one did. The remaining maids, housekeeper, and hall boys all thought it was a good thing that Lucy was taking Charlotte's baby with her. Without Lucy, where else would she go? Most likely to an orphan-age. They hugged Lucy and Annie, and wished her luck. She promised to let the housekeeper know when she found a job. But no one would be writ-ing to her in the meantime. The only people she knew were the staff at Ainsleigh Hall. All of her school friends had died in the bombing of London, and she'd had few friends anyway, working at her father's cobbler shop every day.

The toddler was fascinated by the people on the train, and Lucy sat watching the countryside slide by, remembering when she had come to Yorkshire four years before, at fifteen, and now she was returning to London to make her way and find a job, with a baby of her own. The war had been good to her, after four years at Ainsleigh Hall, and the kindness of the Hemmingses. She had all of Charlotte's papers in her suitcase, and life as a war widow would open new doors for her. There were plenty of girls pretending to be war widows, who had never married, and had babies by the men they met during the war. But none, she was sure, were absconding with a royal princess, pretending it was their own. She had won the prize with little Annie, and no one would ever know that she hadn't given birth to Annie herself. She had everything she'd ever dreamed of. Now all she needed was a job, and a home.

She checked in to a small hotel in the ravaged East End. The streets were still littered with rubble and debris, and everything was dusty as she walked around holding Annie. She went back to see the building where she had lived with her parents, and there was no sign that anything had ever been there. It was a sad, empty feeling, as though further proof that they were gone. The apartment building had vanished the night it had been bombed and the explosion had killed her parents. She clung to Annie for comfort as she walked around the neighborhood for a while, and then went back to her hotel. The memories were too powerful and the sense of loss in their wake. It made her even more grateful that she had Annie now. None of the neighbors had survived the bombing and her father's shop was gone.

The next day she went to the agency she'd read about in **The Lady,** to look for a job. She explained that she would have to take her daughter with her. Before the war, no one would have hired her with a child, now there were many girls like her who had no other choice, and employers would have to make allowances for it. The widows with children had no one to leave them with, and had to bring them along. Employers desperate for help in their city and country homes had to find a way to accommodate them, and many were willing to be creative and give it a try. The woman who ran the agency suggested three jobs to her. One employer wasn't willing to hire anyone with a child, the other two expected her to find someone to care for her baby by day, but were willing to let the child sleep at their home at night. One was in the city, in Kensington, and the other was at a country estate in Kent, which sounded more similar to the life she had led at Ainsleigh Hall, on a grander scale, and seemed more interesting to her.

The woman at the agency called the potential employer, and arranged for an interview for Lucy the next day. The position was as a housemaid, at what the agency claimed was a magnificent estate. Ainsleigh had been more of a manor house, and nothing had been formal there with so little help during the war. The estate in Kent was much more elaborate, with a separate house for the servants, and cottages for the married ones, if both spouses worked for them. The woman at the agency said that they'd been hiring people in droves for the past month, to re-staff their home after the war. They wanted footmen, both a senior and under butler, a fleet of maids. They had excellent stables with experienced grooms and a stable master, and had just hired three chauffeurs and a chef.

Lucy was excited when she took the train to Kent from Victoria Station for the interview the next day. She had paid a maid at her hotel to baby-sit for Annie, but had made it clear to the agency and employer that she had a little girl. She had mentioned that her husband had been killed at the Battle of Anzio, and she had lost her own family in the London bombings as well. The war had taken a heavy toll on many young women like her, and her story was entirely believable, although much of it wasn't accurate. She hadn't been married, she wasn't a widow, and Annie wasn't her child. She almost believed her own story now, and it had the ring of truth.

One of the chauffeurs picked her up at the train station in a Bentley, and they drove through the imposing gates of the estate twenty minutes later.

The interview was conducted by the head housekeeper, a daunting looking woman with a thin, sharp face, wearing a severe black dress, with a heavy ring of keys on her belt. The head housemaid appeared at the end of the interview to walk Lucy through the house, which was as elegant and grand as the agency had said. The owner of the estate was the proprietor of one of the largest and finest department stores in England. They were commoners and extremely wealthy.

Some experienced servants who had been in service before the war preferred working for titled families, but Lucy didn't care. Her potential employers had four young children, two nannies, and a nursery maid, but Lucy had applied for a job as a housemaid, which she knew she could do well. She wasn't afraid of hard work.

She was told that the wife of one of the tenant farmers was willing to babysit for the housemaids' children for a small fee during the day. It sounded like a perfect arrangement to Lucy. She would get one day off a week from morning, after her employers' breakfast, until just before dinnertime, and she would be handsomely paid. It was exactly what she needed, and when they offered her the job before she left, she accepted immediately. She didn't want to lose the opportunity, and it seemed like the ideal household for her to bring up her child. The chauffeur told her how much he liked working there on their way back to the train station. They had asked her to start the next day and she'd agreed.

She packed when she got back to the hotel, checked that the leather box with Charlotte's papers was still in her suitcase, and felt for the key around her neck. The box of Princess Charlotte's papers was Lucy's insurance for the future, if it ever became advantageous to her to share the information in it with the queen. But for now, it was safe, and she was only going to use it if she had to. All she wanted now was to start a good job, and lead a good life.

They had told her that Annie could sleep in a crib in her room, or on a cot later when she outgrew it. Two of the housemaids had young children there as well. Their employers were supposedly modern and very flexible, but expected them all to work diligently and for long hours. They gave house parties nearly every weekend, dinner parties frequently, and balls in their grand ballroom several times a year. Unlike the more distinguished, aristocratic Hemmingses, with diminished funds, they seemed to have unlimited money to spend. It sounded like a very pleasant life and work experience to Lucy, and she could hardly wait to start the next day. She would be given her uniforms when she arrived, and a seamstress would fit them to her.

She took the train to Kent the next morning, and was picked up again, this time by a different chauffeur, who was even more pleasant than the first one. They stopped at one of the farms so she could drop Annie off for childcare, and once at the main house, he took her to see her room, on the top floor of the house. The chauffeurs and stablemen had already filled the rooms in the staff building, and the cottages were only available to couples, of which there were several on staff.

"What about you?" the young chauffeur asked her. "A husband or boyfriend?" He had looked her over thoroughly before he asked. She had an ordinary face, but a voluptuous figure, which would definitely appeal to some. She was a buxom girl and looked well in the black uniform and lace apron their employer expected them to wear. It made her look older than her nineteen years, very serious and professional, with a little white lace cap.

"All I have is my little girl." Lucy answered the chauffeur's question in a neutral tone. "My husband died in the war."

"Oh, I'm sorry to hear that," the chauffeur said kindly. "Maybe you'll meet a new man here," he commented, and she smiled.

"That's not what I'm here for. I'm here to work." And she meant it. By nightfall, after working all day, every inch of her hurt and felt strained, as it never had before, but she knew she had done a good job, cleaning, scrubbing, waxing, and polishing all day. She had helped two footmen carry tables, had vacuumed several large reception rooms, and set the table impeccably for an informal dinner for twelve. She learned quickly from her coworkers, and liked their employers' style. She hadn't met them yet, although she had been told that the lady of the house was very fashionable. "Informal" to them meant the silver service, not the gold one they used for formal events.

The housekeeper had checked on Lucy several times throughout the day, and corrected her whenever she thought it necessary. She didn't like the way Lucy fluffed up the cushions on the small drawing room couch, or the way she arranged the curtains after she opened them, and she reminded Lucy to wear a fresh uniform and apron every day, and if she got one dirty, she was to go to her room and change. Lucy was startled at the end of the day when she went outside for some air and bumped into one of the stable boys walking a horse back to the barn. He smiled as soon as he saw her.

"When did you arrive?" the stable boy asked, clearly admiring her. He was taller and broader than she was. He had piercing blue eyes, brown hair, a strong face, and a warm smile.

"About six hours ago," she answered him, slightly out of breath. "I haven't sat down all day since I arrived."

"They'll work you hard, but they're fair employers," he informed her. "She can be difficult, but he's a great guy. He made a fortune and she spends it lavishly. He doesn't seem to mind. He's a generous man. He's got a few dollies on the side, but you never see them unless she's away with the children."

"That must get interesting," she said, enjoying the gossip with the stable boy. He was a nice-looking man with a warm, outgoing personality that made him even more attractive.

"I'm Jonathan Baker, by the way, and I'm going

to run these stables one day. My boss is twenty years older than I am, and he's going to retire before long. I want to be there to pick up the pieces." She could easily believe he would. He seemed like an enterprising guy, and had a bold upbeat way about him, without being offensive. Just the way he looked at her and smiled made her like him. He looked to be a few years older than she was, he wasn't handsome in a classic sense, but he had a kind face, and she liked his powerful broad shoulders. She introduced herself, since he had, and they went on chatting for a few minutes. It was easy to feel comfortable with him.

"Do you like horses, Lucy?" he asked her.

"Not really," she said. She had wanted to learn to ride while she was at Ainsleigh in order to get closer to Henry, but he had never offered to teach her, and she felt foolish asking him. And then Charlotte had arrived, with her remarkable skill as a horsewoman, which had impressed him, and Lucy had retreated to the kitchen. "They look like big, dangerous beasts to me. I never learned to ride when I was younger. The cobbler's daughter doesn't get riding lessons." She smiled at him.

"Neither does the blacksmith's son usually. I fell in love with them as a boy. They're not frightening once you get to know them, the good ones. I can teach you about them."

"I doubt that I'll have time for riding lessons. It looks pretty busy to me around here. And I have a daughter. I'll need to spend my time off with her. She's thirteen months old. I'll be leaving her at Whistlers' farm while I work."

"War widow?" he asked her, "or do you have a husband tucked away somewhere?"

"He died right before she was born, three months after he joined the army."

"There are too many stories like that one. I was in France myself on D-Day. They died like flies all around me, the poor devils. I got lucky, I guess. I just got back a month ago. I grew up here. My grandfather was a tenant farmer to the previous owner, and my father was the blacksmith. We've been here longer than the current owners. They bought the place seven years ago, right before the war. The previous ones went broke, after the last war. They hung on as long as they could, and finally sold. All three of their sons were killed in the Great War. I like working in the stables. I want to run them one day." The horse he'd been leading started to get restless then, and they both had other things to do. "It's been nice talking to you. I'll keep a lookout for you. The stable hands don't eat in the servants' hall. We have our own kitchen here, and cook our own food."

"See you again sometime." She smiled at him

again. He led the horse back to the barn, and she went to pick up Annie after work. She was crying and fussy when Lucy got there in her uniform, and she walked all the way back, holding her, thinking about what a good place this was going to be for Annie when she got a little older. The Markhams' estate in Kent was a perfect place for a child and anyone who didn't mind being in service, which didn't bother Lucy. She had a roof over her head, plentiful meals three times a day. The Markhams treated their servants well, and everyone said that the wages were better than they had been before the war. There were forty or fifty employees in various positions around the estate, gardeners, chauffeurs, stable hands, as well as those who worked in the house. The newcomers had more staff than most of the original owners, except in the days before the Great War. It had changed everything on the big estates, as money began to run out and the order of things changed.

The new owners could afford to maintain the properties the way the old owners no longer could. It was new money, which the aristocrats looked down on. They had no titles unless they bought them, which some did. Some of the more desperate landowners sold their titles along with their estates, but the Markhams were commoners and didn't mind it. They made up in wealth what they lacked in blood and ancestry. But Lucy knew she trumped them all. She had a royal princess as a daughter, and her grandparents were the King and Queen of England. It didn't get better than that, even if no one knew it. Lucy did, which was all that mattered to her. It always thrilled her when she thought about it. It was so surreal, and an enormous secret. Her baby was a Royal Highness, and Lucy was going to give her the best life she could, worthy of any princess, to the best of her ability. Working for the Markhams was the first step. Maybe she'd rise to housekeeper one day, with a ring of keys on her belt like Mrs. Finch, who ran the Markhams' home with an iron hand, but despite her odd, stiff ways and stern face, Lucy liked her. She was from the northern border of Yorkshire, and had the accent that had become familiar to Lucy while she stayed with the Hemmingses at Ainsleigh.

She settled into her job, determined to work hard, and had a letter from the housekeeper at Ainsleigh a few months later. She had let her know where she was, and told her she'd found a good job. The housekeeper from Ainsleigh reported that the estate had been sold to an American. The old servants had all been let go. The new owner was going to spend a year or two remodeling everything and modernizing the place, and would hire a new staff after they did, probably some of them American. They had bought the place for very little.

Her big news was that two palace secretaries and the queen's equerry had come from London shortly after Lucy left. They had exhumed Charlotte's casket and taken her remains back to London for a service there, and it turned out that Charlotte had been a royal princess. It had all been arranged very quietly, and the palace emissaries hadn't said much about it. No one at Ainsleigh had suspected that Charlotte had apparently been a member of the royal family. It made what they thought was her illegitimate love child even more shocking. And out of respect for the Hemmingses, sympathy for Charlotte, and loyalty to Lucy, no one had breathed a word about Annie. The housekeeper wrote that they hadn't asked about the baby, and she had the strong feeling they didn't know about her, which was probably just as well. Henry and Charlotte were both dead. Annie was illegitimate and she was in good hands. The whole matter was better left buried and forgotten. There was no point maligning the dead and causing a scandal. She also mentioned that they had taken her big horse back to London with them.

Lucy still believed she had done the right thing, taking her because she loved her, particularly since they didn't know about Charlotte's clandestine marriage to Henry Hemmings. It would all be forgotten now, and she and Annie could go on with their lives. She had left just in time, which was providential. She didn't write back to the housekeeper, and didn't want to pursue a friendship with them and maintain a connection. She wanted to put Ainsleigh behind her. It was history now. And they could have exposed her. Fortunately they didn't know about the marriage, which would have changed things if they did, Lucy had turned the page and started a new life where no one knew her. At the Markhams', she was just another war widow with a child. There were thousands of them all over England, some of whom had truly been married, and some not and only claimed to be. There were too many of them to ask questions or garner much interest. The Ainsleigh servants were happy for Lucy and Annie.

And no one at the Markham estate had questioned Lucy about Annie. They just thought she was a pretty little thing, and they never commented that she looked nothing like her mother. Lucy was a tall girl with a big frame, and despite her size at birth, Annie already had the delicate frame and features of her natural mother. Lucy could already see how much she looked like Charlotte. She had the face of an angel and white blond hair, with sky blue eyes. She was going to be a beauty one day, and she was already small for her age, which Lucy blamed on rationing and how little food they'd had in Yorkshire at the end of the war. The restrictions of rationing hadn't been lifted yet, but they ate well at the Markhams', who managed to feed their employees plentifully. And Lucy gave whatever treats she had to Annie. She never minded depriving herself for her baby. Lucy had convinced herself by then that Charlotte's family would have rejected her because of how her birth came about, and everyone at Ainsleigh believed it too. Annie would have been the child of a regrettable mistake, a disgrace they would have buried and probably put her somewhere with people who didn't love her as Lucy did. Lucy had no trouble justifying what she'd done by taking her. Her love for the child made it seem right to her. In her mind, love was stronger than blood or ancestry. She might not have a royal life, or live in a palace, but little Annie had a mother who loved her deeply. What more could she want or need? Lucy had no regrets. She never let herself think about it now. Annie was her baby. And anything she'd had to do to become her mother seemed right to her. And like Charlotte, she would go to her grave with her secrets.

*   *   *

The service for Princess Charlotte was a private one with only her sisters and parents present. They buried her at Sandringham because she had loved it. The queen was devastated when they brought her home, and Victoria mourned her even more deeply than the others, remembering every unkind word and criticism she had ever uttered, which cut through her now like knives, each time she remembered one of them. She had even accused her of fakery with her asthma, and in the end it had killed her. It was a sad day for all of them when Charlotte came home at last. The king felt it acutely. She had been his most favored child because she was the youngest and had such a light spirit and gentle manner. It was hard to imagine that she would never dance through their palaces again, and her delicate little face wouldn't make them smile.

It was more than a year after her death when they buried her at Sandringham, and seeing her casket lowered into the ground tore at their hearts. She would be forever mourned by the family that loved her. The queen blamed herself for sending her to the country, but how could they have known what terrible fate would befall her there? It still shocked them that the earl and countess had died as well, and their son. It was a tragic story, and a loss none of the Windsors would forget. Her mother visited her grave every day, until they went back to London. Then life went on, with their duties to their war-torn country, but Princess Charlotte would live in their hearts forever. And the joy she spread around her in her short life would burn brightly. And none of them imagined even for an instant that she had a child who was the image of her, living as the daughter of a housemaid in Kent. The child was unknown to them, and lost forever.

Chapter 6

By Annie's second birthday, Lucy felt as though they had lived on the Markham estate forever. They were exemplary employers, and Lucy had worked for them for a year by then. She was diligent in her duties, and Mrs. Finch, the housekeeper, had increased them. Lucy was twenty, and was mature beyond her years, with the added responsibility of being a mother so young, and having no family of her own. Annie was the darling of the other servants, who loved to play with her and spoil her. She had a sunny, loving personality, and they frequently said she looked like a little fairy, dancing around her mother with her big blue eyes and light blond hair. Lucy always said she looked just like her father, to explain why she looked nothing like her. She looked remarkably like Charlotte, and it appeared that she had inherited her diminutive size as well. Lucy was big-boned and solid.

The rest of the house staff was always knitting something for her, or making a bonnet, or carving little pull toys she could drag along behind her. She would clap her hands and chortle with delight whenever they gave her something or hugged her. They loved seeing her when Lucy brought her back from the farm at night after dinner. She let her play in the servants' hall for a few minutes and then took her upstairs, bathed her, and put her to bed. Lucy sang to her as she fell asleep, and would look at her adoringly in her crib during the night. She still seemed like an angel who had dropped from the sky to Lucy, and she thanked heaven every day for the gift of this child. Annie was her passion and the love of her life. She loved her as she would have Henry, if he'd let her. But now, that no longer mattered. He was gone, and she had Annie, for the rest of her life. What she felt for her was better than the love of any man.

She ran into Jonathan Baker from the stables from time to time, when she had reason to leave the house on an errand for Mrs. Finch, or for their employers. Annabelle Markham was spoiled and expected a great deal from her employees, but she was also a fair and generous woman and rewarded them when appropriate. They gave all of their employees handsome gifts at Christmas from the store they owned. She loved her home, her husband, and her children, took no interest in the business, which her husband ran so efficiently, and was so lucrative. It was the most successful store in London. She had a fifth child a year after Lucy had come to work for them, and Lucy saw the baby nurse walking in the gardens with the fancy pram. She let Lucy bring Annie to see the new baby, and commented on how prettily Annie was dressed. Lucy had made the dress herself, copied from children's clothes she saw in magazines.

"She looks like a little princess," Annabelle Markham remarked one day, as Lucy smiled proudly.

"She **is** a princess," Lucy always said firmly, as though she believed it. And Jonathan gave Annie rides on the pony the Markhams had bought for their children. She always squealed with delight when Jonathan set her on a horse of any size and held her. She had no fear of horses or anything else, and she would cry when he took her off. Lucy worried that she'd be horse mad like her mother, which was a luxury she couldn't indulge in and didn't want to. She still thought them dangerous beasts.

Jonathan took them to a nearby lake to go

swimming that summer when he had a day off, and taught Annie to swim like a little fish. She had no fear of water either, and it touched Lucy to see such a big man so gentle with a child as young as Annie. He loved the time he spent with her, and with Lucy, and he said it made him dream of having children of his own.

"Do you ever think of marrying again and having more?" he asked her shyly when they were at the lake.

"No, I never think about it," she said, not wanting to talk about it with him. "Annie keeps me busy, and I've had to bring her up alone."

"You wouldn't have to if you married again." She had just turned twenty-one, and marriage was the farthest thing from her mind, or so she claimed. He was twenty-six, and had just gotten another promotion. It was clear now that when the stable master retired, Jonathan would take over for him. It was no longer just a wish, it was a sure thing. He was the most responsible man Lucy had ever known, and in many ways he reminded her of her father, who had been a good husband and father and a good man. But she didn't want any man interfering with her relationship with Annie. She had assiduously avoided any involvements or entanglements with men. She had years ahead of her to bring up Annie, and Jonathan said he didn't want to think of settling down until he was the stable master, and then he would have a cottage with his job. There would be plenty of time to think about marriage then, but not before that.

In spite of their determination not to marry, and caution about getting too involved in a romance, Lucy and Jonathan's attraction to each other evolved slowly into a deep mutual respect, and a long, slow romance that became harder and harder to deny. When Annie was four and he had at long last become the stable master and earned one of the better cottages, he proposed. Lucy was twenty-two and he was twenty-seven, and he told her it was time. He wanted to marry and have children with her, which worried Lucy more than she wanted to admit.

"I'm not sure I could ever love another child as much as I do Annie," she said when he mentioned children to her. "Everything about her is perfect, and I love her with my whole heart."

"I think all parents feel that way, until they have the second child in their arms, and realize that they can love another baby as much," he said sensibly.

"I'm not sure I could," she said thoughtfully. To make up for the royal life Annie would never have, Lucy had devoted her whole life to her, heart and soul.

"It would be good for Annie to have a brother or

sister. It will be lonely for her growing up as an only child," he said, trying to convince her, but Lucy wasn't sure. He kissed her to seal the deal then, and Lucy felt stirrings she had never felt before, which frightened her too. She wasn't going to let passion run away with her as Charlotte had, and end up with an unwanted pregnancy. And what if she died in childbirth? Who would take care of Annie then?

"I would," he said without hesitating when she shared her fears with him. He was surprised by how frightened she was of going through childbirth again. "You're not going to die," he said gently. "You're a strong girl, Lucy. You've been through it before and survived. Women have babies every day and come through it. I'm sure it's not easy, but it can't be that bad or no one would ever have a second child. Was it very bad when you had Annie?" he asked, and she was touched by the compassion in his eyes. She couldn't tell him that Annie's mother had bled to death, but Charlotte was a tiny woman, and Annie had been a big baby. And the medical care was excellent in Kent. There were several very good midwives in the area, a number of fine doctors, and a hospital, they were close to London, and to reassure her, Jonathan said she could see a specialist there. "And I'd be with you." He knew that her husband had already been dead before Annie's birth, which must have made it hard for her too.

She was young. Now he felt she could endure it, with good medical care and his help. He wanted desperately to marry her and have children of his own, although he loved Annie as though she were.

"How would you feel about her if we had other children? Would you love her as much?" Lucy questioned him, and he didn't hesitate.

"Of course I would. I wouldn't stop loving her, or love her less because we had another child. Will you think about it? We don't have to have a baby right away. But I want to be married to you." He had an excellent job as stable master, and their employers were pleased with them. "It would be wonderful to live together in our cottage. My mother could take care of Annie when you're at work. And any other children we have." His mother still had a cottage on their old farm on the estate. He made it sound very appealing, but Lucy wasn't sure. She had her life in perfect balance and control. She made a good salary and could provide for Annie. Adding a man to it, and possibly other children, sounded complicated to her. But Jonathan was so gentle and convincing, so loving, calm, and reliable that he eventually wore her down, and won her heart.

They were married at the local church just after Annie turned five, and Lucy twenty-three. She felt ready to take on a husband and all that it entailed. They fixed up his cottage together, and he painted a bedroom pink for Annie, who said it was her favorite color. They were married in the presence of their coworkers and employers, and everyone was happy for them. He was such a lovable man, and Lucy was a good woman, even though she was quiet and not as gregarious as he was. The wedding breakfast afterward in the church hall was a lively occasion. They left Annie with his mother, and went to Brighton for the weekend for their honeymoon. Rationing had finally eased up, and life had almost returned to normal, so traveling was possible. Lucy was nervous about their wedding night, because she didn't want Jonathan to realize she was a virgin. She told him it was her time of the month when they got to the room, and he said he didn't mind, and hoped she didn't either. She gritted her teeth and didn't let herself make a sound. The pain was sharp and brief, Jonathan was unaware that she'd lost her virginity to him, and when they made love again in the morning it was easier.

The war had ended four years before. The memories of tragedy had dimmed, and the scars had begun to heal. She no longer had nightmares about her parents dying in the bombing, which she never spoke of but were very real. She'd had them all during the war. She still dreamt of Charlotte sometimes too. Lucy's worst fear was that Charlotte's family would find out what had happened, learn of

Annie's existence, find them, and take her away. She couldn't have survived losing Annie. They had lived with the story Lucy told for four years now, and Lucy had almost come to believe it herself. She knew she could never say anything to Jonathan about it. He would never understand, and he would be shocked. He still knew nothing of the real circumstances of Annie's birth, and Lucy had no intention of telling him. It would be too difficult to explain, and he didn't need to know. He still believed the fantasy of her being married to a man named Henry, and Annie being their child. He could never have imagined that Annie was a royal princess and another woman's child. It was a secret Lucy intended to take to her grave. As Lucy planned it, no one would ever know, not even Annie when she grew up. Lucy was afraid that one day, if Annie found out, she might feel that Lucy had cheated her of a better life. She had done it purely out of love for her, and to some degree out of love for Annie's father, but Annie might not understand it and long for everything she'd missed, grandparents, aunts, cousins, a family, and a royal life.

After their honeymoon, they settled into real life, as a working couple. His mother came to take care of Annie every day, or they dropped her off at her cottage. Jonathan's mother loved having a grandchild.

Lucy had spoken to a local doctor about how to avoid getting pregnant at first. He had recommended condoms or a diaphragm. Jonathan agreed to use condoms for a while, and she tried to avoid conception with the rhythm method, avoiding sex at times. But six months after they married, fate intervened. They enjoyed a particularly energetic night of lovemaking, when Annie stayed with her adopted grandmother, and Lucy discovered afterward that the condom had broken. Her greatest fear was realized a month later when she missed her period and realized she was pregnant. It seemed so unfair to her that with only one slip she had conceived, and she cried when she told him. Jonathan could see how frightened she was, which made no sense to him since she'd been through it before. And all Lucy could think of was Charlotte bleeding to death hours after the birth, and she was terrified it would happen to her, perhaps as retribution for taking a child that wasn't her own. But she had given her a good life, and a wonderful father in Jonathan, which she told herself compensated for what she'd done.

Jonathan had found her locked leather box when she moved into his cottage, and he asked her what it was. He wasn't a nosy person, but it was an imposing looking box and beautifully made. She responded brusquely that it was some old letters, and mementos of her parents, and she put it on a high shelf at the back of a closet and left it there. He forgot about it. She kept the key hidden and no longer wore it around her neck. She thought of destroying the papers and letters in it at times so no one would ever see them, but for some reason never did, and gave no further thought to the contents of the box. There was no question in her mind now, no matter who had given birth to her, Annie was hers. And her other family ties were irrelevant, since Lucy had chosen to keep her away from them, for life. And she had convinced herself that Annie's life was happier the way it was now, with Jonathan and her, and a brother or sister on the way.

Lucy's fears about the pregnancy abated slowly over time, with Jonathan's loving reassurance. He was excited about the new baby, and both of them were surprised by how fast it grew. By the time Lucy was three months pregnant, the baby looked huge. She wondered if something was wrong and compared it to Charlotte's pregnancy with Annie, where nothing had showed for several months. But Charlotte was so tiny, she had concealed it easily. By the time Lucy was five months pregnant, she looked as though she was about to give birth. She was a big woman, and the baby was too. Annie was excited at the prospect of having a brother or sister. It was due at the end of the summer, which seemed a lifetime away to Lucy, carrying a heavy load. A month later, when she saw her doctor for her six-month checkup, he looked concerned and sent her for an X-ray, which explained the way she looked. She was having twins. Jonathan was beside himself with joy at the prospect of having two babies, and Lucy had nightmares about it, and was even more terrified of the birth. She couldn't imagine surviving it, in spite of all her husband's reassurance, and his mother was going to help take care of them. Mrs. Markham was understanding about it, and they gave them double supplies for a layette, and she told her to take as much maternity leave as she needed. Lucy was a valued employee, and head housemaid by then.

Annie was even more excited about twins, and wanted to help name them and take care of them. She was hoping for twin girls, while her parents liked the idea of one of each. Jonathan told her that it was fine with him if it was boys since they already had the best little girl in the world. He let her help him get the nursery ready, and paint the crib a friend had given them.

Lucy continued to work but was miserable all through the summer. They had a series of heat waves that made it even worse, and she lay in their cottage at night, feeling like a beached whale, but she wanted to work for as long as she could. She tried to do things with Annie too, but she was exhausted all the time, so Jonathan took Annie out on special outings. When Lucy wasn't working, the three of them went to the movies. Annie loved being with them. And Jonathan took her to the stables with him whenever he could, which was always a thrill for Annie, and what she loved best, even more than movies.

Jonathan had a busy summer at the stables. John Markham had bought six new Arabians that Jonathan was training for him. Annie would sit and watch him for hours. Annie was six, and said she wanted to train horses like him one day. He had been giving her riding lessons for the past year, and he told her mother she had a gift. She had a remarkable way with horses, and was utterly fearless. Lucy knew where it came from, both her parents, and made no comment. But she went out to the ring one day in the barn, and was struck by how graceful and elegant Annie looked on horseback. She was a natural like her mother. Jonathan had her jumping obstacles by the end of the summer, and with Lucy's permission, put her in a local horse show, where she won a blue ribbon. He went riding with her whenever he had the chance. She was an extraordinary rider, even at the age of six. She always said she wanted to be a horse trainer like him when she grew up.

"That's not a job for a girl," he said gently. "You should be a mother and a wife, or a teacher or a nurse." She made a face when he said it and he laughed.

"Nurses hurt people and give them shots. And I don't want to be a teacher. I hate school," she said staunchly. Nothing ever swayed her from wanting to work with horses when she grew up.

"I hope you don't hate school. It's very important," he said as he put her through her paces, which she accomplished with ease. She had real skill going over the jumps he set for her. Nothing frightened her as long as she was on horseback, and she wanted to ride the bigger horses, which he said she wasn't ready for yet, and she was so small. She looked like a four-year-old in the saddle, which made her ability even more startling. She had the hands of an adult while handling the reins, and an unfailing eye for the jumps. She never missed one, and rarely knocked one down.

"Someone in your family must have been an expert rider," he said to Lucy one day after Annie's lesson. "It's not possible to ride the way she does at her age. She has an uncanny knack for anything to do with horses. Are you sure no one in your family rode? A grandparent maybe?"

"Positive," she said and changed the subject, but it struck her too that Annie looked more like

Charlotte every day. The Windsor genes were strong. If possible, she was even smaller and more ethereal looking than her mother. People always guessed she was younger than she was, until they spoke to her. She was very bright, and Jonathan gave up trying to keep her out of the stables.

Annie headed for the barn like a homing pigeon, and was never happier than when she was on a horse. Riding with her, when he had time, was a pleasure. She kept up with him, galloping across the fields and jumping streams. Her horse was smaller than his, but she had no trouble matching his speed, and got the best out of every horse she rode. She had an uncanny communication with them, and seemed to sense their every thought and anticipate every move. He loved riding with her, and her lessons were a pleasure for him. He was very proud of her, as though she was his own.

It was a long hot summer for Lucy, the babies were due in September, and in the last week of August, she could hardly move anymore, and their employer sent her home to rest. She would have continued to the end, but even the doctor had told her to slow down. There was a chance the twins would come early. She'd had no problem with the pregnancy so far, but the delivery was likely to be more difficult with twins. Once she stopped work, she hardly got out of bed, and Jonathan was cooking their meals at night, with Annie's help. He made bangers and mash, and shepherd's pie, stew, and all the things he liked to eat and his mother had taught him to cook. Annie loved assisting him in the kitchen, and everywhere else. She was his shadow in the barn, and he would turn around and find her beside him as he checked on the horses, or called the vet for a horse that had been injured or seemed sick, and when he couldn't find her, she was either currying a horse, taking one a treat, or in their stall.

The nursery was ready. They had a tiny third bedroom in their cottage that was barely bigger than a closet. It was going to be the twins' room. Jonathan didn't want to take away Annie's bedroom that she had had since they moved in, and he had painted pink for her. He treated her as their firstborn, with all the honor and respect that went with it.

Lucy was at his mother's cottage the night she went into labor. It started off with a bang when her water broke, and by the time they got to the hospital, she was unable to speak through the pains. The doctor examined her when they arrived, and spoke to them as Lucy clutched her husband's hand and tried not to scream.

"If this was a single baby, I'd have said it was going to be very fast. But it never is with twins. We can give you something for the pain, Lucy, but we need your help. I can't give you much. We can put you out when it's over, but we're going to need your cooperation, so you'll need to be awake and alert, especially for the second twin. We don't want too much time between the two deliveries. How long did your last labor take?" he asked, and Lucy looked stunned for a minute and didn't know what to say.

"I can't remember," she said vaguely, and the doctor looked surprised.

"It can't have been too bad then." He smiled at her. "Most women remember every minute of it. It won't be long now for the first one. I can feel the baby's head." He examined her again, and that time she screamed, and the doctor asked Jonathan if he wanted to leave the room and he shook his head and didn't move.

"I've helped a lot of mares give birth," he said calmly, and although he said it was unusual, the doctor let him stay. He was worried at how severely Lucy was reacting, and thought she'd need all the support she could get. Jonathan was quiet and calm, and didn't seem inclined to panic. He sat next to Lucy, while she cried, until they took her to the delivery room, and Jonathan stayed near her head. The doctor was right. Lucy sounded like she was dying, but the doctor had the first twin in her arms after half an hour of strenuous pushing. It was a boy. Then the contractions stopped for a few minutes, before they started again with a vengeance, and Lucy begged them both to do something to stop it. They put an oxygen mask on her while she pushed. The second twin took an hour and was much more difficult. He was bigger and gave a powerful cry when he was born. Jonathan held him for a few minutes, while the doctor tended to Lucy, and then he cut the cord. They gave her a shot for the pain the moment both babies were out, and she was groggy as she looked at Jonathan and seemed dazed. But everything had gone well. The first twin had weighed nine pounds, and the second twin weighed just over ten. She had been carrying nineteen pounds of baby, and felt as though she had given birth to twin elephants. They were strapping, healthy baby boys, no matter what they had cost their mother.

"I'm not going to die like Charlotte, am I?" she asked Jonathan with glazed eyes.

"You're not going to die, my love. I'm so proud of you. We have two big beautiful boys. Who's Charlotte?" he asked her then, and she shook her head and cried, as the doctor put another mask over her face and gave her a whiff of chloroform to put her out.

"She'll sleep for a while now," he said softly to Jonathan. "She did very well. Twins aren't easy. And you have two great big boys there. I'm surprised she went full term." They were fraternal twins, not identical, but they looked very similar to their father. "You can go to the nursery now if you like. We're going to clean her up, and take her to a room. The nurse will call you when she's awake." Jonathan thanked him, and followed his sons to the nursery. It was the happiest day of his life, and he couldn't wait to show the twins to their big sister.

He took turns holding them in the nursery, and he was sitting at Lucy's bedside when she woke up. She looked as though she had been through an ordeal, and she had. He kissed her as soon as she was awake.

"I thought I was going to die," she said in a hoarse voice.

"I wouldn't have let you. We all need you too much." He had never thought there was a risk of that, and the doctor seemed calm throughout. "Who's Charlotte?" he asked her again, now that she was awake.

"Why?" She looked panicked at the mention of her name.

"You asked if you were going to die like her."

"She's a woman I used to know, who died a few hours after she gave birth."

"That's not going to happen to you," he said firmly, as a nurse came in and asked her if she was going to nurse her babies. Lucy said she was, although it seemed daunting with twins, but she wanted to try. Now that she had survived it, she wanted to enjoy her baby boys to the fullest. She had been terrified for nine months.

"Did you nurse last time?" the nurse asked her, since she was listed as a second-time mother on her chart.

"No, I didn't," Lucy said, and seemed awkward about it. "But I want to this time." The nurse told her how to do it with twins. It sounded complicated and she was going to need all the help she could get when she went home. But her mother-in-law had promised to be there, and Jonathan would help her at night.

She spent five days in the hospital, and the babies were nursing well by the time she went home. Annie couldn't wait to meet them. They let her hold them, sitting down, one at a time. Jonathan was a natural father, and managed to make Annie still feel special too. He even cooked her favorite dinner of shepherd's pie, and ice cream. Overnight they had become a family, with a mother, father, and three children. Their cottage felt as though it was bursting at the seams, and Jonathan enjoyed it thoroughly. Lucy was overwhelmed, but Annie did little chores for her, and her mother-in-law was a huge help. Three children were a lot for Lucy to cope with, and it was even harder than she expected. In comparison, Annie had been so easy. Twins were a lot to deal with. One was always hungry and crying, and sometimes both of them.

A month after their birth, Lucy was relieved to go back to work. All of her colleagues had come to see the twins while she was at home, and Mrs. Markham had sent them lovely gifts, in duplicate, with little matching outfits. But it was nice getting out of the house and going back to her job. She stopped nursing when she did, and she went home at lunchtime to help her mother-in-law give the twins their bottles. After the terror of the last nine months, thinking she would die like Charlotte, she hadn't, and Lucy felt complete with the family she and Jonathan had. She was emphatic about not wanting more children. Annie remained special to both of them, and the twins were like whirling dervishes going in opposite directions as soon as they could walk, which one of them did at nine months, the other at ten. Annie was the perfect big sister, patient, loving, responsible. She told her parents she would teach her brothers to ride one day, and she admitted to her grandmother that as much as she loved her baby brothers, she still liked horses better.

"She certainly doesn't take after you," Jonathan's mother commented to her daughter-in-law, laughing. Blake, one of the twins, was the image of Lucy and looked just like her, and Rupert was identical to his father. And Annie looked nothing like any of them. She was fine-featured, tiny, and seemed to float when she walked. She had a regal air and grace even at six. And looking at Lucy's large frame, and plain facial features, at times it was hard to imagine she was Annie's mother. They looked and acted nothing alike.

"The fairies must have left you on your mom's doorstep," her grandmother teased her. Annie loved that idea, and Lucy didn't comment when she heard her say it.

Chapter 7

When Blake and Rupert were eighteen months old, they were running everywhere, and it took Lucy, Jonathan, Annie, and their grandmother to control them. They knocked things down, pushed over lamps, climbed up on tables. They got into mischief everywhere, and the only time Lucy and Jonathan had peace was when the boys were asleep at night in the crib they shared. They slept in one crib, and cried when they didn't, so whichever of them woke first invariably woke the other, and then the fun began.

Jonathan and Lucy had no time for long, lazy mornings, or romantic nights. The twins were like a tornado that hit the cottage every day, as soon as they got up. Jonathan thoroughly enjoyed them, and Lucy loved them too, although Jonathan had more patience with them. They wore Lucy out and she told Jonathan that the twins and Annie were enough for her. He would have liked one more, but she said he'd need another wife to pursue that plan, and he graciously conceded, and settled for three children. In his opinion, Annie and the twins were the best things that had ever happened to him. He was a happy man. He loved his wife, his family, and his job. He loved working on the estate where he'd grown up, even with new owners. He had never hungered for distant shores or great adventures. He had exactly the life he wanted and was content.

Three months after the twins turned two, he gave Lucy a Christmas present that she said was the best one she'd ever had. He bought her a television, one of the big fancy floor models with the widest screen they made. It came in a piece of furniture, and was the pride of their living room, even though the images were black and white. They hadn't invented color TV yet, but he promised to get Lucy one whenever they came out with it.

Lucy had favorite programs she turned on every night when she came home from work. Jonathan watched sports matches on the weekends, and there were even suitable shows for Annie early in the evening. She was eight years old. Whenever there was a horse show on TV, she ran to see it. It really was the best gift he'd given the entire family. The boys were still too young for it, but soon they'd be able to watch it too. The gift was particularly meaningful that year because King Frederick had died in February, and his oldest daughter, Alexandra, had become queen. Her coronation had been postponed for sixteen months, for assorted political reasons the public wasn't privy to, and her coronation had been set for June of the coming year. For the first time in history, it was going to be televised, so millions of people could watch it in their homes around the world. Lucy was going to be one of them. She had been saying for months that she was going to take the day off from work to watch it, wherever she had to go to find a television, and now, thanks to her generous husband, she had her own.

It had always amused Jonathan that Lucy was obsessed with royalty, and in particular the British monarchy. She subscribed to **The Queen** magazine, and any publication that wrote about the royals. She read every news report about them. The coronation of Queen Alexandra was going to be the high point of her obsession with the monarchy. Jonathan's well-timed Christmas gift would allow Lucy to watch Queen Alexandra's coronation at home in June.

The new queen was a young woman, the youngest to ascend the throne since Queen Victoria
had become queen at eighteen in the nineteenth
century. Queen Alexandra was twenty-nine years
old when she became queen, had been married for
five years, and was expecting her third child when
her father died. She gave birth to her third son the
week after her father's funeral. So the succession was
now assured with an "heir and two spares" as the
British liked to say. Queen Alexandra's three sons
were in line for the throne after her, with her oldest
son first in line. Fourth in line to the throne was
Queen Alexandra's younger sister Victoria, a year
younger than the new monarch, and unmarried.
She had always been somewhat wild in her romantic choices, and had the personality to go with her
flaming red hair. Alexandra and Victoria had had a
younger sister who had died tragically at seventeen
during the war, in 1944. She'd died of complications from pneumonia. Queen Alexandra's mother,
Anne, was now the Queen Mother since the death
of her husband, King Frederick.

Jonathan had always been ignorant about the
royals, and somewhat indifferent to them, until
Lucy filled him in on all the details. She seemed
to know everything about them and read up on
them constantly. Queen Alexandra had a German
husband who was prince consort, His Royal

Highness Prince Edward, just as her great-great-grandmother Queen Victoria had had in her husband, Prince Albert. Although allegedly very much in love with their husbands, neither queen had ever requested the government to make her husband king, and both men had remained with the more limited status of prince consort. But as both were German-born, it was unlikely that the cabinet would have approved of their being made king. So both queens reigned alone. Queen Alexandra's coronation in June promised to be a dazzling affair, complete with the legendary historic golden coach in which she would travel to the ceremony, while wearing an ermine robe over her coronation gown, and her heavily jeweled crown was said to weigh forty pounds.

Monarchs from all over Europe and dignitaries from every country would be in Westminster Abbey, by highly coveted invitation, to see her crowned. And now Lucy could see every last detail of the ceremony too, sitting on her couch in her own home.

Jonathan had often teased her about her fascination with the monarchy, and now he had made her dreams come true. Her new television was her proudest possession.

Annie didn't share her mother's obsession with the royals, and at eight years of age, she was still much more interested in horses than Royal Highnesses. She would turn nine in a few weeks before the coronation and Lucy correctly suspected that her daughter wouldn't bother watching it, although she was slightly intrigued by the horses that would be part of the ceremony, and those that would be drawing the golden coach. Other than the horses, Annie had no interest in it.

In June, the coronation, which Lucy watched on TV for several hours, from beginning to end, lived up to all her expectations. It was the high point of her passion for all things royal.

It was not lost on Lucy, although no one else in the world knew it, that Annie was now fifth in line to the throne, though it was unlikely the succession would ever get that far down the list. The young woman who had just been crowned Queen of England was Annie's aunt, and the late Charlotte's oldest sister. The young queen's three sons were Annie's cousins, and the Queen Mother, Anne, was her grandmother. They were Annie's family by blood and birth, although she didn't know it, and they had no knowledge of her existence. But it was a thrill for Lucy to know it, as she watched them on her television screen. The child she considered her daughter, and always would, was part of the royal family because of her mother, the late Royal Highness Princess Charlotte, who had died hours after giving birth to Annie. And the only person who knew was Lucy herself. The proof of it was still locked in the leather box that had belonged to Charlotte, and Lucy had taken from her room before she left Yorkshire with Annie when she was a year old. All the pomp and ceremony in Westminster Abbey, the golden coach, the fabulous horses and gowns and glittering crowns were all part of Annie's heritage. She was a Royal Highness too, just as her mother had been. Lucy never allowed herself to think that she had deprived her of it. She had given her love instead. The thought that the royal family might have loved her too, although they knew nothing of her existence, never occurred to her. She had never regretted her decision, or doubted her judgment, even once.

Annie headed for the stables to find her father while her mother was still watching the coronation on television.

"What's your mom up to?" he asked Annie when she climbed under the fence. She was still noticeably small for her age, having just turned nine, and looked more like a six-year-old, but she rode like a man, her father liked to say. Her riding skill was as much part of her birthright as the ceremony in Westminster Abbey, but no one except Lucy knew that either. Lucy had kept her dark secrets for nine years now, ever since she had left Yorkshire and Ainsleigh Hall with Annie as a baby, and had pretended that she was her own, and had erased all trace of Annie's existence so the royal family would never find her.

"She's watching that thing on TV," Annie said with a roll of the eyes. "The coach was pretty cool though. And the horses are gorgeous."

"I think your mom is more interested in the crowns and gowns." They both laughed, but Jonathan was happy for Lucy that she was enjoying it, and was sure she would talk about it for days. Televising the coronation had been a stroke of brilliance and had brought it into the common man's living room. Women like Lucy could have a front row seat, on the couch, with a cup of tea.

By the time Annie was twelve, she had won ribbons at every horse show Jonathan entered her in. She was much more interested in speed than in the precise maneuvers of dressage or jumping competitions.

And at thirteen, she and her father had several serious arguments, and he had banned her from the stables for a week, after she snuck out with John Markham's wildest new stallion, not even fully broken yet, and rode him hell for leather across the fields. Her father noticed the horse was missing a short time after she'd taken him, and he'd gone looking for her. What he'd seen was heart-stopping. He was sure she'd broken some kind of speed record, but she could easily have broken her neck or lamed a horse who over his lifetime might prove to be worth millions. He had brought her back looking chastened and mollified. She begged every day to be allowed to come back to the stables, and he had stuck to the week restriction to teach her a lesson. To his knowledge, she never did it again, but he wasn't entirely sure. Annie was smart as a whip, and in love with horses, the faster the better.

At fifteen, to complicate matters further, she saw a horse race on television. Instead of aspiring to be a horse trainer or a stable hand, she announced that she wanted to be a jockey when she grew up. The televised horse race had convinced her. She was the right size, but the wrong gender, her stepfather informed her. Women were not allowed to be jockeys. Horseracing was a man's sport, and he told her it was much too dangerous. It was 1959, and the idea of women jockeys was unheard of. Jonathan told her that females were allowed to compete in some amateur events, but in his opinion they would never be allowed to race in professional ones.

"I want you to grow up to be a lady," her father

told her, "not an amateur jockey at sleazy, second-rate events. I love what I do, but you have to aspire to more than just being master of the stables, a job no one is ever going to give a woman anyway. Your mother wants more for you too." Lucy had been a housemaid, and more recently housekeeper for the Markhams, but she had greater ambitions for the daughter she always referred to as her "princess." Oddly enough, Annie looked like one when she wasn't riding at full speed. She had a natural grace and elegance and a strangely aristocratic look to her in spite of her small size.

"All I want to do is what you do, Papa. Train horses and work with you, unless I can be a jockey one day."

"You can't," he repeated. And Lucy wanted her to be more than a mere housekeeper. A teacher, a nurse, any respectable profession for a woman, and eventually a wife and mother. Annie told her that her aspirations were pathetic. And the only thing that interested her was anything involving horses. Nothing had changed.

At eighteen the battle raged on, when Jonathan insisted she go away to school and further her education. She'd attended the village school. She'd never been interested in her studies, only in horses. But she lost the battle and went away to university to please him and her mother. Her grades were

less than stellar and Jonathan eventually discovered that she had lied about her age and ridden
in several minor amateur horse races as a jockey.
He went to visit her at school to discuss it with
her, and all she wanted was to drop out and come
home to work with him in the Markhams' stables.
She'd been hanging around the local stables and the
only friends she'd made were there, which her parents considered unsuitable. She had no interest in
pursuing school.

Despite mediocre grades, she managed to gradu-
ate in three years under duress, and in the end,
came home to work as an apprentice stable master
and trainer. John Markham commented frequently
to Jonathan about how talented she was.

"It doesn't matter what we do, I can't keep her
away from horses," Jonathan told his boss, sounding discouraged. Markham laughed at him. He had
his own problems with six spoiled wild children by
then, and an expensive wife.

"Maybe you should stop trying to keep her away
from horses," John Markham said with a wry smile.
"Give her her head and see what she does with it."

"She wants to be a female jockey, which isn't
even legal. She'll break her neck and my heart one
of these days." He worried about her. In contrast,
the twins, who were fifteen by then, had showed
very little interest in horses. They took after their

mother. Blake wanted to be a banker and Rupert wanted to go to vet school, which was at least closer to his father's interests. Jonathan hadn't been able to get Annie interested in veterinary school either. All she wanted was speed, although she admitted that one day she might be interested in horse breeding, though not yet. She followed the bloodlines of several stables, including the queen's, which was her only interest in the royal family, unlike her mother, who was obsessed with everything about them, from what they wore to the kind of tea they drank.

"Kids do what they want to in the end. So do wives," John Markham said before he drove off to London in his new Ferrari. He was as obsessed with speed as Annie, but it was more appropriate for him than for a twenty-one-year-old girl.

But a month later, they had other things on their minds. Lucy suddenly fell ill with severe stomach problems, and lost a shocking amount of weight. She lost fifteen pounds in a month, and Jonathan took her for tests at the local hospital, and then to see a specialist in London, at the Markhams' suggestion. They were worried about her too.

The tests were inconclusive at first, and the diagnosis vague. She lost another ten pounds, and looked like a shadow of her former self when the doctors finally told them she had stomach cancer.

It had metastasized to her liver and her lymph system, and the prognosis was not good. Jonathan was in shock when they told them. They suggested exploratory surgery, but as soon as they opened her up, they closed her up again. The cancer had spread too far and too quickly. There was nothing they could do. It didn't seem possible. She was thirty-nine years old, and the twins were only fifteen. What would they do without their mother, and Jonathan without his wife?

They administered a round of chemotherapy followed by radiation to slow things down. And after the treatment, she seemed better for a while, and they gave her morphine for the pain. Jonathan wanted to cling to her to keep her with him. He had loved her for twenty years and couldn't imagine his life without her. He was desperately in love with her. She was such a good person, and a decent woman, and her illness and suffering were so unfair. She still went to work, directed the Markhams' housecleaning staff, and supervised household repairs. She could only manage a half-day now, and some days she couldn't go to work at all. They had nurses come to the house when she needed them, and the nights were hard when she was in a lot of pain. Jonathan gave Annie more responsibility in the stables so he could spend more time at home with his wife, and nurse her himself. At other times, Annie stayed home with her so Jonathan could work. She sat with her mother for hours, watching TV with her, and prepared meals she thought she'd like. She didn't want to lose her mother either and was afraid she would. She took care of her brothers, did the family laundry, and tried to do as much as she could. To thank her, Lucy took a small box out of a drawer one afternoon and put a gold bracelet on her wrist, with a gold heart dangling from it. Annie remembered her mother wearing it many years ago.

"I want you to have it," Lucy said in a tired voice, and Annie smiled.

"I love it." She kissed her mother and went to check on her brothers.

The Markhams were very understanding, and heartbroken for them. Everyone on the estate was aware of how sick she was. Whenever Lucy was at home, she sat staring at the TV. She had her favorite shows, and particularly one about the royals. She watched it one night and Jonathan could see that she was in pain. He was tempted to have a drink himself to calm his nerves, but he wanted to be alert for her, in case she needed him in the night. She had trouble sleeping, and he often stayed awake all night to keep a watchful eye on her, and give her morphine when she needed it.

She seemed agitated when he put her to bed. She

was having trouble breathing, and he was terrified that the cancer was spreading, and he could see that she had lost more weight.

"I have to talk to you," she said in a whisper, as she looked intently at him. She seemed worked up about something, and he was afraid that she wouldn't sleep. She was often anxious now, as the illness progressed at a rapid rate.

"We'll talk tomorrow. You need to rest," he said gently.

"No, I don't. It's important. We need to talk." He could see that arguing with her would only make things worse. He couldn't imagine what was so important that it couldn't wait till morning, and he wanted to give her a morphine pill for the pain. "Listen to me," she said sharply and then closed her eyes for an instant.

"I'm listening to you." He didn't want her to get upset, but he could sense that she already was. There was an urgency to everything now, as though she were fighting for more time. But he was afraid it was a fight she couldn't win. "What is it, love?" he said gently, fighting back tears. She looked so ill.

"It's about Annie. I've never told anyone, but now I think maybe I should have." He suspected that she was about to tell him that she had never been married to Annie's father during the war, and wasn't a proper war widow, which was something he had wondered about anyway. So many women who had had babies during the war had never been married to their children's fathers. And afterward, they just claimed to be widows. There were so many that no one ever questioned it. It didn't matter now, and never had to him. He loved her whether she'd been married to Annie's father or not.

"It's not important," he said kindly.

"Yes, it is." She stopped talking for a long time, a full five minutes, and then whispered to him. "She's not mine." He hadn't been prepared for that, and suspected that she was confused. The doctors had warned them the cancer might spread to her brain. He wondered now if it had.

"Of course she is," he said gently.

"No, she isn't. I didn't give birth to her. Her mother died a few hours after she had her." He wondered if it was true or some kind of delusion she was having. "Her name was Charlotte. She was staying at Ainsleigh Hall at the same time I was. I didn't find out who she was until after she died," she said, and he recognized the name from what she'd said the night the twins were born, and for an instant he wondered if it was true. "She was royal," Lucy said with eyes like daggers staring into his. She seemed very intense and anxious to tell him. "Annie is royal too. Charlotte was the youngest sister of the new queen." He vaguely remembered that one of the young princesses had died during the war, but he was convinced now that Lucy was hallucinating and confusing it with one of her TV shows. "Charlotte's parents sent her to the Hemmingses, to get away from the air raids, the way mine did, and she fell in love with their son. She got pregnant, and they never told the king and queen. I read the queen's letters to her after she died. The queen didn't know about the baby, she never mentioned her existence. I think the countess was probably going to tell them later face-to-face, but with the war still on, she never got to it. I think they didn't want to tell the queen in a letter. The Hemmings boy was Annie's father, they were both seventeen. He turned eighteen and left for the army, and was killed before Annie was born. I thought they'd never married and she was illegitimate, so they hid the whole story. But after Charlotte and the countess died, I read all the letters from her mother and from Henry. I found their marriage certificate. So they were married in secret. But by then, everyone had died, Annie's parents and the earl and countess, an old cousin had inherited the estate and was selling it. And the Windsors, Charlotte's family, didn't know about her, I thought they wouldn't have wanted her, because she was born of a disgrace. And I loved her. I thought the Windsors would have sent her away. I was nineteen, and I took all the letters and documents, so they wouldn't find out about her when they came for Charlotte's things. I said the baby was mine and I was a war widow. She was only a year old when we left Yorkshire, and I came here. She's mine now, Jon, as if I gave birth to her. But sometimes I wonder if I should have told her. She's a Royal Highness, a princess, the queen's niece. I'm not sorry I took her. She's had a good life with us, and you're a wonderful father. But she's not really ours, she never was. Her mother was as horse mad as she is." Lucy smiled and closed her eyes to catch her breath. "The Windsors never knew that she existed, that Charlotte had a baby, or that she married the Hemmings boy in secret once she was pregnant. So I took Annie and raised her as my own. They still don't know that she exists. The Queen Mother is her grandmother, and was Charlotte's mother. The death certificate says she died of complications from pneumonia, but she didn't. She died after childbirth. Jonathan, Annie is a royal princess, and they know nothing about her. I think now that maybe what I did was wrong. I loved her, and I didn't want to lose her. When they all died, I just took her. I talked to the housekeeper and the maids about it. They didn't know she was royal or legitimate, but I did when I left. It's all in the leather box with the crown on it. I want you to read it, and tell me what I should do. You have a right to know too. I don't want to lose her, but she has the right to a life we can never give her. Read it. Read it all. The key to the box is in an envelope in my underwear drawer." She was clearly out of her mind, and Jonathan spoke to her firmly, as he would have to a child.

"You need to rest. I want you to take a pill."

"The leather box," she said again, her voice fading. "You have to read the letters. I should have told you years ago. The box is in my closet, on the shelf."

"It doesn't matter now," he insisted. "Annie is your daughter. Our daughter. I love her too."

"They must have been heartbroken when they lost Charlotte. I read all the letters from her mother to her for the entire year. The queen loved her, and they don't know she had a daughter. Maybe they deserve to know and so does Annie." She was getting increasingly wound up, and Jonathan couldn't distract her. "Promise me you'll read what's in the box." She fixed her eyes on him almost fiercely and he nodded. Her eyes were sunken deep in their sockets with dark circles under them.

"I promise." It killed him to see his wife in this condition, and now she was losing her mind either from the pain or from her illness. She suddenly looked like an old woman, and nothing she had told him made sense. He loved Annie too, and she was a wonderful girl, but she wasn't royal. If she was, they would have known about her. Their daughter would have told them about her, or the countess would have. He was sure that she couldn't have gotten married and had a child without her family knowing, particularly the royals. It just wasn't possible. The royal family didn't go around losing princesses. He knew his wife. Lucy would never have stolen someone else's child, even at nineteen. She was the best mother he'd ever seen to Annie, whoever her father had been, and to their sons, who were devastated over their mother's illness too.

He gave Lucy some of the drops for pain then, since she refused to take the morphine, and a few minutes later, her eyes closed and she drifted off to sleep.

He went to sit in the living room for a while to gather his thoughts. It broke his heart to see how mentally disordered she had become. She had never been irrational before, and now suddenly she was caught up in some kind of obsessive fantasy about Annie being royal, and the circumstances of an allegedly royal princess's death, who probably wasn't a princess at all, and just some young girl from London staying in the country to avoid the air raids, as Lucy had done. Nothing she had

shared with him made any sense. He wondered if
the box she was talking about was empty. He had
seen it once, years before, when Lucy first moved
in, and never since. To put his mind at ease, he
went to look for the box, and found it where Lucy
had said it would be. Then he looked for the key
in the envelope in her underwear drawer, and
found that too. He brought it back to the living
room, took the key out of the envelope, and fitted
it into the lock. He noticed the gold crown on the
leather, as the key turned easily, and he lifted the
lid and glanced inside. The box was crammed full
of packets of letters tied with ribbon, and there was
a sheaf of documents. He saw a birth certificate, a
marriage certificate, a death certificate, and some
photographs. For an instant, he stared at it, not
wanting to read through the letters, but at least this
much was true.

He picked up one packet of letters and untied
the ribbon to get a sense of what they were, and
immediately saw the Windsor crown, the queen's
initials, and her elegant hand, dating the letter,
with the words "Buckingham Palace" under it, and
he frowned. Maybe there was a kernel of truth to
something Lucy had said, and the rest was hal-
lucination from her illness. He wondered again if
the cancer had gone to her brain. He read the first

letter, saw that it was to someone named Charlotte, obviously her daughter, and the letter was signed "Mama." And as he set it down in the box again, his heart was beating faster. Without meaning to, or wanting to, he had opened Pandora's box, and he was afraid of what he would discover next.

Chapter 8

Jonathan went in to check on Lucy several times while he read through the contents of the box. It was late and everyone in the house was asleep. It was a quiet time for him. Lucy was sleeping soundly from the drops, and made an occasional noise. He would watch her for a minute, gently touch her or stroke her hair, and then he went back to the living room to continue reading.

He had read all of the queen's letters to her daughter, and, like Lucy, he had no doubt that they'd been written by the queen.

He remembered now the royal family sending their youngest daughter to the country during the war, to set an example to others and get her away from the air raids in London. And her tragic death at seventeen a year later, of an illness, he thought. It was also remarkable that the princess and Lucy had ended up in the same place. War was the great equalizer. There was also no mention of a baby, a pregnancy, a marriage, or even a romance, so whatever had gone on in Yorkshire, Charlotte's parents had apparently been unaware of it. Perhaps, as Lucy said, they were going to tell her all of it when they saw each other again, when Charlotte returned to London. But she seemed not to have shared any major news in the meantime. She also couldn't tell her mother anything shocking on the phone, since phone lines were not secure during the war, and the palace switchboard would have been equally unreliable, with others listening in on conversations and talking about it afterward. For government business and military intelligence, they had used scramblers and codes, but Charlotte wouldn't have had any of that available to her. Her news would have been that of a seventeen-year-old girl. In this case, one who had gotten pregnant, and then secretly married. News that would not have been easy to share with her parents at a distance, particularly as a royal princess.

Jonathan read Henry's letters to Charlotte after that, which referred to both the baby before it was born, and their marriage in haste and secrecy before he left. They were obviously deeply in love with each other, and had gotten themselves into a very awkward spot.

The official documents in the box told their own tale. Their marriage certificate by special license, signed by the countess and earl, which Charlotte's parents knew nothing about, under the name she must have been using to guard the secret of her identity for a variety of reasons. But it seemed reasonable to believe that Charlotte Elizabeth White was in fact Charlotte Elizabeth Windsor. It was also reasonable to believe that they might not have been too upset about the Hemmings boy in other circumstances, but a marriage at seventeen due to an unwanted pregnancy was enough to upset any parent, royal or not. They sent her away for a year, for her safety, to respectable people, and she got both pregnant and married in that order. It would have been a lot for them to swallow.

He could see why neither Charlotte nor the countess had told them, and were probably waiting for the right time to do so, but that time had come and gone, with the death of the baby's father in wartime, the deaths of both the earl and later the countess, and Charlotte's own death after the baby was born. The entire situation had gotten out of hand, which left an infant whom they knew nothing about an orphan of the royal family. The circumstances had been perfect for Lucy to simply sweep the baby up, tuck her under her wing, and take off with her, with no one more mature to reason with her and stop her. Her ill-judged though well-meant action at the time had resulted in a royal princess who had been deprived of her family and her birthright, and a royal family who had been deprived of their late daughter's child. Knowing that Princess Charlotte had left a daughter behind when she died might have offered them some comfort in their grief at the time. It wasn't too late to set things right, but it was going to be awkward now. Their suddenly coming forward with a lost princess was going to be highly suspect and not easy to pull off without causing a major uproar, or Lucy even being accused of a crime, child theft or something worse, on her deathbed. And there was no one left to corroborate the story.

Jonathan suspected that Lucy no longer knew where the Hemmingses' servants were, since the property had been sold, or even if they were still alive since more than twenty years had passed. Also, who knew if the doctor who had delivered Annie was still alive, or the vicar who had married them? Twenty-one years was a long time, and Henry Hemmings and his family were all dead. The entire mess was not going to be easy to unravel, but Jonathan was convinced it had to be, for the Windsors' sake, and also for Annie's. She had a right to know who she was, and what had happened, and that Lucy loved her, but was in fact not her mother. Jonathan had no idea how Annie would react to the news, not to mention the Windsors' reaction. And he wanted to clear Lucy's name and protect her. What she had done was very wrong, but also naïve, and she had been suffering from the loss of her own family, and clinging to the infant for love and comfort, however misguided.

It was a most unusual story. Lucy was not delusional, she was trying to repair the mistakes of the past at the eleventh hour. They were not small mistakes. Whether she meant to or not, Lucy had stolen Annie from the Windsors for more than two decades, her entire life so far, and had deprived Annie of the life she had been born to and had a right to, with her royal family, in a palace, not the life of the child of a housemaid and a stable master in Kent. The biggest question of all was how to get the information to the queen now, without causing a scandal, and catching the attention of the press, and then leaving the royal family to handle it as they wished. Jonathan didn't want Lucy to be punished for an enormous error of judgment she had committed at nineteen. And what would Annie think of Lucy once she knew, and found out that the mother she loved in fact wasn't? She had lived with a lie all her life, and was someone else entirely than she thought she was.

One thing was certain in Jonathan's mind. The Windsors would want to see Annie. And the other thing he felt sure of was that Lucy had made a terrible mistake, and taken it too far. He was grateful she had told him, and he lay awake thinking about it all night. He was sitting next to her on their bed, when she woke up the next morning. In spite of the drops that had made her sleep, she remembered immediately what she had asked him to do, and she searched his eyes as soon as she woke up.

"Did you read it all?"

He nodded, with a serious look. "I did. That's quite a story. You got in over your head through a series of unusual circumstances, and some bad decisions on your part, made from the heart."

"I don't regret it, I love her. But now I wonder if she'll hate me for keeping her from the life she was born to. We should tell her, but I don't want to just yet."

"We both love her, and she won't hate you," he said quietly. "But she has a right to know where she comes from." He was the only father she had ever known, and Lucy the only mother, but in fact she had an entire family of aunts and uncles and cousins, a grandmother who had loved Annie's rightful mother. She was a royal princess, and no matter where she had grown up, that could not be denied. He wasn't sure how Annie would feel about it. She was hard to predict at times, and could be stubborn too. He didn't know if she'd be angry or only shocked, and it was shocking, even to him. It was hard to believe that his wife could do such a thing, and had gotten away with it, but she had. For almost twenty-one years.

They were still talking about it when Annie came in with a breakfast tray for both of them, and her stepfather stared at her as though seeing her for the first time. Suddenly her natural grace and elegance made sense, as did her skill as a rider, even her passion for horses, which the royal family was famous for. She was heavily influenced by her bloodline. He was looking at her intently, thinking of what they would all have to face when the truth surfaced, and Annie stared back at him, confused.

"What? Do I seem weird or something? You're looking at me as if I have two heads."

"Not that I'm aware of." He smiled. She left the room then and he glanced at his wife. "Do you want to tell her?" But Lucy shook her head. She knew she had to, or thought she should, but she was exhausted and didn't feel up to it. Jonathan didn't want to press her, but he didn't know how much time they had, and he thought

Annie should hear it from Lucy first, so she could understand why she had done it. Only Lucy could truly explain what had motivated her to do such a thing.

"Don't tell her now. I will," she said weakly, and he nodded and went to take a shower and dress for work. When he came back, she was asleep. He told Annie he was leaving, so she could check on her mother. And when he returned to see her at noon, she was weaker, and that night she felt too ill and was in too much pain to think or speak. The next morning she was worse. Annie came and sat beside her, while her mother slept. Lucy seemed to be sliding downhill quickly. Jonathan sat with her all the next day and didn't go to work, and by that afternoon, Lucy was in a coma. The doctor had come several times and left a nurse. And Annie was in her room crying all afternoon. There was nothing she could do and the boys were at their grandmother's. Jonathan had sent them there.

He lay next to her holding her hand, as the nurse checked her and Annie came and went. That night, the boys came home, and Annie sat with them, and as Jonathan lay beside his wife, she silently slipped away without ever regaining consciousness. They never got to say goodbye. And she never got to tell Annie the story that was essential now.

The pain of the loss was shocking, and more brutal than he could have imagined. He went through the motions of making the arrangements while trying to console his children, who had lost their mother. Annie was devastated, and the boys couldn't stop crying. Jonathan held himself together for their sakes, and two days later, as they left for the funeral in the church where he and Lucy had been married, he thought about the contents of the box Lucy had revealed to him before she died. He was grateful she had told him about it, but now it was up to him to try to reach out to the Queen Mother, and tell her what had happened to her daughter and granddaughter. And after that, he would have to tell Annie. But he wanted to know the royal family's reaction first. And this was not the right time to tell Annie. She was shattered by her mother's death. She needed time to catch her breath, before another shock. He had loved Lucy unconditionally, but she had left him the hardest job of all at the end. How was he going to explain it to Annie, and the Windsors? He had no idea where to start.

He thought about it all through the funeral, and for days afterward. He missed Lucy like the air he breathed. She was his lover, wife, best friend, and companion of twenty years. Now he had to find a way to return a lost princess to the Windsors, without breaking Annie's heart or dishonoring Lucy's memory. It was the hardest task he'd ever faced. Without Lucy now, he had to keep his family together, while tearing them apart.

Chapter 9

The weeks after Lucy's funeral were like a fog which enveloped Jonathan and the children. He felt as though he was swimming underwater and everything around him felt surreal. He kept telling himself he had to put one foot after the other, go through the motions of his daily life, and be there for his children. But nothing made sense without Lucy. He felt now as though he was in a free fall through the sky with nothing to stop him, no parachute.

Annie was no better. She barely spoke, except to talk to her twin brothers. They argued with each other constantly, which was their fifteen-year-old way of coping with the loss of their mother. They took it out on each other. Annie took care of them as best she could. Jonathan's mother came to cook for all of them. Their nightly meals were deadly silent. No one talked and they hardly ate. Jonathan was inconsolable and Annie looked shattered, although she pulled herself together for the twins.

All Annie felt able to do was exercise the horses. It was usually the stable hands' job, but she was grateful to have something to do that she could cope with. Sometimes she walked them slowly through the fields and let them graze when they wanted, and sometimes she rode them at full speed. Jonathan saw her do it, but for once he didn't say anything about it to her. He knew she needed the release.

It was weeks before he was able to focus again on what he had read in the leather box two days before Lucy died. He knew he had to do something about it. If he didn't, Lucy's secret, and the secret of Annie's very existence, would die one day with him. He couldn't let that happen, for Annie's sake, and the Windsors'. Not knowing what else to do, he tried the simplest way first. He got the number from information for Buckingham Palace, which was ridiculously easy, like calling the White House in Washington. Getting the number wasn't difficult. It was what happened after that that mattered.

He asked for the queen's private secretary, and got the runaround from start to finish. The names they gave him were for inconsequential underlings who put a smokescreen around the queen's secretary. His attempt to get through to the Queen Mother was equally fruitless. And after nearly an hour of waiting for half a dozen people, he got nowhere, and finally hung up. He should have known better, but it was worth a try. He realized now that he had to be more ingenious and find another way to gain access to the queen, or her personal secretary. He needed to be put in touch with her, on a deeply personal matter, like the fate of the sister she had lost more than twenty years before, and the niece she was entirely unaware of.

After thinking about it for several days, he decided to try channels he was more familiar with. He couldn't just march up to the gates of Buckingham Palace and demand to see the queen, or even send her a letter which might never reach her, and end up in a file of crackpot mail she'd never see. Instead, he asked John Markham if he was acquainted with the queen's horse trainer, and his employer looked instantly worried.

"Are you looking for a job?" He was seriously concerned. Jonathan was the one employee he didn't want to lose. Jonathan shook his head.

"No, not at all. It sounds crazy, but I'm trying to get access to either the queen or the Queen Mother, about a matter that happened twenty years ago. I spent an hour on the phone yesterday, trying to get through to her secretary. I thought I might have better luck through her horse trainer. At least it's a world I understand. Do you know him personally?" Jonathan asked, and Markham seemed relieved.

"I've met her royal racing manager a few times. He's an important man. He's responsible for all her racehorses. He's a little grand and my name probably won't get you far, but you can give it a try."

"I thought I'd tell him we're interested in their stud services, to get my foot in the door. I don't really want to talk to him, I need the name of the queen's private secretary. It's a personal matter." John Markham gave Jonathan the number, and later that afternoon, Jonathan called, and reached a secretary who wanted to know what it was about. "I run John Markham's stables. We're interested in stud services for several of our mares, and John asked me to discuss some possibilities with him." The secretary sounded more interested, and a moment later, he put him through to Lord Hatton directly. It went a lot more smoothly than his futile call to the palace previously.

He spent a few minutes mentioning the mares they allegedly wanted services for, and the stallions that might be available. Lord Hatton was interested, and talked for some time about the virtues of the various stallions they were using for stud at the moment. At the end of the conversation, Jonathan casually mentioned that John Markham had asked him to get the name and direct line of the queen's private secretary, about an event he wanted to invite her to on his yacht. Hatton took the bait and gave Jonathan the name and number he had been unable to discover before when he called the palace. It had all been so simple in the world he was accustomed to, in the language he spoke well. Jonathan was respected in horse circles, and his employer was well liked. He thanked Lord Hatton for the information, and said he would get back to him about the studs they preferred, after he discussed it with John Markham.

He took a deep breath when he hung up, and dialed the palace after that. He got straight through to the queen's personal secretary this time, Sir Malcolm Harding, who answered the phone himself on his direct line. Lord Hatton had given him the secretary's private line, and for an instant Jonathan was a little shocked. He tried to stay calm, and not get flustered or he'd sound like a freak.

"I'd like to request a private audience with the queen, at her convenience. My wife died recently, and entrusted me with some documents which I believe belong to Her Majesty, or the Queen Mother, and date back to the war. They're of a personal nature, and I would like to return them personally. They relate to the queen's late sister, Charlotte. She and my wife were personal friends, and my wife held on to the documents out of sentiment for a very long time." There was a pause at the other end of the line, while the queen's secretary digested what Jonathan had said to him. He didn't want to turn him away, nor did he want to give him instant access to the queen.

"Would it be possible to entrust the documents to me and allow me to have a look at them? If the queen feels an audience is warranted, I'll be happy to arrange it. We don't want to waste your time." More to the point, they didn't want him to waste theirs. "You could send them to me by post if you like."

"I'd rather not. I'd rather put them in your hands. Lord Hatton gave me your name and number, and I'd be happy to give them to you to have a look at. There's a personal side of the story as well, I'm afraid. I won't take up much of her time, but I believe it's a matter that would be of great interest to Her Majesty." Jonathan wondered how many people said that to him every day. Dozens probably, but in this case it involved a long lost relative who had been stolen from them. He couldn't say that to him, but he intended to write up a brief summary of what had happened, what had remained hidden for such a long time and what remained. He had no idea what their reaction would be after so long, or if they would suspect him of trying to blackmail or extort the royal family. They might refuse any further contact with him entirely, but at least he had to try, for Annie's sake and theirs.

"Could you bring the documents to me tomorrow, sir? Say at two o'clock? I promise to put them in the right hands." The mention of the queen's horse trainer's name had greased things along, as Jonathan hoped it would.

"I'd be delighted to." The secretary told him which entrance to come to, who to ask for, and the inside line for his office, and they agreed to meet at two the next day. As soon as Jonathan hung up, he sat down to write a brief summary of the facts, to simplify things. It was almost painful to write the details.

He mentioned the romance between Princess Charlotte and Henry Hemmings, before he left for the army, and the unexpected result that the princess had gotten pregnant, but didn't have the opportunity from Yorkshire to share the information with her mother. He then gave the date of their marriage by special license, and the subsequent date of the young man's death. He said that she had given birth to a baby girl, and had died three hours after delivering her. He listed the dates of both the earl's and the countess's death, which left no one to care for the infant, once orphaned, and no one knowing what to do with a child who was in fact legitimate but whose existence was entirely unknown to Their Majesties, Charlotte's parents. And for better or worse, a young girl who had been staying with the Hemmingses to escape the bombing raids in London had cared for the child herself, and had then taken the infant to live with her as her own. Jonathan did not deny that poor decisions had been made by the young person involved, whom he had subsequently married. He had said that the information had only fallen into his hands two days before his wife's death, several weeks before. And the most important piece of information of all of it was that Princess Charlotte's child was alive and well, living with his family in Kent. She currently had no knowledge of the circumstances of her birth, or her connection to the royal family, of which she was in fact a member, as the niece of the current queen, and the granddaughter of the Queen Mother.

Jonathan said his only interest was to reunite Anne Louise with her family. He would be happy to bring her to meet them, if they were so inclined. It was confusing at best, but the story was familiar to him now, and he tried to make it as simple as he could. He made copies of everything that was in the box, made a package of all of it, put it in a large envelope, and sealed it, with the information on how to reach him, should they wish to. He respectfully thanked Their Majesties for reading the material he sent, hoping that they would. It occurred to him that he could get arrested for interference or blackmail, or if they thought he was trying to extort money from them, or had sequestered the girl against her will for over twenty years, or worse, was trying to pawn off an imposter on them. There was risk involved in trying to be the go-between, and set things right, after Lucy had let it lie in the shadows for so long. He made no attempt to excuse his wife's behavior, and said she had died with deep remorse for keeping Her Highness Princess Anne Louise away from them for so long.

He took the train to London the next day and asked Annie to cover for him. He said he'd be back that night.

"Where are you going?" she asked, curious.

"To London, to see the queen," he said, sounding as though he was teasing her, but he wasn't. "Just like the nursery rhyme says."

"Very funny," she said.

He caught the train on time, and arrived promptly for the appointment with Sir Malcolm Harding, shook hands with him, and handed him the package.

"These are all copies. I have the originals, but I don't want them to get lost. I'll be happy to turn them over to you, if it's of interest to the queen, or the Queen Mother." The secretary thanked him politely and set the bundle on his desk, and a moment later, Jonathan was back on the street, looking up at the palace where Annie's mother had grown up.

He took the train back to Kent and arrived in time for dinner. He was very quiet, and Annie noticed that he had worn a suit to go to town, and he seemed very formally dressed for a simple errand, but Jonathan volunteered nothing about how he had spent the afternoon. He wasn't ready to tell her yet.

The phone rang in his office in the stables, at nine o'clock the next morning. Jonathan was startled to hear from Sir Malcolm so soon. He went straight to the point.

"The queen would like to meet with you tomorrow, at eleven in the morning, and she would like you to bring the girl." They weren't dignifying her with her title yet, and weren't sure if she was for real. Jonathan hesitated for only a fraction of an instant, thinking that he would have to tell Annie the whole story sooner than he was ready to, but now there was no choice. He had until eleven A.M. the next day to do it.

"Of course," Jonathan responded about bringing Annie with him. He wondered if he was going to be arrested when he got there, and wind up in jail. Anything was possible, but he was too far down the road to back out now, and he didn't want to. He had a bumpy stretch of road ahead of him, when he told Annie about her history, and tried to explain why Lucy had taken her in the first place, and never contacted the Windsors until now.

He waited until he saw Annie return from exercising one of the horses, and then asked her to have lunch with him as she walked the horse back to his stall.

"Something wrong?"

"Not at all. I just have something I want to discuss with you," like the fact that you're a royal princess and part of the royal family, just a little thing like that.

He made two sandwiches, put them on plates, and set them down on a picnic table near the barn, where they could talk.

"Something's up," she said, looking suspicious after they had both sat down. "Is it something to do with Mom?" she asked.

"Yes, and no. It's actually old news, but your mom only told me about it two days before she died. I think you should know about it too."

"She left each of us a million pounds," she teased him, and he laughed.

"That would have been nice. Actually, it's more complicated than that." He wasn't sure how to broach the subject with her, so he just plunged in and told her the story and the circumstances surrounding her birth. It got complicated here and there, but Annie followed, and at the end of his recital, she sat and stared at him, as though she'd seen a snake.

"Stop. Let me see if I got this right. Mom was not my real mother, she didn't give birth to me, and the woman who did died a few hours after I was born. She was a royal princess, and her mother was the queen when I was born. And the woman who is the queen now is my mother's sister, and my grandmother is now the Queen Mother. If any of that is true, it sounds totally crazy to me. And what does that make me, if it is true?" she asked, visibly confused and more than a little overwhelmed.

"It makes you a Royal Highness," he said quietly. And it made Lucy, the woman Annie knew as her mother, an infant thief, a young girl who had stolen a baby and kept it a secret for more than twenty years. But Annie hadn't absorbed that part of the story yet, and she loved the woman she knew as her mother, and the memory of her, no matter what.

And Jonathan hoped she always would. Annie had been suffering terribly from her mother's death.

"Wait a minute," Annie said holding a hand up, as though to stop traffic. It was all coming at her too fast. "You're telling me that I'm a princess, that I'm royal, and related to the queen and the royal family." He nodded and then she stared at him in disbelief. "And how did Mom get away with that for so long?"

"Because no one knew that you existed. Tragically, everyone died, your mother, your father in the war, and both his parents. The only other family you have are the royals. And me, of course." He smiled at her. "And I want you to know that I think what your mother did was wrong. She did it because she loved you, but just taking a child is not the way things should be done. She told me about it two days before she died. I think she would have told you herself if she hadn't been so ill. I'm not judging your mother, but what came clear to me is that you have a right to meet your relatives, and at least know who they are. And your mother felt that way too at the end, which was why she told me the whole story. What you do after that is up to you."

"What if I don't want to be a princess, Papa. I don't think I'd like it. And what if they hate me on sight? Or don't believe you?"

"They might not. But why would they hate you? You're the daughter of their beloved sister and daughter. They owe it to her to be civil to her child, and welcome you after you've been lost to them for so long. They never knew that you were born."

"I wasn't lost. I was with you and Mama, where I belong. I don't want to be a princess, Papa," she said, sounding like a little girl.

"You don't have that choice. That's who you are, and who you were born. We don't get to pick and choose our families, although being related to the Royal House of Windsor is a pretty cool thing to be."

"When am I going to meet them?" She looked afraid.

"Tomorrow at eleven A.M., at Buckingham Palace."

"Oh my God," she said and immediately looked panicked. "I don't think I want to be a princess, Papa. It sounds hard. I think I'll renounce my title. Can I do that?"

"Technically, yes. In real life, I wouldn't. Why not enjoy it and try it out for a while? And get to know your Windsor relatives first. You might all love each other, and somehow I think it would make Lucy happy."

They threw away their paper plates from lunch then, and Annie left him to walk slowly back to

the house. She needed time to think about everything her father had said. She was a royal princess,
and had been stolen at birth by the woman she
knew and loved as her mother. It sounded like a
fairytale, and Annie didn't know what to believe.

Jonathan saw her walk into the barn later that
afternoon and saddle up one of the horses. She took
a horse he had discouraged her from riding before.
He was a stallion who was barely broken, skittish
and hard to manage, although she had never had
any trouble with him. He saw her leave, heading
toward one of the trails at a slow trot, and then
he saw her take off across the hills at a blistering
gallop, riding as hard as she could. He stood watching her for a minute, hoping no harm would come
to her, as she flew across the meadow at breakneck
speed, and for once, knowing what she was wres-
tling with and had to face the next day, he didn't
blame her a bit, or try to stop her. She was riding
like the wind.

Chapter 10

Annie was almost silent on the brief hour's train ride from Kent to London. She sat staring out the window, thinking of the only mother she had ever known, trying to understand who she had been at nineteen, to take a baby she believed no one wanted, and claim it as her own for twenty years. Annie couldn't fathom why Lucy had never told her the truth. She had done it out of love for Annie, and in time, the lie had become too big to admit. She had in fact been a wonderful mother, and perhaps she had been right and saved her from an orphanage, if the royal family had rejected her as an infant. She would never know now what they would have done.

Annie could even less understand her place in

the family she had inherited overnight. She was suddenly a royal princess with all the burdens, responsibilities, expectations, and confusion that entailed. She had no idea what was expected of her, if they would accept her, or accuse Jonathan of having concocted a lie, and Annie of being an imposter. What if the royal family didn't believe them? Annie still couldn't believe it herself.

And what had her "real" mother been like? Princess Charlotte, who died at seventeen, hours after Annie was born. She didn't know what to think, or believe, or who she was now. It was all so confusing, and she wondered if they would treat her like a fraud at the palace. Why would they believe a history as complicated as hers? She was twenty-one years old, and it was a lot to absorb. Whatever would happen at Buckingham Palace, both of her mothers were dead now. She felt like the motherless orphan she was as she stared out the window, and then turned to Jonathan with an unhappy expression.

"I want to go to Australia," she said in a dead voice.

"Now? Why? What brought that on?" It was an odd idea to him.

"Female jockeys can ride in amateur races there. I want to see what it's like and sign up."

"How about an apprenticeship at the queen's

stables here instead? She has some fabulous race-horses and the best stables in the country. You could do worse." They might be open to that idea, if they believed her story at all.

"I'd rather go to Australia," she said, trying not to think of the meeting they were going to. She had worn her only appropriate dress to meet the queen, who was supposedly her aunt. It was the black dress she had worn to her mother's funeral, and Jonathan recognized it immediately. It suited Annie's somber mood, as they headed for their fateful appointment in London. He was nervous too, but tried not to show it. He wanted to give Annie the courage to face whatever came next. His worst fear was that they would be blamed for Lucy's youthful but very grave mistake. However innocent her intentions, she had robbed them of a child. It explained to him some of Lucy's obsession with the royals.

"I can't afford to send you there," Jonathan said apologetically about Australia. "I think you should stick around here for now, until you get things settled."

"What if they think I'm a fraud?"

"They might. But then you'll be no worse off than you were before." He had brought the original documents with him, at their request, and all the letters, and kept handwritten copies and photographs of the documents and letters for himself, and a set made for Annie too. He had brought the leather box with him in a bag too, in case it added to their credibility.

"Do they pay you to be a royal princess?" she asked with a mischievous look and he laughed.

"They give you an allowance. The entire royal family gets an allowance. It would be nice for you." There was an upside to this for her, if Lucy's story was true and they believed her.

"Is that why you did this?" She was worried when she said it.

"No, I did it because they're your family, and you deserve to know them, and they have a right to know about you." It had crossed his mind that if they accepted her, she might not want to live with him anymore. He wasn't her father and he had never adopted her officially. It hadn't seemed necessary, but he might lose her in the process. Even if he did, he knew that what he was doing was correct, for her. She had a right to a life he couldn't give her, and they could. He wanted the best for her. And in her own naïve way, Lucy had too. Jonathan was just grateful that Lucy had told him the truth before she died. Otherwise, they would never have known.

They were both quiet as they got off the train, and he could see that Annie was anxious, and so was he. People probably tried to claim that they were part of the royal family every day. He wasn't sure who would be there, the queen or the Queen Mother, or only the queen's secretary.

They took a cab from the station to Buckingham Palace, to the same entrance he had used two days before, when he had dropped off the copies of the letters and documents.

A security guard checked their ID papers at the desk and called Sir Malcolm and told him they were there. "Miss Walsh and Mr. Baker." She hadn't been accepted as royal yet, and a moment later Sir Malcolm hurried down a hall, and they followed him into an elevator after Jonathan introduced Annie. He saw the secretary staring at her, as Annie gazed at the floor, and then they walked down a long carpeted hallway with portraits of members of the royal family all the way back through several centuries. They stopped at a tall door, where two uniformed palace guards opened the door and announced them, and Jonathan could feel his heart catch as he realized that at the end of the room Queen Alexandra was sitting at her desk. She stood to greet them as Jonathan bowed and Annie curtsied, and she invited them to sit down. An older woman walked into the room, and they both recognized Queen Anne the Queen Mother, for whom Annie realized now she had been named, since she was her grandmother. She was wearing a simple black suit. Jonathan and Annie stood and bowed and curtsied again. The Queen Mother had a photo album with her, and after a few moments of polite superficial conversation, she handed it to Annie.

"Would you like to take a look?" she asked, and Annie nodded, almost too intimidated to speak. "They're photographs of your mother as a little girl and before she went to Yorkshire. You're only a few years older than she was then." Annie's eyes grew wide as she carefully turned the pages. The photographs were old, but it was easy to see that Annie was the image of her. They looked like twins. The Queen Mother had seen it too when she walked into the room, and Queen Alexandra spoke to Jonathan and Annie then. She noticed the leather box that Jonathan was still holding, and she asked to see it. He handed it to her, and she opened it carefully, moved some of the contents aside to look for the initials, and stared at Jonathan with amazement when she found them.

"My father gave me this box on my eighteenth birthday. I gave it to Charlotte for her correspondence when she left for Yorkshire," the Queen Mother said quietly. She looked deeply moved when she said it. "It's a very unusual story," the queen admitted. "But wartime can create some very odd situations. Our phone lines weren't secure then, and Charlotte and our mother communicated entirely by letter during the time she was away. The news of her early marriage, and your impending arrival," she smiled at Annie as she said it, "is not the sort of thing you want to write about to your mother at seventeen. She was meant to stay in Yorkshire for a year, to get away from the air raids in London, and she suffered from severe asthma. But things apparently got out of hand while she was away. It must have been an awkward situation for the countess too. It was a heavy responsibility shepherding young people that age. I don't envy her." She smiled at both of them again. "The tragedy for us was when she died, whatever the cause, whether from pneumonia, or . . . other causes in the circumstances. We knew nothing about you, Anne, until two days ago," she said solemnly, and Annie nodded. "It's been a shock for my mother." The Queen Mother appeared to be fighting back tears when Annie handed the album back to her. "And for my sister, and for me as well. Charlotte died twenty-one years ago, but it seems like yesterday to us. We're going to authenticate the documents your stepfather brought to us. Her Majesty, my mother, recognized the letters, and the leather box with the crown. They're genuine. And once we verify the documents, so there can be no doubt about who you are, and if indeed you are my niece, and Her Majesty's granddaughter, we'd like to introduce you to the rest of the family. But we need to be sure first. I trust that's agreeable to you," she asked, looking at Jonathan, and he immediately agreed.

"I'd like to make one thing clear, Your Majesty," he said to the young queen. "There is nothing I want from this for myself. If in fact everything checks out, your niece should be restored to you. You all lost a great deal and it was a tragedy when Her Highness Princess Charlotte died, and Anne should know who she is and who her relatives are. There is nothing more we want from any of it."

"Is that true for you as well?" she asked Annie directly, and she nodded, in awe of the woman who was allegedly her aunt. She looked every inch a queen in a navy velvet suit with a string of pearls around her neck.

"Yes," Annie confirmed in barely more than a whisper, and then, "My father says you have wonderful horses. I would like to see them one day."

"That can be arranged." The monarch smiled at her. "Do you like horses?" Annie beamed and her father laughed and relaxed a little. The meeting had been very formal so far.

"It's the **only** thing she cares about," he answered for her. "She's been horse mad ever since she could walk. She's a bruising rider, and extraordinarily skilled."

"I want to be a jockey," Annie added bravely, "but women are not allowed."

"Maybe you will be one day. And I'd be happy to arrange a tour of our stables in Newmarket with Lord Hatton, the royal racing manager." She smiled at them both. "We have some rather famous horses there. I'm horse mad myself. And your mother was too. She was just about your size. If the papers are genuine, you both take after my great-great-grandmother Queen Victoria, who was no taller than you are. You're the perfect size for a jockey if they ever change the rules."

"I hope they do," Annie whispered and the queen smiled and stood up, and then something caught her eye.

"You'll be hearing from us as things proceed," the queen said formally, but she was staring at Annie's arm. She was wearing the gold bracelet with the heart that Lucy had given her. "May I look at your bracelet?" she said in a voice softened by emotion as Annie extended her wrist. Queen Alexandra recognized the bracelet immediately as the one she had taken from her own wrist and given Charlotte when she left for Yorkshire. "May I ask where you got that?"

"My mother gave it to me. My mother Lucy," she explained. There were tears in the queen's eyes when she nodded. "I gave it to your mother, my sister Charlotte. It was mine." There was silence for a moment, as the Queen Mother cried silently and Jonathan spoke up.

"Thank you for seeing us, Your Majesty. I know it's a visit we'll never forget," he said with a bow, and Annie curtsied deeply to both Majesties, her grandmother and her aunt.

"If things go well, the first of many visits, I hope," the queen said generously, and her secretary appeared from nowhere, and all three of them backed out of the room, and the two palace guards in livery closed the door, as the queen turned to her mother with a sigh. They had left the leather box, and its contents, with them to authenticate.

"She looks just like Charlotte, doesn't she?" The Queen Mother nodded and wiped the tears from her cheeks. "Don't get too excited, it could all be a trick. People are too clever sometimes. They may have noticed the resemblance and decided to take advantage of it. It could be purely coincidental. I hope that's not the case, but it's possible. It would be lovely to have Charlotte's daughter in our midst. She seems like a very sweet girl." Seeing the bracelet had shaken the queen and gave her hope that Annie and the strange story were real.

"Her stepfather is a simple man, but polite and without pretension. He seems to care about her a great deal. I thought he was sincere," the Queen Mother commented in a serious voice. The meeting had been deeply emotional for her.

"Let's hope they're honest people and it all turns out well."

They had spent half an hour with her, which was longer than the queen normally spent with non-cabinet visitors, but she and her mother had been anxious to see the girl. Princess Victoria was in Paris, so hadn't come, but had wanted to meet her too when the queen told her sister about her. Nothing like this had ever happened to them. Long lost relatives didn't just turn up, or never had before. She was hopeful that they were telling the truth. It was like having a piece of Charlotte back after so many years.

Annie was smiling broadly when they got into a cab and headed for the station, after thanking the queen's secretary for his help. He had been charmed by Annie, who looked more like an elf or a fairy than a girl her age. She was so small and delicate, and looked like the photographs he had seen of Princess Charlotte in the Queen Mother's rooms. He had worked for her before when she was queen.

"They were so nice," Annie said, looking awe-struck, and Jonathan was impressed too. It was the high point of his life so far. They had been to Buckingham Palace to meet the queen.

"Maybe if she's really my aunt, she'd let me ride one of her horses one day," she said with dreams in her eyes.

"Oh Lord," Jonathan said. "She has racehorses worth millions. You'd be a lucky girl if that ever happened. Just seeing them at close range would be a gift."

She smiled at him then. "I'm lucky anyway. I love you, Papa. Thank you for bringing me here." All he could think of as they rode toward the station was again how grateful he was that Lucy had told him about the leather box, and let him see its con-tents, before she died. Whatever she had done, for whatever reason, and no matter how wrong it was, she had redeemed herself. With luck, Annie would be restored to the family where she belonged. Even if he lost her as a result, it was his fondest hope for her. To atone for his wife's sins, out of love for his stepdaughter, was a sacrifice he was willing to make.

Chapter 11

Their visit to the queen and Queen Mother at Buckingham Palace had a fairytale quality to it. Even if nothing came of the authentication of their documents, and whatever investigation they were sure to conduct, it was exciting to have been to see the queen. No one knew that they had been there. Their life in Kent on the Markham estate seemed like drudgery after that. Annie exercised the horses as she always had, and Jonathan was working with the new horses to break. Their life was hard without Lucy, and their evenings sad. Annie missed Lucy terribly, her warm contact and their brief conversations when they saw each other at the end of the day. Annie took over from her grandmother and cooked dinner for her father and the twins every night, and the boys complained about her cooking. But Jonathan and Annie agreed that family meals were important.

The house seemed so dreary without her mother. And it was a rainy spring, which made it worse. They felt as though they hadn't seen the sun in months.

There was no word from Sir Malcolm Harding, the queen's secretary, for nearly two months. Jonathan wondered if that meant the documents had been discredited or rejected, but they heard nothing either way. It was almost as though nothing had happened, and they'd never been to see the queen. Annie began to suspect she wasn't royal after all. It didn't really matter. She was happy as she was, living with her father and brothers. She had more work to do than before, trying to step into her mother's shoes, doing the laundry and the cooking, picking up after them. They tracked mud into the house, grumbled about doing homework. She felt like the mother of two teenage boys since her mother's death. There were days when it all seemed like too much. Too much energy, too much work, too much complaining, too many men in the house who messed everything up as soon as she cleaned it. There was no woman she was close to. She saw only the grooms in the stables, who were her age, and her father and brothers at night.

They went to dinner at a local restaurant in Kent on her birthday, and the day after, Sir Malcolm called to tell them that all of the papers appeared to be authentic.

The handwriting on the Queen Mother's letters had been verified. The letters from Henry Hemmings appeared to be all right. The town hall county record office near Ainsleigh had registered all the documents. Charlotte's cause of death on her death certificate had been a discrepancy, and the doctor who had attended the birth was long dead, but a nurse who had worked for him remembered how distressed he'd been when Charlotte had hemorrhaged shortly after the delivery. She had died after childbirth, but the nurse recalled that the countess had asked the doctor to list the cause of death as pneumonia to spare her parents embarrassment, since neither the pregnancy nor her marriage were known to her parents at the time, so the doctor had agreed. The marriage certificate was genuine. The vicar was still alive and had verified it, and said they were lovely young people and very much in love on the eve of his going to war, and Henry died shortly after, so the vicar was glad that he had married them, and had therefore legitimized Annie's birth. And Her Majesty the queen had instantly recognized the little gold bracelet Annie was wearing, that the queen had given to her sister

Charlotte. Annie could have gotten it from someone else, which all of them thought unlikely. It was credible that she got it from Lucy, who probably found it among Charlotte's things after she died, along with the papers and letters. And the Queen Mother had acknowledged the brown leather box as hers as well.

Everything was in order, so far, and MI5 was doing some further investigation, but Sir Malcolm did not explain it. He promised to stay in touch and call when the investigation was concluded.

Annie wondered after she hung up if Lucy would have felt betrayed by their trying to have Annie recognized as a member of the royal family, or if she would have been pleased. She had gone to such lengths to make Annie her own, that Annie felt guilty about it at times, but Jonathan kept telling her that it was her birthright, and encouraged her to see it through to the end. And Lucy had told him the story herself and wanted to right the wrong she'd done. Nothing had been leaked to the press about it. The royal family was keeping it quiet in case she turned out not to be related to them after all. None of them wanted the embarrassment of discovering that Princess Charlotte wasn't her mother, in which case Annie didn't know who was, maybe Lucy after all. It was hard to guess the truth after silence for so long. And if Annie wasn't Charlotte's daughter, what had happened to the infant born to Charlotte at Ainsleigh Hall, now that they knew the rest?

It was another two months before Sir Malcolm called again. None of the Ainsleigh Hall servants were still alive, but they had spoken to the daughter of one of the maids, a hall boy, and the doctor's nurse again. Blake and Rupert were screaming over a soccer match on TV when Sir Malcolm called. Annie could hardly hear him, and shouted at the boys to turn it down, and stop screaming. They were rooting for opposing teams and driving her insane. They had just turned sixteen, and the cottage seemed too small now for four of them. They were turning into big, brawny men, and they left a mess in their wake everywhere, which Annie constantly cleaned up for them.

"I'm sorry," she apologized, "I couldn't hear you. My brothers were behaving like savages." She glared at them as she said it, and turned off the television. "Could you repeat that?" she said to Sir Malcolm, as her brothers left the room, grumbling.

"Your Royal Highness." It struck her as odd when he said it. "The investigation has been concluded to everyone's satisfaction. Her Royal Highness Princess Charlotte was your mother, and you bear a remarkable resemblance to her." He was smiling as he said it, and much to her own surprise, Annie had tears in her eyes, and sat down suddenly, feeling dizzy. She had wanted this result and didn't even know it. It was now confirmed that she was Her Majesty's niece and the Queen Mother's granddaughter. "Her Majesty is very pleased. We will be releasing a statement in the next few days. You might want to prepare for some media attention. They can be quite intrusive, no matter how discreetly we frame the news. It's liable to cause considerable excitement." Her heart was pounding as he said it. She was a member of the royal family after all. And she had no idea what would come next.

"What are you going to say in the announcement?" She was curious about it.

"Her Majesty's press secretary is handling it. We want to keep it as discreet as possible, so it doesn't raise too many questions of a delicate nature. It will say that you've been living abroad with distant relatives who brought you up, since your parents' tragic deaths during the war, you've completed your education, and you have now returned to England to take your rightful place with the royal family. Her Majesty is immensely pleased at the return of her youngest sister's daughter. It's hard to make much of that, but the press will always try.

"Her Majesty also wanted me to let you know that the cabinet will be deciding on your allowance next month, and she'd like you to come to

Balmoral for a few days this summer, to meet the rest of the family. Her boys are close to your age, and they'll be home from school then. And Her Royal Highness Princess Victoria always spends a week or two there on her way to the South of France, where she spends the month of August. It's a bit chilly in Scotland, but I'm sure you'll enjoy the palace. The Queen Mother and Her Majesty have always loved it. The Queen Mother would like to have you to tea in the coming days. And Her Royal Highness Princess Victoria would like to meet you when she returns from the trip to India she's on now." Annie felt dizzy when she hung up, her head was spinning, and she sat staring into space for a minute. Her father came in from the stables in time for dinner, and saw the look on her face, as though she'd seen a ghost.

"Did something happen? Did the boys break something?" Jonathan asked, looking worried. They'd come back into the room and were screaming at the soccer match and threatening to kill each other again, as she shook her head and stared at her father.

"I've been authenticated," she whispered. "It's all true, Charlotte is my mother. The cabinet is voting on my allowance next month, and the queen wants me to come to Balmoral this summer to meet the others. Oh my God, Papa, I'm for real!" He put his arms around her and hugged her with tears in his eyes.

"You've always been real to me," he said gruffly.

Then her face clouded for a minute. "Do you think Mama would be upset about it? Or pleased? It seems so disloyal after everything she did for me." Suddenly Annie had two mothers, but both were dead.

"She must have wanted this to happen or she wouldn't have told me," he reassured her. "This was meant to be. She had you to herself for twenty years. They're your family. I think she thought it was time to make a clean breast of it, before she left us. I think she would be happy for you. I suppose this means that you don't have to play Cinderella for me and your brothers anymore." He smiled at her. "Will you be moving to one of the palaces?" he asked her innocently. But Sir Malcolm hadn't said anything about it. Only about tea with her grandmother and aunt.

"Of course not. I'm staying here with you. But it would be nice if those two Neanderthals could pick up after themselves occasionally, and stop screaming when they watch a match on TV," Annie said, exasperated.

"Good luck with that, and you don't have to stay here, Annie, if you don't want to."

"Where else would I go? You're my papa, and I

want to live with you." He looked pleased. He hadn't lost her after all. He had been afraid he might, but it hadn't stopped him from pursuing the truth for her. He had done what was right.

She put dinner on the table a few minutes later. The hamburgers were overcooked and she had burned the potatoes, but her hungry brothers ate it all anyway. She sent them upstairs after that, so she and her father could enjoy a peaceful end to the meal. "I'm so happy for you, Annie. And I really think Mama would be too."

"I hope so. I'm not sure I'm ready to be a princess yet. They're going to make an announcement to the press in the next few days."

Neither of them was ready for the onslaught of photographers and TV cameras that assaulted them, invaded the stables, and generally drove everyone nuts for a week following the announcement. They tried to get pictures of Annie doing her chores, with her father and brothers, on horseback. The announcement was as discreet as Sir Malcolm had said it would be, but the press was wildly excited. A lost princess was big news.

It said simply that Her Royal Highness Princess Anne Louise, daughter of Her Royal Highness Princess Charlotte and the son of the late Earl and Countess of Ainsleigh, the late Lord Henry Hemmings, had returned to England after living abroad since her parents' tragic deaths during the war. It referred to the fact that Princess Charlotte had died in Yorkshire at seventeen, that she had married and had a daughter during the year she spent in Yorkshire, and that due to the war and constant bombings, the family had waited to announce it after the war and by then, the young couple were both dead, and their daughter grew up in seclusion, under the supervision of the royal family, until she came of age. And she was now brought home to her aunts, uncle, grandmother, and cousins, and she would be publicly presented soon. In the meantime it said that the queen was extremely pleased to have her niece home in England again. And she was residing at an estate in Kent, which was how the press found her. They checked every large estate until they did. They reported that before that, she had been living with distant relatives on the Continent, and having completed her studies and reached her majority, she had returned to take her place with the royal family, as Her Majesty's niece, as well as the niece of Her Royal Highness Princess Victoria, and the granddaughter of Queen Anne the Queen Mother. It said everything pertinent about who she was related to, and where she'd been for the last twenty-two years without bringing up anything that might prove to be controversial or embarrassing. It was all very clean and direct and established her as a Royal Highness. And it acknowledged her father as having died a hero's death at Anzio at eighteen.

The Markhams saw it in **The Times** the next morning at breakfast and were stunned and recognized who it was instantly. Annabelle Markham dropped by to congratulate Annie on her newly elevated rank, and recognition as a royal princess. It was an extraordinary story that had taken them by surprise.

"Will you be moving to London now?" she asked her. At twenty-two, as the newly recognized niece of the queen, she couldn't imagine Annie wanting to hang around in Kent in their cottage for much longer. She had the world at her feet now, or would soon.

"I'm staying here, as an apprentice to Papa in the stables," Annie said firmly. "Where else would I want to be?"

"Silly girl, dancing your feet off at a disco in Knightsbridge, if you had any sense," Annabelle teased her.

"My father and the boys need me here, or the house will look like the stables." But two days later, she got a call from Lord Hatton at the queen's stables, with an offer that was seriously tempting.

He was inviting her to tour the stables and view Her Majesty's racehorses, and he offered her a summer internship if she was interested. It was an offer that was nearly impossible to resist, and her stepfather insisted she had to take it. He said she'd never get another offer like it, and she was inclined to agree. So she called Lord Hatton back and said she would be delighted to work for him for August and September if he wanted her. July was already almost half over. He said he could use the help, and was sure that she'd enjoy it. Who wouldn't? With the queen's racehorses all around her. She hoped he would let her exercise them.

Her recognition by the royal family had brought nothing but happy changes to her life, in spite of the brief furor in the media, which calmed down within a week after the paparazzi got enough pictures, which Annie hated. She didn't like being a media star. She wrote the queen a note to thank her for the internship at her stables. She was sure that Her Majesty had put in a word for her with Lord Hatton. Lord Hatton reported that the queen was very pleased with Annie's dignified handling of the press.

"This is going to be a seriously fun summer," Annie said, beaming at her stepfather, as she walked into the stables. Balmoral to meet her family, and an internship at the royal stables. The queen wanted to give her time to adjust to the changes in her life, which suited Annie too. She wasn't ready to leave home yet, except to work at the queen's stables instead of the Markhams'. And all the current excitement balanced some of the sadness of Lucy's death.

She took one of their stallions out to exercise him that morning and rode like the wind across the meadows. She was inheriting the life she had been born to. It was almost too wonderful to be true.

Jonathan delivered Annie to the queen's stables in Newmarket himself. It had taken just under two hours from Kent, and they chatted on the way. She was excited by the internship Lord Hatton had offered her. She didn't care if she had to muck out stalls, or curry horses, or simply sponge them down after a run. Just being there was an honor, surrounded by the kind of horses the queen owned.

Newmarket was the center of Thoroughbred horseracing, and the largest racehorse training center in Britain. Five major races took place there every year. Tattersalls racehorse auctions were held frequently, and there were excellent equine hospitals. The queen had five main horse trainers to train her horses in different locations. The famous trainer Boyd-Rochfort was one of them. She kept horses at the Sandringham Estate too, and in Hampshire before they were sent to Newmarket to train. There were more than fifty horse-training stables and two racetracks in Newmarket. A third of the town's jobs involved horseracing. Most of the stables were in the center of the town. The top trainers in England were there.

Lord Hatton was very gracious to Annie and her father when they arrived, and he already knew that Annie was the queen's long lost niece who had recently turned up. Jonathan was the stepfather who had brought her to them, the only father she'd ever known, and was the stable master for the Markhams, who had impressive stables too. Though the queen's horses surpassed them all. While Lord Hatton and her father talked about the stud services for the Markhams' mares again, Annie walked around, and stopped to admire each of the queen's racehorses. She had some of the finest horses in England.

She was halfway through her quiet private tour going from stall to stall, when she noticed a striking-looking young man leaning against a wall and staring at her. He was wearing white jodhpurs, a crisp white shirt, and tall black riding boots. He had jet-black hair, and a surly expression as he watched her. He didn't greet her or approach, and then finally when she reached the last stall, he ambled over. He seemed very pleased with himself.

"How old are you?" he asked when he got to her, without introducing himself or asking her name.

"Why?" she asked him, annoyed by his bad manners, supercilious style, and arrogant attitude.

"Because you don't look tall enough to ride a decent-sized horse. Do you ride ponies?" He was almost laughing at her, and she was furious but didn't show it.

"I'm twenty-two, and I can ride anything you can. I'm going to be a jockey one day," she said, sticking out her chin.

"Oh please, not another feminist. It's my personal belief that women aren't made to be jockeys. They don't have the nerves for it."

"Really? When was the last time you saw a successful male jockey taller than I am by the way? At least we know you'll never be one." He was six feet three or four, and irritatingly good-looking, in a kind of studied way. He looked as though he considered himself God's gift to women, an opinion Annie didn't share.

"I have no desire to be a jockey, and spend my life with a mouth full of mud, my face covered in dirt as I cross the finish line." He looked immaculate in his white jodhpurs, and Annie had taken an instant dislike to him.

"I suppose the white pants work well for you.

Do you play polo?" He looked the type, a spoiled rich boy whose main interest was showing off to women. He looked vaguely familiar but she didn't recognize him, and she didn't think they'd ever met before.

"Yes, I do play polo. I take it you don't?"

"It's not my sport. It's too tame."

"Don't be so sure. Polo can get rough too."

"Mostly at cocktail hour when you talk about it."

"Are you visiting?" he asked her.

"I'm going to be working here for the next two months," she said proudly.

"That should be interesting. I'll be working here too. Maybe we can have some fun, and exercise the horses together, if you think you can handle them."

"What makes you think I'm such a sissy?"

"You're such a little girl. I'd be afraid you'd get hurt."

"Let's have a race sometime. It would be fun to see if I can beat you," she said, smiling at him.

"Trust me, you can't. I've got the biggest horse in this stable. He's the only thing here that has longer legs than I do." She wanted to slap him just listening to him.

"I accept the challenge. Little People against Big People. The difference is I'm not afraid to get mud in my hair or my teeth, as you pointed out earlier."

"You must look charming when you race."

"I'm not interested in how charming I look. All I care about is winning."

"At least you're honest about it. Most women like to pretend they don't want to compete with men." She looked too small to him to be a man-eater, but she sounded like one. Normally she wasn't, but she hated men like him. They put women down constantly, and thought themselves superior. "What's your name by the way?"

"Anne Louise," she said simply, and it didn't ring any bells for him.

"No last name?" he asked, supercilious again, and this time she let him have it.

"Windsor. Your Royal Highness to you." She laughed at him then and walked away, as he blushed purple. Lord Hatton and her father found her then, and the queen's stable master glanced at the tall young man in the white jodhpurs.

"I see you've met my son, Anthony Hatton. I saw you talking to each other. No mischief together please. Tony likes to ride the fastest horses we have here, and your father tells me you're a demon when it comes to speed too. I expect you both to behave and not egg each other on, if you exercise the horses together. This is not a racetrack." He was serious and Annie promised to act responsibly, while his son rolled his eyes and looked amused.

"The horses need real exercise, Father, you can't just trot them around a ring when they're used to racing."

"Let's just be clear about it. If you lame one of our horses, I'll shoot you, and have you hanged for treason." He looked at Annie then, appearing demure as she admired the horses. "I'm shorthanded this month, and Anthony offered to help me out. That usually means he does exactly what he pleases and rides anything he wants. Your father tells me you're a hard worker and I can count on you, Your Royal Highness. I need someone like you around here."

"You can call me Annie while I'm here." She was still getting used to being a Royal Highness, and she didn't think it necessary while she was working for him, although it was her title now, and people were obliged to use it.

"I'm not uncomfortable using your title, ma'am. Her Majesty and I are old friends, since her childhood. My younger brother went to school with her. I knew your mother too," he said gently, and Annie smiled at him. She liked him a great deal better than his son, who had sauntered off without saying goodbye and disappeared.

She had been assigned a room in the luxurious guest quarters behind the stables, and they'd given her one of the best rooms. Her father carried her bags upstairs for her, and she had a large comfortable room, with antique furniture and a desk. But she was dismayed to see from his open door that Anthony Hatton was two doors down from her. He was standing in the middle of the room, and had just added a well-cut blazer to his outfit with the white jodhpurs and still had his boots on for a sporty look. He was obviously going somewhere. He hurried down the stairs and a few minutes later, she saw him drive off in a red Ferrari.

"Handsome guy," her father whispered and winked at her.

"He's a jerk. He acts like he owns the place."

"Actually, his father does." Her father laughed at her. "He's partners with the queen on these stables, and they buy most of the racehorses jointly. He and the queen are close friends. There have been a few rumors about them."

"How would you know that?" She looked amused. Her father almost never repeated gossip.

"Your mother kept me well-informed about the royals. She read everything about them." He missed her now more than ever. She had made a colossal mistake in her youth, absconding with Annie, but other than that, she had been a wonderful wife to him, and a devoted mother to their children, including Annie. "Well, don't get into any mischief," he warned her as he hugged her and kissed her goodbye. Her dinner was going to be brought to her on a tray. They had a chef especially for royal guests and VIPs, and she was both now, and she'd been told the food was delicious. The chef was French, and she was looking forward to it.

"I love you, Papa," she whispered when she kissed him goodbye. He waved and headed down the stairs, and five minutes after he left, her dinner arrived. The first course was caviar and blinis, followed by lobster salad, with profiteroles for dessert. She felt like she was at a dinner party all by herself as she sat in the handsome room, enjoying the meal. She was excited about spending the next two months here. The only fly in the ointment so far was Anthony Hatton, but she was sure that she could beat him any day, no matter what he rode. She was determined to prove it at the earliest opportunity. There was a man who needed to be put in his place, and she would have given her right arm to do it, or whatever it took.

Chapter 12

Annie was up and dressed and in the stable at six the morning after she got there. She wanted some quiet time to familiarize herself with the horses. There were three large horse barns, with state-of-the-art facilities and equipment. One was for breeding, another was for their most illustrious racehorses, and the third was a mixture of the very fine horses they owned, some that had already won several races, others that were ridden but had never raced, and perhaps never would, or might someday but weren't ready yet. Some horses the queen kept there because she enjoyed riding them. She was an avid and talented rider and had been all her life, as was her mother before her, and most of her relatives for generations, even centuries. It was in their blood, both on the German and British sides. The queen knew as much about breeding horses as her business partner Lord Hatton did, and sometimes she knew more, as he readily admitted. He was one of her greatest admirers and closest friends, and valued the companionship they shared.

Annie made her way quietly through the three horse barns, patting a neck or a muzzle here and there when the horses in their stalls stuck their heads out to see her. Sometimes she just stood and admired them. They were each the finest of their breed. In the racing barn, she was in awe, reading the names on each stall. Some of the greatest racehorses in history were in that barn. Just being near them felt like having an electric current race through her. They were not only incredibly valuable, they were horses with spirit and history and the best possible bloodlines, and also heart to win the races they had. It made her eyes water thinking of some of their victories. She was admiring one of them, when she heard a step behind her and turned. It was Lord Hatton, enjoying his universe before the day began. He was impressed to find her there. He could see in her eyes what it meant to her to be there, and was moved by it.

"They're so beautiful," she said, awestruck.

"Indeed. There is some extraordinary horseflesh in these barns. I'm fortunate to have the partner I do." Annie knew he meant the queen. "Her father was one of the finest riders I've ever known. He picked some of the greatest racehorses we've had. You can't learn that kind of judgment. It's a gift. She and I have spent years trying to figure out some of his decisions. I've never known him to make a mistake. I can't say the same for myself." He smiled at her. "It's not just about speed, it's about heart and courage and endurance. You have to believe in them. They know it when you do and they rarely let you down." He pointed to some of the horses she'd been looking at, as examples of what he meant. She felt grateful to be there, and wanted to learn all she could. Most of her feelings about horses were based on pure instinct, not always on what you could see. Jonathan had taught her that too.

"You have to love them. People are like that too," he said wisely, as they walked out of the last barn. "Is there any horse you'd particularly like to ride today?" he asked generously, "except for the queen's. She's particular about that." He smiled tenderly, and Annie could see both respect and affection in his eyes. "She has a keen eye for horseflesh. We've made some interesting choices together. We balance each other. Horses can teach you a great deal about life. Your stepfather tells me you want to be a jockey. Why is that? It's a tough business. Most men think women aren't suited to it. I disagree. I think women will be better at it, once they're allowed to ride professionally. That day will come. It's not far off, if you're serious about it."

"I am," she said, as they stopped at a coffee machine and he filled a mug and handed it to her. "I like the excitement and the speed," she said, taking a sip of the strong brew. "But I like the calculation and the theory along with what you have to know about the horse you're riding. There's so much soul to great racehorses, maybe that's what I love about it. They try so hard and they're so brave. It's not just about winning, it's about how you get there. Everything about it appeals to me. And the combination of rider and horse is so important. I think jockeys lose races, not horses." It was a fine point, something he always said himself. You could put some jockeys on a mule and they'd win a race, and give others the finest racehorses in the world and they'd lose every time.

"You'll be a fine jockey one day if you think that way," he said, getting to know her better. "Horses are a lot less complicated than people," he commented, and she remembered that he had been married three times. "We have a new horse you might like to try. I'd be interested to hear what you think of him." In theory, he was much too big for her, but instinct told him that she could manage almost any mount, her stepfather had said the same, and she liked a challenge. She was an amazing girl, and with her history, something of a dark horse herself. She had come from nowhere, and was suddenly the surprise of the hour. It was all about breeding and courage and bloodlines, and perseverance, and she had them all. The queen had said as much when she recommended her to him, and he trusted her judgment implicitly. And she had turned out to be a fine monarch.

He led Annie to the stall of the horse he was thinking of for her. He was a magnificent stallion, and her eyes lit up as soon as she saw him.

"I'm not sure he'll ever win a race for us, but he's an interesting ride. We've had him for about a month. I don't know him well enough to tell. He doesn't trust us yet. He has a slightly dodgy history, but fabulous bloodlines." She could see it in the way he stood and moved, even in his stall. "You can take him out now if you like." She finished her coffee, put the mug in a sink, and went to get a saddle. She walked into his stall with confidence, and led him out. His name was Flash, and she looked ridiculously small beside him, which didn't occur to her at all. She had him saddled in a few minutes, led him to a mounting block, swung up easily, and let herself into one of the rings, as Lord Hatton watched. She had a light hand on the reins, and her legs were short but powerful. She was guiding him with her knees as much as her hands, and had a fluid grace that blended with the horse. She rode him around the ring to get a sense of him, changed directions several times, and then eased him into a gallop. The horse seemed to be enjoying it as much as she was. He balked at a sound nearby which didn't faze her, and her confidence and poise calmed him, as Lord Hatton watched her, fascinated. She had all the instincts he looked for in a rider, and was unaware of them herself. She had the powerful horse in her full command, and he could tell that the stallion trusted her, which was half the battle.

"He's a beautiful ride," she said admiringly.

"Yes, he is. Inconsistent, though. He's a moody guy. Everything has to line up just right for him. He threw one of our best riders the other day, and we couldn't figure out why." But he was as docile as a lamb with Annie astride him. She took him through his paces again and Lord Hatton left them and went to his office. He liked getting an early start, when everything was calm. Once he left, Annie rode Flash for an hour, and then dismounted and took him back to the barn. Both rider and mount were pleased with the time they'd spent together. After she'd removed his saddle, she put him back in his stall, and went to join the trainers she saw gathering outside the racing barn. They were handing out assignments for the week, and she was assigned to shadow one of the head trainers.

They were busy after that until lunchtime. There were a dozen assistant trainers, each with special skills that were suited to the functions they performed.

She didn't see Anthony again until after lunch. He looked as though he had just gotten up, and had had a rough night. He'd been assigned to exercise one of the horses who had had a pulled tendon for several weeks, and was told to go easy on him. As soon as she saw him riding the horse around a ring, she saw that he had heavy hands. He had no instinct for the horse he was riding, just impeccable training, and an elegant style, but he wasn't at one with the horse. She didn't comment. She walked over to the rail, and he stopped to chat with her for a minute.

"I hear my father let you ride Flash this morning. Scary devil, isn't he?"

"He was a gentleman with me," she said noncommittally.

"Don't count on his being like that again. He tried to kick me when I walked into his stall the other day, and bucked when I rode him."

"A personality clash perhaps," she suggested, smiling at him.

"Would you like to have dinner with me tonight? There's an amusing pub nearby. It's pretty quiet here at night." She didn't mind that, but she could sense easily that he did. She didn't want to be rude, but she would have preferred having dinner in her room.

"That would be nice," she said politely, and she had the feeling that he was as insensitive with women as he was with horses. It was all about getting them to do what he wanted, not figuring out who they were and what they needed.

She went back to the trainer she'd been assigned to then, and he had her exercise two of the horses. Flash was the high point of her day, and Anthony stopped by and told her he'd pick her up at seven.

She changed into slacks and a sweater before they left for dinner, and was surprised when he turned up still in his riding clothes with a rakish look. "You don't mind, do you?" he asked as they got into the Ferrari she'd seen the night before. She had no experience with men like him, and far more with horses. Her romantic life had been nonexistent so far. She'd spent all of her time around stables and with her father, except for the boys she'd gone out with at university, but had never fallen in love with any of them. They just seemed young and foolish to her, and she didn't flirt the way the other girls did, nor did she play games with them. She was simple and direct, and without artifice. She spoke to Anthony like one of the guys at the stables when they got to the pub, and he laughed after she talked about the racehorses she'd seen in the barn.

"Do you ever think of anything except horses?" he asked her after they ordered dinner and a bottle of wine.

"Not often," she admitted with a smile. "I was a disaster in school. I rarely went to class at university. I begged to come home the entire time. All I ever wanted to do was train horses and work with my father. You don't need a degree for that. I thought about vet school for a while, but it takes too many years. I'm basically lazy," she said modestly, and he laughed.

"I doubt that. You're just not an academic. Neither am I. My father studied physics and psychology at Oxford. I don't know how he wound up in a horse barn. He can quote Shakespeare for hours. He says he wanted to be an actor. He's a Renaissance man."

"And what about you? What are you passionate about?" she asked. She had a feeling it wasn't horses, although he had been around them all his life because of his father. But it wasn't a love affair for him. It seemed more like something to do between parties.

"I just invested in a nightclub with a group of

friends. It's a lot of fun. I like people more than horses, and women in particular." He gave her a look that was meant to melt her heart, or her knickers, but it didn't. "I'd like to own a restaurant one day. Or a small hotel, maybe in the South of France. I lived in Paris for a year. It was a fantastic experience. I'd like to live there again one day."

"I've never been," she said innocently. She hadn't been anywhere, although that was about to change in her new life. Until then, she had spent most of her life in Kent on the Markham estate, and Liverpool where she went to college. "I'd like to go to the States one day. It seems so exciting." There was something about her openness to new experiences which touched even him. She was very young, and seemed even younger than her years. There was an Alice in Wonderland quality to her, which was accentuated by her girlish looks and tiny size, and at the same time there was something very old and wise in her eyes.

She was an odd mix of naïveté and experience. She was different from the women he knew. They all seemed so jaded and sophisticated compared to her. He liked the childlike quality about her, much to his own surprise. She had a lot of growing up to do, and a lot of the world to see. "I've been thinking about going to Australia to race there. And I'd like to see the Kentucky Derby one day."

"I went with my father once. We had a horse in the race. He didn't win though. Kentucky is an odd place. We bought a horse there. I like New York better." America was a mystery to her, as was his way of life. He had mentioned that he was thirty years old, and the difference in their ages and life experience was enormous. He had gone to Eton and Cambridge, had traveled extensively, and moved in a fast crowd. They had nothing in common. "So when are we going to race?" he asked her halfway through dinner. "It should probably be sometime when my father's not around. There will be hell to pay if he catches us. He's going to an auction in Scotland next week. Maybe then, if I'm not in London. I'm going to Saint Tropez for a weekend. I have a friend who has a yacht there." He would have asked her to come, she was pretty enough, but it would be like taking his little sister. There was nothing racy about her, and he could sense that she had no interest in the fast life of fashionable beach towns and yachts. All she cared about was horses, and her dream of being a jockey. "And after horses, what?" he asked her. "Marriage and babies?" She seemed like that kind of girl. He had no interest in either one for now.

She looked blank when he asked her. "I never think about it. I just think in terms of horses right now."

"I have a half-sister like you, from my father's second marriage. She breeds horses in Ireland. She and her husband have a big operation there. My father helped them set it up. They have seven kids. Scary thought," he said and she laughed.

"I have twin brothers. They're sixteen, and they drive me crazy. I've been helping my dad with them since my mother died . . . my stepmother," she corrected, in her new life. "Actually, my world is a little confusing right now. I thought she was my mother all my life, and I loved her that way, and now it turns out she wasn't. My real mother died when I was born, but I never knew about her until after this mother died, and it all came out. Now suddenly I'm a Royal Highness, and the queen is my aunt. I haven't sorted it all out yet. I'm going to Balmoral to meet the rest of the family for a weekend at the end of August. I suddenly feel like two people, or one person in two worlds, my old life and my new one. The only constants in my life at the moment are horses and my stepfather. He runs the stables for John Markham. Most people in horse circles know John." She was so honest and open about everything that he didn't know what to say. There was no artifice about her. She was a straightforward person who had been cast into a new life that would have daunted most people. It forced him to be real with her too, which was new to him and unfamiliar. He was used to much more complicated girls who always wanted something from him. She didn't, which was refreshing.

"It must be a little strange to suddenly be a Royal Princess."

"The queen and her mother were very nice to me when I saw them. I haven't met Princess Victoria yet." And the queen had gotten her the highly coveted internship.

"She's more exciting than her sister. She's never married or had children, but she's had some exotic romances, with the Aga Khan, an American senator, a few married men no one talks about, except the tabloids. She was in love with someone who died when she was young. I think she decided to pursue a different life after that. She's very amusing," Anthony volunteered. "I see her in nightclubs a lot. She actually went out with one of my friends a year or two ago. She and her sister are chalk and cheese. She's the racy one. The queen is all about duty and the job. I think the crown is heavier to wear than one thinks. It can't be a lot of fun."

"I wonder what my mother was like in the midst of all that. She died when she was so young."

"So did mine," Anthony said quietly. It was the first serious side of him she'd seen.

"I'm sorry, I didn't know."

"You wouldn't," he said with a forgiving look.

"You haven't been around for all the scandals. She left my father for another man when I was eight. They were killed in a car accident in the South of France shortly after. I went off to boarding school a few months later, and that was the end of family life as I knew it. She was my father's third wife, and he never married again. He's always had women in his life, but no one he's serious about. He's probably closer to the queen than anyone else. She's his best friend. I'm not sure he ever got over my mother. He doesn't talk about it. He's a decent father, though he probably likes his horses better than his children. Very British, you know." It made her realize how lucky she was to have Jonathan in her life. He was warm and loving, and the only father she had ever known, and she would always think of him as her father, even though they weren't related by blood. "I can't really see myself settling down, not for a long time anyway. I have no role model for it. I hardly remember my parents together before she left. They were always out somewhere. He didn't start his horse operation until after she was gone, and that's really his first love now. I don't think he'll ever marry again."

"I'm not sure I will either," Annie said, looking pensive. "My parents had a good marriage and they loved each other, but it seems complicated. I grew up in a tiny cottage with them and my brothers. My mother was the housekeeper on the estate where my father works. Marriage doesn't seem to work out for most people. I'm not sure it's for me. Horses are a lot easier," she said, smiling at him.

"Or wine, women, and song. That works for me," he teased. But underneath the glib exterior, the good looks, and the charm, she had the feeling that he was afraid of getting close to anyone, maybe because his mother left when he was so young, or he was having too much fun now. The kind of life he led was a mystery to her and didn't seem very appealing. But he wasn't as arrogant as she had thought when she met him. There was a soft side to him. Outwardly, he was just the stereotype of the handsome playboy. She couldn't imagine going out with someone like him, or with anyone for now. The hub of her life and her only interest were the stables.

He drove her back to the horse farm after dinner, and they walked into the guesthouse together. He invited her to his room for an after-dinner drink, and she didn't think it was a good idea. She was worldly enough to be cautious about going to men's rooms with a bottle of scotch for easy sex. She was still a virgin, and had no intention of changing that for him.

"I have to be up at five-thirty," she used as her excuse. "I promised to exercise Flash again at six."

"You're the only girl I know who'd rather be with a horse than with me," he said, laughing, and she thanked him for dinner, and went to her room. It had been a nice evening, and for some reason, even with all the trappings, the fancy car, his good looks, and the racy life he seemed to lead, she felt sorry for him. He'd had a lonely childhood and no mother to love him. She'd been better off growing up as the daughter of a housemaid and a stable hand who both adored her. It had been a simple life, but they were real, and she knew how much they loved her. She never doubted it. The life he led seemed empty to her. He was a lost boy in a glittering world that had no appeal at all to her.

In his room, Anthony poured himself a glass of scotch and wondered what would become of her. She was like a child, and a breath of air. A little too much so for him. The women in his world were more exciting, and what they wanted from him was easy to give. What you'd have to give a girl like her was beyond him, and would have terrified him.

Annie was back in the stables at six o'clock the next morning, and had Flash in the main ring ten minutes later. He was more skittish than he had been the day before, but her steady routine and soothing voice calmed him, and by the time she brought him back to his stall at seven, he was peaceful and easy to manage again. She saw Lord Hatton go to his office as she walked Flash back to the barn. She was at the trainers' meeting on time, and got her assignment for the day. She heard a rumor from the other trainers that there were photographers lying in wait for her, and then was told later that Lord Hatton had chased them away. He didn't want Annie harassed by anyone, nor their collective privacy invaded. It was a great relief to Annie.

She'd exercised five of the horses by the end of the afternoon, and passed Anthony in the hall of the guesthouse. He was on his way out, looking very dashing. He obviously had a date or was going to a party.

"My father's going to London tomorrow. Shall we race?" he said enticingly, and she hesitated.

"Will we get in trouble?" she asked him with wide eyes.

"We might," he admitted, "but not if you don't tell him." The challenge was too great for either of them to resist, and they agreed to meet at seven the next morning. She was tempted to ride Flash, but knew he wasn't stable, although she could have run any race with him. She didn't want to win badly enough to damage a horse that wasn't settled yet, and decided to ride a horse she'd exercised that afternoon, that was tried and true and easier to predict.

They settled on the meeting place, and she hoped no one would see them and tell Lord Hatton. It was a risk that seemed worth taking and she was looking forward to it.

She exercised Flash the next morning, and switched horses in time to meet Anthony. The idea of racing him was exhilarating. He was a good rider, but his skill was more mechanical, without passion. He had learned about horses and had been taught well, but didn't "feel" them in his gut the way she did, or love them. She was smiling when she met up with him, in anticipation of what was to come. They left the more populated area sedately, and didn't start the race until they were well out of sight. She gave her horse its head, and coaxed everything out of him he had to give. She wasn't going to let Anthony beat her, and she calculated her horse's strengths well, and won easily. Anthony looked angry when they finished, but got control of himself quickly.

"You're a hell of a rider, Your Royal Highness," he said grudgingly. "Rematch tomorrow?" he pressed her and she laughed. It had been an easy victory for her.

"Where will your father be?" They were like

two naughty children, but she was pleased with beating him, and wanted to do it again. She'd outsmarted him as much as outrun him.

"He won't be back till tomorrow night," Anthony said.

"Then you have a deal. Same time, same place," she said, and they headed back to the barns, with no one any the wiser for what they'd done.

She met him again the next day. She had chosen a different horse this time, one that was faster and more spirited. He danced around a bit on their way to where they had raced the day before. They were both wearing helmets, which would have been a tip-off to anyone who knew either of them that they were up to mischief, but no one had seen them leave the barn and ride off.

She got a good start on him as she had the day before, and they pounded across the meadow, and raced toward the cluster of trees that had been their finish line the day before. They were almost there when her horse shied from something he'd seen. She kept control of him, but he almost stumbled, and with no warning, she came off and flew through the air like a doll and landed hard, as Anthony reined his horse in, and raced to where she lay, suddenly realizing how foolish they had been. She lay lifeless on her back when he got there, and he grabbed her horse's reins on the way, and tethered the two horses to each other as he jumped down and knelt next to her. She was breathing, but looked deathly pale. He took her helmet off and tried to decide what to do, and as he started to panic, she opened her eyes and couldn't speak for a minute. She was badly winded, and when she tried to sit up, he stopped her.

"Stay still for a minute. I was an idiot to suggest this. Can you move?" he asked her. She gently moved her arms and legs and smiled up at him as she caught her breath enough to speak to him.

"It was fun, until I fell. I haven't come off in years."

"I should have known better. I'm older than you are." He took off his jacket and folded it under her head, looking deeply concerned. "Do you think you can sit up?" He could tell that she wasn't paralyzed but had difficulty moving. She'd had a hard fall.

"Should we finish the race?" she asked as she sat up and saw stars for a minute, and then her head cleared. She had a slight headache, but nothing serious, and nothing was broken. She had been lucky. She'd been going at breakneck speed, but the ground had been soft enough to cushion her fall.

"You're insane. Do you think you can ride back, or do you want to ride with me?" he asked as he helped her to her feet. She was as light as a feather.

"I'm fine," she said gamely, but she looked

unsteady to him. He held her arm until she seemed solid on her feet, and he gave her a leg up back into the saddle, and he watched her closely to make sure she wasn't dizzy, and stayed close to her. He knew she had to be feeling badly bruised from the fall, but she was steady in the saddle, and never complained. She was much tougher than she looked.

"You are one hell of a rider, and damn brave. I thought you were dead for a minute," he admitted, still shaken by the sight of her flying through the air like a leaf on the wind.

"So did I," she said and grinned at him.

"You could have broken your neck. I'm not racing you again." She was too daring to be safe.

"You're just afraid I'll beat you. I probably would have if the damn horse hadn't tripped."

"You were not going to beat me this time. I was two lengths ahead of you."

"One, and I was catching up. I hadn't gotten Mercury up to full speed yet."

"Don't be a sore loser," he teased her with a broad grin, grateful that she hadn't been injured. It seemed like a miracle that she wasn't. "You probably came off just to get sympathy. That's women riders for you. And you want to be a jockey? In what, the powder puff races?" He teased her all the way back, but he had unlimited respect for her now. She was the ballsiest girl he'd ever met. "You're a hell of a lot stronger than you look," he complimented her, and even he could recognize that she was a better rider than he was. She was at one with the horse at all times, even if she'd flown off. If the horse hadn't stumbled, she would have won in the end, and he knew it. "Let's ride again sometime," he suggested, "but no racing."

"That's no fun." She looked disappointed and he laughed at her.

"I happen to like you, Your Royal Highness. I don't want to kill you. I think you're the craziest damn rider I've ever seen, and the bravest girl I've ever met. I'd rather not see you dead if you come off again."

"Thank you," she said for the compliments and smiled at him. She'd had a hell of a fall, and knew she'd be hurting by the end of the day. She already was but wouldn't admit it. But she'd won something better than she had the day before when she'd beaten him. They were friends now. And she needed one in her new world. He was different from the men she had known in her previous life. More complicated, more spoiled, and surprisingly more interesting. She liked him better now than she had when they met.

They smiled at each other and walked the horses the rest of the way home, and he saw her wince when he helped her dismount, but she didn't say a word and marched into the barn and unsaddled the horse herself.

"Good exercise session?" one of the trainers asked them as they put the saddles away.

"Not bad," Annie answered and smiled at him, and Anthony watched her as she walked out of the barn. She was a devil on horseback, but he liked that about her. He liked her better than any girl he'd met in years. Maybe she would be a jockey one day. She had the guts for it, and the heart. And she was the best damn rider he'd ever seen. His father had thought so too. He had plans for her, but hadn't told her yet. He wanted to speak to Her Majesty first. And then they would see.

Chapter 13

August flew by as Annie settled into her duties at the queen's stables. She wasn't aware of it, but Lord Hatton observed her whenever possible, and frequently asked for reports from his other trainers. All reports confirmed what he'd glimpsed from the first. She had a rare talent and a gift, a passion for horses, and a sixth sense of them that even her ancestors and new relatives didn't have. And the queen was pleased with what she was told. The new addition, and previously undiscovered princess, was conscientious, hardworking, modest, and well liked by all. She expected no special favors because of who she was, and was tireless in accomplishing the tasks she was assigned.

She seemed to have no special friends among

the people she worked with, but was polite and respectful to all, which was how she had been at the Markhams' too. She kept her distance and was unfailingly dignified and discreet, even more so now. As a royal princess, she felt an even greater obligation to be responsible and private at all times. She felt she owed the queen her good behavior. Her only friend at the queen's stables was Anthony, and she called Jonathan to say hello several times a week. And from what Lord Hatton had heard, she never went out at night, except once or twice with his son. She appeared not to have a wild side, unlike some of her new relatives, and Lord Hatton knew it wouldn't go far with Anthony, who was a rake of the first order, occasionally to his father's chagrin. At thirty he had already been involved in several scandals, and had a penchant for married women who were as outrageous as he was when it suited them. He liked showy women and had little respect for the rules governing polite society, whereas in contrast Princess Anne Louise was fearless with horses, but demure and somewhat shy in the world. She proceeded with caution and a careful step, and was respectful of her new role, however unfamiliar to her.

Annie took criticism well, which no one would have said of Anthony Hatton. If nothing else, his father thought Annie would be good for him, even as a friend, just as his own friendship with the dignified Queen Alexandra had tempered him. They were good contrasts and counterpoints to each other.

The queen was pleased with everything she'd heard, both from her old friend, and others who encountered the princess. It was difficult to believe that she'd grown up as simply as she had, brought up by people who were essentially servants, but her stepfather was known to be of high moral character. The royal family thought less of his late wife after what she'd done. And it amazed everyone in the family that Princess Anne Louise had gone undiscovered for so long.

She was excited and nervous about her upcoming weekend at Balmoral Castle in Scotland, to meet the rest of the family. The queen had purposely moved slowly to include her to give Annie time to adjust to her new life, and not overwhelm her, and she had convinced the Queen Mother to be patient too. And it made sense to her as well. This wasn't Charlotte returning from the dead. To Annie, everything and everyone around her was brand new.

Balmoral was said to be the most relaxed of the queen's homes, where she enjoyed a proper vacation every summer, with family picnics and barbecues, and fishing for all, which was why she had chosen it for Annie's family debut. Annie spoke to Jonathan about it, and was anxious about what it would be like, and how she should behave. It was all new to her, and no matter what her lineage, she was the stranger in their midst. Everyone had been gracious to her so far, particularly the Queen Mother, her grandmother, and the monarch herself, who treated her like any other young girl, with ease, and chatted with her when they met at the stables.

The queen was a frequent visitor at the stables when she had time, in order to discuss recent and future purchases, which of the stallions they were using for stud services, which was a lucrative business for them, and upcoming races. It was a going concern and did well, and a serious business interest of the queen's, although the rumor was that the prince consort didn't share her passion, and only came to major races under duress. He was never seen at the stables with her, but he would be at Balmoral when Annie was there. She hadn't met him yet, or her aunt Victoria, who would be staying there on her way to or from the South of France for more hedonistic pursuits.

Annie gleaned whatever information she could from Anthony about Balmoral, since he and his father were frequent visitors there, but he was much more excited about his own trip to Saint Tropez. He wished Annie luck when she left for Scotland by train. Jonathan's best advice had been to just be herself, which didn't give her much help. She wasn't even sure what kind of clothes to bring, and had no woman to ask. All Anthony said was to bring some nice dresses and you'll be fine.

"What kind of 'nice'?" she pressed him over dinner at the local pub a few days before she left. "Fancy nice? Or sundress nice, or shorts and a blouse in the daytime?" She hardly ever shopped, had never gone without Lucy, and until now didn't need fancy clothes, but she forced herself to visit the shops in the town near the stables and bought herself a few simple things that looked like good basics to her. She showed them to Anthony and he approved.

"Why not wear something sexy?" he suggested. She had a great figure she never took advantage of to show off. "You're a girl." He had never known a woman like her, so totally without artifice or vanity.

"Until now I only owned one dress, to wear to church on Christmas. All I need is riding gear, and I can't wear that to dinner," she said, still nervous about her wardrobe even with the new additions.

And Lucy had never been helpful in that department either. She was used to wearing her housekeeper's black dresses, and housedresses and slippers on her days off when she sat in front of the TV watching her favorite shows. Annie still missed her, and her unconditional love, and Jonathan said that he and the boys missed her terribly too. She'd been gone for less than a year, and so much had changed. Everything had, for all of them, especially in Annie's life.

She had an allowance to spend now, which the cabinet had approved. It seemed extremely generous to her, and was put in an account for her every month, but she had no expenses living at the queen's stables, and she'd never been extravagant. She did wish she'd had time to shop more when she packed her meager summer wardrobe for Balmoral. She saw Anthony briefly the morning she left. He was rushing to the airport for his flight to Nice, and what he referred to as Sodom and Gomorrah with French subtitles in Saint Tropez, on his friend's yacht. He couldn't wait.

"Good luck!" he called over his shoulder as he hurried down the stairs. She left a few minutes later, and Lord Hatton had one of the grooms drive her to the train station, where she boarded with her single battered suitcase, feeling like an orphan again, and not a royal princess.

The trip to Aberdeenshire in Scotland took eight hours, changing several times, and the scenery was beautiful along the way. The area around the castle was very rural, which was what the queen and Queen Mother loved about it. She had already spent most of the summer there, and was now at Sandringham in Norfolk with friends. And she was leaving this time in August to the young people. Annie knew that the family usually spent Christmas there, and only went to Balmoral in the summer, for a proper holiday. Of all of them, Balmoral was the queen's favorite castle. It had a romantic history. Victoria and Albert had rented it in 1848, and had liked it so much, they continued to lease it for four years, until Prince Albert bought it as a gift for Queen Victoria in 1852. They had built an entirely new castle there, and it remained their favorite holiday home. The rest of the time, they used Windsor Castle as their main residence, and preferred it with their nine children when they were growing up. They lived at Buckingham Palace for part of the time, but Windsor was the main seat of the monarchy during Victoria's reign.

Balmoral was on the bank of the River Dee, near the village of Crathie, and the queen's private secretary picked Annie up at the station, and was surprised to see she had come with only one very small bag, which he carried for her, and put in the queen's Rolls for the short drive to the castle.

"Did you have an easy journey, Your Royal

Highness?" Sir Malcolm asked pleasantly. He was happy to see her again, and she was relieved to see a familiar face.

"The scenery was beautiful." She had brought a picnic lunch to eat on the train, prepared by the excellent chef at the stables.

"Dinner will be at eight o'clock," he informed her. "Family in the drawing room at seven." A wave of panic washed over her as he said it.

"Is it formal dress?"

"Never at Balmoral. Her Majesty prefers to keep things informal here. A simple dress will do nicely. There's a picnic lunch planned tomorrow, and a barbecue the day after. Her Majesty's children love barbecues. They visited a ranch in America last summer, and the queen enjoys barbecues too." He smiled at her, and a few minutes later they reached the castle. It was more of a large estate house, and was less daunting than Buckingham Palace, or the other residences like Windsor, which was a real palace, and one of the oldest castles in the world, and rivaled Versailles in France. Balmoral was far more human scale.

A flock of corgis greeted them when they got out of the car, and the queen herself appeared a few minutes later to welcome her, and escort her inside. She hugged Annie when she saw her. Annie was wearing a navy blue linen skirt, which was sadly crumpled from the trip, a white blouse, a blazer, and sandals, and looked like a schoolgirl as she followed her aunt into the house.

There was a striking redheaded woman playing the piano and singing, with a crowd of young people around her, and Annie recognized her immediately. It was Her Royal Highness Princess Victoria, her other aunt. She waved from the piano with a broad smile, and three handsome young boys glanced at the new arrival and went on singing. They were singing American show tunes, and knew all the words, as Annie approached cautiously, the queen went outside with the dogs, and the head stewardess took Annie's bag from the secretary, who followed Her Majesty outside for a brief conversation before he left.

The song ended a few minutes later, and Princess Victoria stood up and came around the piano, observing her niece closely, and looking deeply moved. Annie looked so much like her mother that there were tears in Victoria's eyes when she hugged her.

"At last! I was in India for a month when you met my mother and sister. I've felt quite cheated not to meet you before this. Do you sing? We do a lot of it here," she said, and the boys laughed. "I have no voice at all, but that never stops me," she said easily and laughed. But she played the piano beautifully, and sang better than she admitted. She did a lot of it at parties. "I'm your naughty aunt," she said happily. "The queen is the good one. And these are your cousins, my dear." She introduced her to the queen's three sons, who were eighteen, seventeen, and fourteen, close to the ages the three princesses had been during the war. They were Princes George, Albert, and William and were good-looking boys. They had the Teutonic blond looks of their father, who appeared a few minutes later to welcome her as well. He was Prince Edward. He had renounced his German nationality when he married Alexandra and exchanged his German title for a British one.

They all went out on the terrace after that, and half an hour later, Princess Victoria offered to show Annie to her room.

"You're a brave girl to come and meet all of us at once. I hear you're a smashing rider. Your mother was as well, dangerously so, I fear. She was about your size, and fearless on a horse. Our father was always afraid she would break her neck and kill herself riding." She looked wistful as she said it. "I'm afraid I was the wicked older sister who always scolded her. Jealous, I suppose. It seems so stupid now. I'm so glad you're here." She didn't say it, but it had occurred to her that Annie gave her the chance to do things better now, and make up for how mean she had been to Charlotte in their youth. "You look just like her, you know," she said softly as they reached the top of the stairs and she walked Annie into a splendid room, all decorated in yellow satin, and floral silks, and filled with antiques. "This is my favorite guest room of all," she said, as Annie caught her breath and looked around. She had never seen a bedroom as beautiful in her entire life. There was a portrait of Queen Victoria in her youth on one wall, and a huge canopied bed. "This was her favorite house," Victoria said, pointing to the painting. "Prince Albert bought the original house for her as a gift and then built her a new one. They were a very romantic couple, and madly in love. I suppose all those children were testimony to that," she said and laughed. She had a very light spirit and seemed like a lot of fun, as Anthony had said. She was much more frivolous than her older sister, although they were only a year apart. Princess Victoria was forty-two but didn't look it. She seemed very young, in white linen slacks, with a starched white shirt and silver sandals. The queen had been wearing a linen skirt and pale blue twin set, and her traditional double strand of pearls, which she wore every day, wherever she was. "And don't worry about dressing for dinner. We don't bother here. It's all very casual," she added.

"I didn't really know what to bring," Annie said

in a soft voice, feeling nervous with this dazzlingly attractive woman who seemed so at ease in her own skin and so full of life. It had shocked her how much Annie looked like her late mother, they were almost identical, but she tried not to let it show. It was a knife in her heart, and almost as though her younger sister, Charlotte, had returned to them in the form of this shy, pretty young girl.

She could see why her mother and sister liked her. She was so unassuming, and so sweet and direct, with no artifice or pretense. Her manner was like Charlotte's too, and even the way she moved. "Don't let us overwhelm you, my dear," she added before she left the room. "There are a lot of us, but we mean you no harm, and your cousins are wonderful boys. We're all going fishing tomorrow. And you can ride if you like. Alexandra keeps some very nice horses here. I hope you'll enjoy it." She smiled and left the room, closing the door behind her, and Annie lay down on the huge bed and looked around, smiling. Everything was so beautiful, and they were all so nice. She still couldn't understand how all of this had happened to her. She wished Jonathan was with her, so he could see it all too. She would tell him all about it after the weekend.

She bathed before dinner. The bathroom was old-fashioned and had an enormous tub. She wore a plain black skirt and a white silk blouse, one of her few choices. She made up with youth and beauty for what she lacked in fashion, and the queen looked as though she approved when Annie entered the room in her simple skirt and blouse and black high heels that were new too, and hard to walk in, but looked pretty on her. Victoria came downstairs a few minutes later in a Pucci dress she'd bought in Rome, which the queen thought was too loud and too short, in a bright paisley pattern in turquoise, yellow, shocking pink, and black with shoes to match. Victoria had famously great legs and liked to show them off, although the queen disapproved. Annie looked like a schoolgirl in comparison, but a very proper one, and resolved to go shopping soon with her new allowance, for future family occasions. She had almost nothing to wear, and they all looked so fashionable to her. She wouldn't have dared to wear a dress like Victoria's, but it looked like fun, and molded her fabulous figure. It all went well with her flaming red hair, which she wore loose down her back, and made her look even younger. Annie could easily see how she'd had an affair with one of Anthony's thirty-year-old friends. She looked barely older than that herself.

The queen had seated Annie next to her at dinner, and they talked about horses all through the meal, which suited them both, and put Annie at ease. She knew little about anything else, but a great deal about horses. And the queen invited her to go riding with her the next morning, before the planned fishing expedition. Annie accepted with delight, and after dinner they all gathered around the piano again, and sang all their favorite songs. Annie even knew the words to some of them and sang along. It was a fun evening, and they all went to bed early.

Annie had agreed to meet the queen at the stables at seven, was up at five and watched the sun come up over the hills. She arrived punctually at the stables. The queen was already there, and had chosen a mount she thought Annie would enjoy. He was a very lively horse, and she'd brought him to Balmoral for the summer to see how she liked him. Victoria had already said he was too nervous and hard to manage, and she preferred one of the older mares. She wasn't quite as horse mad as her sister, although she was an excellent rider. They all were, but Victoria didn't enjoy a challenge as much as the queen had heard Annie did.

Annie got in the saddle with ease, and calmed the big horse quickly. She had him well in hand by the time they left the stable yard a few minutes later, and headed along a path that led into the hills, and crossed a stream, which Annie and her mount jumped with ease.

"Do you hunt?" the queen asked her, and Annie shook her head.

"I never have, but I'd like to."

"We'll arrange that for you this winter. You'll enjoy it. Lord Hatton tells me that you dream of being a professional jockey. It will happen one of these days. They can't keep women out forever," she said calmly.

"I hope so, ma'am. It doesn't seem fair. We're only eligible for amateur events, and most of them aren't very good. I'd give anything to be in a real race," Annie said.

"I believe it will happen one day," she said. "Dangerous though. Be careful, my dear. Lord Hatton said you're a fearless rider. That's not always a good thing. Never forget these are powerful beasts, and we don't control them as thoroughly as we believe. They have a voice in the matter too." Annie smiled. She believed the same thing.

"I respect the horses I ride." She knew the ones that were dangerous, although she had a penchant for those, which Lord Hatton had spotted, and reported to the queen. He had said that it would make her an excellent jockey if she ever got the chance.

They rode for an hour, and then went back to the stables. Before they left to go back to the house, the queen showed her the Shetland ponies she bred there. She was very proud of them. And then they returned to the house for breakfast with the others. The whole group went fishing after that. The queen stayed back to attend to her official boxes and diplomatic pouches that were brought to her even here. Annie caught two fish and squealed with delight when she did. Her oldest cousin, Prince George, took them off the hooks for her. He was four years younger than Annie, and a very serious, polite young man. He was next in line to the throne and would be king one day, which always had a sobering effect on the next in line. Prince Albert was a year younger and full of mischief, and at one point, jumped into the lake fully dressed and climbed dripping back into the boat while everyone complained. He shook the water off himself and onto his relatives like a big dog, but the weather was warm. Prince William at fourteen was very studious and shy and still at Eton and more introverted than his two older brothers. His gentleness touched Annie and she chatted with him.

At lunchtime, they had the picnic that the cooks had packed for them in wicker baskets. Stewards arrived in a van to serve it at folding tables with linens and china. Everything was easy and fun and prettily done, and the following day, they had the American-style barbecue that the queen's sons had requested. Everyone loved it, hot dogs and hamburgers and corn on the cob, apple pie and ice cream.

"I want to work on a dude ranch next summer," Prince Albert announced at lunch. It sounded like fun to all of them. He'd been talking to his mother recently about transferring to an American university, and she hadn't agreed to it yet, but he was adamant. He was fascinated by all things American. He told Annie all about a rodeo he'd gone to when they vacationed in Wyoming. "I hear you're a bruising rider," he commented, and Annie smiled, surprised.

"How did you hear that?"

"My mother told me. She said you'd be a professional jockey if women were allowed to."

"I'd love that," Annie admitted. "I doubt it will ever happen here. Maybe in America one day. They're much more open-minded."

"About everything," Prince Albert confirmed. "I'd love to live there one day. My brother had better never abdicate. I want to be a cowboy when I grow up, not a king." It struck her then that it was a serious concern for all of them, the reality that one of them would be king or queen one day, although she was too far down the line to worry about it. But it was a heavy responsibility for Queen Alexandra's sons, particularly the two oldest. Her own father had become king reluctantly, when his brother had abdicated. So it did happen.

The end of the weekend came too quickly. The others were staying on for a few more days, although Princess Victoria was leaving for London the next day, and the queen was planning to spend another week there. She urged Annie to come again, now that she had met everyone in the family, other than distant cousins who were scattered all over Europe, many of them on other thrones.

"You're a true Windsor," she said to Annie when she left. They all hugged her and hoped to see her again soon. She had another month of work ahead of her at the queen's stables, and Prince George and Prince Albert promised to come and see her before they went back to university, and Prince William before he started the new term at Eton.

The queen touched on the subject of where Annie would live after she finished her internship at the stables. There were apartments available at Kensington Palace, if that appealed to her. Annie had been planning to go back to Jonathan to help him with the twins. She said she'd like to think about the queen's offer of an apartment. It hadn't occurred to her that they would do that and she was pleasantly surprised.

She was far more relaxed on the trip back on the

train than she had been on the way to Scotland. She had managed to stretch her meager wardrobe to its limits. She had been impressed by how fashionable Princess Victoria was, and she was so lively and stylish at everything she did. She lightened the mood wherever she was, but unlike the queen, she had few responsibilities, not even a husband and children. She had been very warm and welcoming to her newest cousin and gave her little snippets of advice throughout the weekend. Publicly, she had a reputation for being flighty and a party girl, but Annie could tell that she was intelligent and much less superficial than she pretended to be. It was simply the style she had chosen for herself when she didn't marry. She jokingly referred to herself as the family spinster, which was not the image Annie had of her at all. She was a very glamorous, beautiful woman.

In contrast, the queen was actually more light-hearted than she seemed publicly. She was a warm wife and mother, and enjoyed the time she spent with her family at Balmoral. She was already regretting that the summer was almost over. From Annie's perspective it had been a very successful weekend, and she had gotten to know a little bit about all of them, and genuinely liked her new family.

She didn't see Anthony until the following evening, when he came back from the South of France a day late, and looked a little worse for wear but said he had had a fabulous time. He had stayed on his friend's yacht, had lunch at the Club 55, danced at all the discotheques, picked up numerous women of assorted nationalities, which he didn't tell Annie, but she could guess. When he asked about her weekend at Balmoral, she said she'd had a fantastic time. He smiled at her enthusiasm.

"It's more your cup of tea than mine," he said. "My father loves it too. I always find it incredibly boring. It's a little too rural and family for me. Did Princess Victoria sing?"

"Every night," Annie said as she smiled at him, "and we had a barbecue." He didn't tell her the details of what he'd been doing in Saint Tropez, but a family barbecue with teenage boys present had not been on their agenda, much to his relief. But Annie had loved it. She was at a very different point in her life than he was and family-style weekends didn't thrill him, even with the royal family. He wanted racier diversions and couldn't see himself ever content with a life like that. And he knew that Princess Victoria was far more like him. But Annie's innocent enthusiasm seemed sweet to him.

She was already busy with the horses by the time he got there. His father was annoyed with him for returning a day late, but Anthony was used to it, and the lecture he got didn't impress him or bother him at all. He'd had a lifetime of them, about responsibility, his least favorite word.

Annie hardly saw Anthony all week, and the following weekend she went home to Kent for the twins' birthday. She had promised to be there, and wouldn't miss it. It was a very different weekend from the previous one at Balmoral. They went out to dinner at an Italian restaurant, and bowling afterward, and the Markhams let them use their pool because they were away. Annie spent hours in the pool with her brothers, and had given one a camera, and the other a stereo for their birthday. She was happy spending the weekend with them, with their father looking on. She had two families now, one royal, and the other, the one she had grown up with, as the daughter of employees on a big estate. The two lives were entirely different, and yet she was at home in both of them. She had adapted surprisingly well to the new one, as the niece of the queen, and the cousin of the future King of England. She was both people now, the simple girl she'd grown up as and a royal princess by birth. The boys teased her about it when she went bowling with them, and they asked if the queen had her own bowling alley at Buckingham Palace. Annie said she didn't, and Jonathan laughed.

"If I were king, I'd have my own bowling alley, a pinball machine, a jukebox, my own movie theater, and an Aston Martin," Blake said, imagining it, and his older sister grinned at him.

"Why an Aston Martin?" she asked him, thinking of Anthony Hatton's Ferrari, which seemed more glamorous to her.

Her brother gave her a look that implied she didn't know anything. "James Bond drives an Aston Martin," he said with a supercilious look, and she laughed again.

"Of course! Silly of me," she said, kissed him on the cheek, and went to buy popcorn for all of them. She was still smiling at the image of Blake as king with his own movie theater, jukebox, pinball machine, and bowling alley. She wondered if her new cousin George had those on his list too. More likely on Albert's, or maybe William's. There was something universal about teenage boys that was very sweet, even if they grew up to be king one day.

Chapter 14

The month of September went by too quickly for Annie. She loved her duties at the queen's stables, and her internship had only been for two months. She was sorry to see it come to an end. Anthony's had been for a shorter time, and he left in the middle of September. He was starting a new job at a public relations firm in London, which sounded interesting to her. He said it would be mostly organizing parties and special events for VIPs, and using his connections to get wealthy new industrialists introduced into society, and helping them get into the right circles. It didn't sound like a serious job, but it sounded amusing and right up his alley, since it involved parties.

"They pay dearly for that kind of service," he

explained to her during dinner at their favorite pub the night before he left. She had enjoyed their friendship of the last month and a half, more than she'd ever expected to. He was deeper than he looked, although he never set the bar high for himself, and having fun was always the top priority to him. It sounded like he had found a job that met that criterion and he got paid for it. It was the best of all possible worlds for him. "What about you? What are you going to do when you leave here in two weeks?" he asked her.

"I'm going to travel for a month, to Australia. I've been dying to see it," she said innocently, and he looked at her with suspicion. It was the first time she had mentioned it to him.

"Why is it that I don't believe you? What do you have up your sleeve? Something to do with horses undoubtedly. Amateur races perhaps?" He grinned at her and she laughed.

"You know me too well. Don't tell your father. He wouldn't approve. He and the queen think that the amateur races in Australia aren't worth bothering with. But it's good experience if they ever change the rules here. I could ride in the Newmarket Town Plate. But I didn't have a mount for it. So, I'm off to Australia."

"And after that?"

"I don't know. I could go home to my father for

a bit, and give him a hand in the stables. He hurt his knee and could use the help."

"Why don't you buy yourself a decent dress and come to London. You could come to some of the parties I organize. I can put you on the list as Her Royal Highness, and you could impress my crude clients with the important people I know."

"It sounds a bit awkward to me." She looked hesitant.

"It's not. They're actually very nice, and I could use some more royals on my list. Victoria will come to any party. But it's a bit slim pickings after that. I need another Royal Highness. Hell, I'll buy you the dress," he teased her. "Something shocking and naked and sexy." He liked the vision of it and she laughed.

"I'd look like a ten-year-old who ran away from a brothel," she said. "Why couldn't I come in my riding clothes?"

"On horseback preferably. You can always join the circus if you're bored."

"Thank you," she said primly.

"Just don't get yourself killed in those second-rate amateur races in Australia. Be careful, Annie. I know you won't be, but I'll worry about you."

"No, you won't." She laughed at him. "You'll be too busy giving parties to think about me."

He looked serious when he answered. "That's

not true. I think about you a lot. And I do worry about you. You need someone to take care of you."

"No, I don't," she said stubbornly, jutting out her chin. "I'm tougher than I look."

"And more vulnerable and innocent than you think. I don't want anyone taking advantage of you." He felt protective of her, which was new for him.

"I'll be fine," she assured him. He remembered all too easily how terrified he had been when he thought she was dead when she fell off the horse during their second race. They had never raced again. She was like his little sister now. She was unfamiliar with the world she had been catapulted into, and the people in it, who would have liked to take advantage of her in countless ways. Anthony was well versed with that world, she wasn't.

"Just be careful." They went to his room after dinner that night, for the first time. But she knew she had nothing to fear from him now. He wasn't a masher, there were more than enough women who were desperate for him, and they had genuinely become friends.

He poured her a short glass of gin, and she made a face when she drank it. He drank a malt whiskey, neat, and they sat talking for a while, and then she got up to leave.

"We got a new horse today. I'm exercising him

tomorrow to get a feeling for him," she said as she stood up. "I'm going to miss this place."

"They should hire you. You're better than any of the trainers they've got." He meant it, and walked her to the door, and she looked up at him with a smile. She seemed so tiny standing in front of him as she looked into his eyes, and for the first time, he wanted desperately to kiss her, but didn't dare. There was a long awkward moment as she looked up at him and felt something too. She thought it was the gin, but he knew it wasn't the whiskey, it was her. But the last thing he needed was a royal princess, and to have his life run by the queen and the Crown and the cabinet, who would have to give their permission for every move he made if they ever got serious. He couldn't think of anything worse or more restrictive. He liked being a free man. He bent down toward Annie then, and kissed her gently on the cheek, with greater tenderness than she had expected, or he had intended to show her. He wanted desperately to put his arms around her, but resisted the urge, and she scampered back to her room with a wave and closed the door.

"No!" he said to himself out loud as he closed his own door. "Never! Don't be ridiculous. She's a child." But she wasn't a child, she was a woman, and there was something so damn enchanting about her. He poured himself another whiskey, and lay down on his bed and fell asleep. He woke when he heard her leave for the stables at six o'clock the next morning, right on schedule. But he had come to his senses by then, and the moment had passed.

He left for London that morning to start his new job, and two weeks later, as she packed to leave, Annie had two surprises. One from Lord Hatton, and the other from the queen.

Lord Hatton offered her a job at the queen's stables as an assistant trainer, and she was thrilled. He asked what her plans were, and she said she was traveling for the next few weeks. He invited her to return when she got back, and move into the trainers' quarters and start her job. He was as pleased as she was, and delighted when she accepted, and he said the queen would be too.

The second surprise she got in a letter from the queen's secretary. Her Majesty wanted Her Royal Highness to be the first to know. Mr. Jonathan Baker was to be knighted. The queen had several discretionary titles that were in her gift, and knighted certain subjects when she deemed it appropriate. For being responsible for returning Her Royal Highness Anne Louise to her royal family, and asking for nothing in return, but doing it merely for honorable reasons, the queen was proposing to knight him at the end of October, as Sir Jonathan

Baker. Annie was even more excited about that, and couldn't wait to tell him when she got home to Kent that night. She was staying with him and the boys for a few days before leaving for Australia for three weeks, to see if she could ride in any of the amateur races open to women there, even as a substitute. Annie had always wanted to go there and try out.

She waited until the end of dinner that night to tell him the big news about his knighthood. The boys were restless and wanted to leave the table, but she told them to wait. Jonathan stared at her when she told him he was going to be knighted, and he had tears in his eyes.

"**Sir** Jonathan? Are you joking?" She handed him the letter from the queen's secretary. "But I didn't do anything," he protested. "At first I was afraid they might put me in jail when I tried to reach the queen," he smiled.

"You did everything, Papa. You found a way to reach the queen. None of this would have happened if you'd stayed silent or lost your nerve. I have two families now, thanks to you, and I'm a princess." She told him about the job at the stables too. Something wonderful had happened for both of them. She was to be paid a salary for her work, and was pleased. And she didn't need an apartment in London now.

"What are you doing in Australia?" He always worried about her.

"Just looking around," she said. He didn't believe her.

"Don't do anything foolish."

"I won't. And I'll be back in time for your ceremony." The twins had been impressed too.

When he told John Markham the next day, he responded with a promotion and a raise. He invented a fancy new title for him, since he was already stable master, and the raise was appropriate. Jonathan had promised to invite him to the ceremony too. And Annie learned while she was home that Annabelle Markham had a new secretary and Jonathan had just started dating her. The twins said she was very nice, and good-looking. Annie was happy for him. He deserved it. He had done so much for her, and always had. He was going to bring his new date to the knighting ceremony too. He still got tears in his eyes whenever he thought about it. He had never expected anything like it to happen to him. He was going to be a knight!

Annie left for Sydney after a week at home. She only stayed two weeks in the end, and was disappointed in the amateur races. She thought they were poorly organized and unprofessional. She was able to sign up for two of them and didn't like her mount in either case. The women were rough and the organizers seemed crude to her. It wasn't what she had hoped for, and she was happy to come home, although she thought the country was interesting.

She was happy to be back in England, and had dinner with Anthony when she returned. He was having one of his first events in the new job that weekend, and wanted her to come. It was to introduce a well-known American into British social circles. He'd rented a fabulous house in Mayfair for the weekend to give the party.

"I feel a bit like a pimp doing this kind of thing," Anthony admitted to her. "These guys want to meet women, mostly hookers in the end, and be seen with respectable women. I draw the line at drugs, but they expect me to do everything for them. And they're powerful men. They don't take no for an answer. Will you come?" he asked her hopefully.

"I'm not going to impress anyone, Anthony. And I have nothing to wear."

"Go to Harrods or Hardy Amies, your aunt Victoria shops there. I need you on my team," he said, nearly begging her.

"I am on your team. Why do I have to be there?"

"To impress them."

"Will Victoria be there?"

"She's going to some ball in Venice. I need **you**."

"All right, all right," she said grudgingly. "What kind of dress?"

"Sexy, slinky, half naked," he said without hesitating.

"That's not me."

"All right. As sexy as you dare."

"Now I feel like a hooker," she grumbled.

"That makes two of us. I feel like a pimp," he said and she laughed.

She went to Harrods the next day and bought a simple black velvet strapless dress and a fake diamond necklace that looked real, black satin high heels and an evening bag. The night of the party, she pulled her blond hair into a neat-looking bun, put on a little makeup, and looked surprisingly regal when she arrived in Mayfair at the address of the house he had rented for the event. He took her aside immediately, and took a leather box out of a drawer. He opened it and held out a beautiful small antique tiara and placed it on her head as she looked at him in surprise.

"I borrowed it from Garrard's. It was Queen Victoria's. Now you look like a princess," he said, looking pleased, and she was startled when she looked in the mirror.

"It's gorgeous."

"You can't keep it. But you can say it was your great-great-great-grandmother's." He was perfect in the role of PR man, and she was impressed when she saw him in operation that night. The party went off seamlessly and his client was delighted. The press was there and took a photograph of her with the host, who was an oilman from Texas, who had just invested a fortune in aeronautics in England, and wanted to make a big splash. He had wanted to meet the queen, which Anthony told him wasn't possible, so Her Royal Highness Princess Anne Louise was second best and an adequate consolation prize for the Texan, who invited her to visit him in Dallas. She looked beautiful that night and every inch a princess, and Anthony thanked her and kissed her cheek when she left and handed him the tiara.

"I thought you did a great job," she complimented him. "You make an excellent pimp."

"And you make an excellent princess, Your Royal Highness." He was glad they were friends now and so was she. "I'm keeping you on my list. And I like the dress by the way."

"I only spent a hundred pounds on it. I can't ride in it, so I didn't want to go nuts," she said, laughing.

His client was beckoning to him then, and he rushed off and she left. She was surprised that she had had fun, but she had. And Anthony looked very handsome in black tie. It had been a glamorous evening, and she liked wearing the tiara. She felt like a real princess in it.

There was a photograph of her with Anthony in the papers the next day. And her aunt Victoria called her when she got back from Venice and saw it.

"Be careful, my darling," she warned her. "Anthony Hatton is charming, but he's a player. Don't lose your heart to that one." She was a woman of the world and wise about men.

"I'm not. We're just friends. He needed a princess to impress his client," she told her aunt.

"Oh God, he'll whore us all out if we let him." She laughed at the thought. "I was at a very amusing ball in Venice so I couldn't be there. You'll have to come with me some time. The Italians are so sexy and handsome. They're all broke but so charming. Everyone is a prince there. It was a divine party. And you looked very pretty with Anthony in the photo. I just worried when I saw it."

"His father is my new boss. He just gave me a job as an assistant trainer at the stables."

"Excellent." They talked for a few more minutes and hung up. The call didn't really surprise her. She knew that Anthony had a reputation as a playboy in London, but he was harmless, and there was no romance between them. They were just friends. He sent her red roses to thank her for coming to the party, which was very nice of him.

After that she turned her attention to the ceremony for her stepfather. The queen did it herself at Buckingham Palace in a small receiving room. It was all very official, with a saber she used to tap him on each shoulder and declare him a knight of the British Empire, and he would be known as Sir Jonathan Baker hereafter. Tears rolled down his cheeks as she pronounced it, and Annie cried too, and was so proud of him. The boys had new suits, their first, for the occasion, and Jonathan did too and looked very proper. His mother was there and was bursting with pride, and she was happy to see Annie. It made Annie miss Lucy too, who would have been ecstatic at the knighting ceremony. The Markhams attended, and the woman Jonathan was dating, who was very polite and nice to Annie, and seemed very smitten with him. There were several officials and the lord chamberlain of the queen's household and her secretary. A round of champagne was served, and then Jonathan treated his family and the Markhams to dinner at Rules, the oldest restaurant in London. At Annie's request, Anthony arranged to have them go to Annabel's to dance afterward. It was a perfect evening. Annie couldn't help thinking how her life had changed in a short time. Her stepfather was a knight now, and she was a royal princess. The headwaiters and manager at Annabel's fawned over her, and she danced with Jonathan. He smiled at her, and she called him Sir Jonathan, and he called her Your Royal Highness . . . but whatever the titles, she knew she would always be just Annie to him, and the daughter of his heart, which was the best part.

Chapter 15

At the end of October, Annie returned from Kent to the queen's stables to start her job as assistant trainer. She'd been staying with Jonathan and the boys and enjoyed it. It felt almost like old times, except for Lucy's absence. Annie still missed her.

As a trainer, she had more responsibilities than she'd had as an intern, and was assigned to the three barns on a rotating schedule. She learned a great deal about their breeding program, which she discussed with Jonathan whenever she visited with them. The process of selection of matching up the horses to be bred was fascinating, and as much art as science. Lord Hatton consulted with the queen about almost every choice.

Annie loved her job, although it was all-consuming and she had no time for anything else. She didn't mind.

In November, she received the queen's invitation to spend Christmas with them at Sandringham, which meant that she couldn't spend it with Jonathan and the twins if she accepted, but he understood, and thought she should spend it with her royal family this year. She was sorry not to be with him in Kent, but Christmas with her royal aunts, uncle, cousins, and grandmother, was appealing too. She didn't know who else would be there, but had the impression it was only family. And this time, she would have to buy some clothes. The only proper dress she had was the one she had bought for Anthony's party for the Texas oilman. She was sorry she didn't have the tiara to wear with it again. It had been the perfect look, and she smiled when she thought of it. It seemed particularly appropriate because people were always comparing her to her own mother and Queen Victoria, since both of them had also been small. The rest of the family seemed to take after the German side and were much taller than she. All of Queen Alexandra's sons were tall like their father, and the queen was tall too.

Sandringham was in Norfolk, much closer to London than Balmoral Castle, and it was where the royal family usually spent Christmas. She shopped for some dresses, most of them black or navy, and a deep red velvet one for Christmas Eve. She bought gifts for everyone when she had a day off. She bought Jonathan a beautiful set of antique leather-bound books and a pinball machine for the twins, which was delivered the morning of Christmas Eve. When she called, Jonathan said they had gone nuts and invited all their friends from school to come over and play.

And she had sent a beautiful warm black coat to Jonathan's mother, her other grandmother. She had seen too little of her since going to work at the royal stables, but she wrote to her whenever she had time. Her new allowance enabled her to make generous gifts to all of them, and she was sorry not to see them over Christmas. She knew they understood that she had new responsibilities now, and two families. It was going to be her first royal Christmas.

Annie was shown to a beautiful bedroom at Sandringham when she arrived, and several footmen carried her bags and all her packages to her room. She was directing them about where to put everything when a familiar face walked past her room, and she saw Anthony Hatton standing in the doorway, smiling at her. His father was there too, and she remembered that the Hattons spent

Christmas with the queen's family every year. She was embarrassed not to have brought something for him. She had given Lord Hatton a bottle of Dom Perignon champagne before she left the stables. She was genuinely surprised to see Anthony. She hadn't seen him since his party for the oilman. They had both been busy with their new jobs.

"I hoped I'd see you here." He smiled at her as he crossed the room to kiss her. "I meant to call you, but my life has been insane. The PR firm I'm working for has really taken off. I've been running parties for them every week with a list of VIP clients an arm long. What about you? Is my father working your tail off?"

"Yes, and I love it." She smiled at him.

"Are you behaving?" he asked her.

"Of course." She wasn't sure what he meant by it, but she had no time to do otherwise. He noticed but didn't mention that she looked suddenly more grown up, and more sophisticated than she had when he met her. She was wearing a red wool suit with a fashionably short skirt, which was part of her recent haul from Harrods when she was buying gifts. She thought it would come in handy at Sandringham. He was admiring her legs with the short skirt. She was small but well proportioned, and he'd never noticed her legs before in her riding clothes, or her evening gown at his party.

"My room is just down the hall if you need any-thing," he said, as he left to check on his own bags.

Christmas at Sandringham was more formal than the family gatherings at Balmoral in the summer. There were no picnics or barbecues, and the queen's secretary had called to tell her that dinner would be black tie, which was why she'd gone shopping, so she was prepared. She had bought three long dresses, and had brought the strapless velvet one, which was the only one she'd owned. She'd bought a kilt, the red suit she was wearing, a black velvet suit, and a white wool dress by a French designer for Christmas Day. She had a full wardrobe and she could fill in with some skirts and sweaters she had brought from Kent the last time she went there. As always, when she went downstairs for cocktails before dinner, Princess Victoria was wearing a very chic French designer black cocktail dress and looked sexy and fashionable, and the queen was wearing a black velvet evening suit with a long skirt, with her pearls, diamond earrings, and a very handsome tiara.

Annie was seated next to Anthony at dinner, and he leaned over and whispered, "I should have brought the tiara from Garrard's that you wore to the party. I meant to give it to you for Christmas, and I must have forgotten it at home." She grinned at his comment, and remembered how much she liked it. "It suited you very well. You should wear tiaras all the time."

During dinner she told him how lovely her father's knighting ceremony had been and how much it meant to him, and Anthony was touched. Somehow, despite everything that had happened to her in a short time, it hadn't gone to her head, and she had managed to stay real.

"What about you? Do you still like the job?" she asked.

"It's a hell of a lot of work, and some of their clients are real jerks, but some are very nice. The Americans mostly. There's kind of a sweet innocence to them. They all want to meet the queen, and think they should. They don't really get how it all works, the protocol, and all the rest. We should get a stand-in that looks like her. They'd never know the difference." Annie laughed. It was fun sitting next to him, he always had something interesting to say and he always made her laugh. "What about you, how does it all feel? Has the protocol gotten to you yet? I know Victoria gets fed up with it."

"I'm not the queen's sister," she reminded him. "I'm only her niece. No one worries about what I do. I'm kind of below the radar and I like it that way."

"Until you put a foot wrong, and then they'll come down on you like bricks, if you go out with the wrong man, or say the wrong thing." That was Victoria's specialty. She was always dating men that her sister and the cabinet didn't approve of, or being too outspoken or critical about the government, the prime minister, or her sister.

"I don't do anything they can object to," Annie said easily.

"You will one day," he assured her, "and then there will be hell to pay." It was why he had never gone out romantically with Victoria, or anyone royal. He didn't care that she was older, nor did she. But he confined his love life to commoners, socialites, debutantes, models, and starlets, which caused comment too, and had won him the reputation of being a playboy, as Victoria had warned her. But Annie was in no danger of falling prey to his charms. She knew him too well now and still only liked him as a brother.

Her cousin Albert was seated on her other side at dinner the first night, on Christmas Eve, and he was talking about college, and a ski trip to France he was planning after Christmas. She had seen in the press that he was dating a beautiful girl, who was a duke's daughter, but there was no evidence of her there. None of them brought their dates to the queen's home for Christmas, not even her sons. It was strictly family, and the Hattons. Lord Hatton was seated next to the queen on one side, and her oldest son, the heir apparent, on the other. She was deep in conversation with Lord Hatton about a horse she wanted to buy, to use for stud services. Horses were her main topic of conversation in private. The prince consort was seated next to his sister-in-law Victoria, and she was making him laugh as she always did, with irreverent stories. She brought out the best in him. Men loved her.

The ladies left the table at the end of dinner, and waited in the drawing room for the gentlemen to join them shortly after, and then they played charades over coffee and brandy, followed by card games. At midnight they all went upstairs. Gifts were to be exchanged the next day before lunch, which would be a sumptuous meal in the main dining room. They followed the same traditions every year.

When Annie went to her room at the end of the evening, there was a fire burning brightly. The room was warm and cozy, and she was relaxing in a chair thinking of what a nice time she'd had, when there was a knock on the door. She went to open it, and was surprised to see Anthony standing there with a bottle of champagne in his hand and two glasses.

"A bit of bubbly before bedtime?" he offered. She wasn't tired and she let him come in, and he sat down across from her in front of the fire and stretched his legs out as he filled two glasses with champagne, and handed one to her.

"I'm glad you're here," he said, looking relaxed. "It's all a bit serious for me, and a little formal. But staying home alone on Christmas would be depressing. So I let my father talk me into it. And to be honest, I hoped you'd be here. I wasn't sure if you'd be in Kent instead."

"I thought I should be here this year."

"Be careful. The royal life is a web you'll never escape."

"You make it sound ominous," she said as she sipped the champagne.

"Not ominous, insidious. After a while, nothing compares to it and you get trapped. Like Victoria. I'm sure there are a dozen places she'd rather be. But she's still here."

"It's home to her," Annie said.

"She'll wind up an old maid if she's not careful. Men are afraid of this, and she won't be young and beautiful forever. She's already forty-two, and I don't think any of the men she's been in love with wanted to take this on."

"Why not?" Annie looked surprised, as he finished his glass and poured himself another. She wondered if he was a little tipsy, but he didn't look it.

"Because the queen makes the rules, my dear, for the entire family. **And** the cabinet. **And** the prime minister. **And** the archbishop. And all the rules and traditions that have existed for hundreds of years. You can't escape that. It's a prison of sorts, a golden one, but nonetheless the walls are thick and the doors are barred, and they let very few people in. Queen Alexandra is a stickler. It will happen to you too if you're not careful. You can't just marry whoever you choose now. They have to approve."

"Are they still that strict?" Annie looked surprised. These were modern times, and the queen was young.

"They are," he answered. "You're far enough down the line, so they may not be as tough on you. But poor George and Albert will have to marry the girls their mother approves of. No go-go dancers for them," he said, and she laughed.

"Well, they don't need to worry about me. I don't want to get married. I just want to be a jockey one day, if they ever relax the rules and let women into the inner sanctum of racing."

"You can't wait for that forever."

"Yes, I can," she said confidently. "That's my only goal for the moment."

"Then God help the racing committee. I get the feeling that you always get what you want."

"Not always, but I'm willing to wait and be patient."

"You'll probably marry and have ten children before that," he said lightly.

"I hope not. I'm not sure I want any," Annie responded seriously. "It certainly didn't work out well for my mother," she said quietly, and he looked at her gently.

"Are you afraid of that happening to you?" he asked, and she nodded. It was her worst fear, dying in childbirth. He had his own demons.

"That was a long time ago, during the war. She was young, and you probably weren't born in a hospital," he said sensibly to reassure her.

"No, I wasn't, but it still happens even now."

"Think of Queen Victoria. She was as small as you are, and she had nine children, all at home, and she was fine. I suppose we all have our terrors. I'm afraid of the woman I love leaving me, the way my mother walked out on my father. It nearly broke him. I don't think he ever recovered. I don't think he's loved a woman since." Although he had dated many, and had a reputation as a ladies' man.

"It's odd how the things in our childhood mark us forever," Annie said. "Once I knew about my mother, I decided I didn't want children. It seems safer not to try." And yet she never played it safe on horseback, and had no fears there. But she guarded her heart. And so did Anthony and his father.

"It's not too late for you to change your mind about having babies. You're young. It will be fine, if you fall in love with the right man. Finding a woman who won't fall in love with someone else and leave you is harder," he said, expressing his own fears.

"Maybe you don't know the right women," she said, and he stared into the fire as he thought about it and then looked at her.

"Probably not. The ones that sparkle like diamonds in the snow are always the most dangerous. I don't trust them, but they're always so damn tempting. I think my mother was like that. She was the daughter of a marquess, and she was a famous beauty. My father was dazzled by her. But she left him for another man, as you know."

"Love seems complicated," Annie said softly, and he nodded.

"It does, doesn't it? It shouldn't. It should be so simple between two good, honorable people. The trouble is, so few people are honorable. And the ones who are can be damn boring," he said and then laughed. "Like your aunt Alexandra. She's a woman of duty and honor, and a profoundly good person, but I don't imagine she's much fun to live with and must be rather dull. Victoria is a great deal more amusing, but I wouldn't trust her. I suspect she can be very naughty, and even wicked. Her love affairs never last and they're never with suitable people. She prefers the high-risk ones, but when you do that, you wind up alone like her." He was in a serious contemplative mood, but Annie suspected that his analyses were correct. "Who knows, maybe your mother would have left your father by now, if they'd survived."

"I don't know much about her. No one likes to talk about her. It makes them too sad. She was so young when she died."

"I can understand that. And one thing I do know," he said, looking seriously at her, as he slid out of his chair across from her and came to sit on the floor next to the low chair where she was sitting. "I know you're an honorable woman, Annie, and you're not boring. I always have fun with you, that's a rare combination." She smiled down at him, and always felt comfortable with him.

"Thank you. I have fun with you too, except for the time I nearly killed myself racing with you."

He winced. "Christ, I thought you were dead. I've never been so frightened in my life."

"Well, I wasn't," she said. "I was lucky."

"We both were." He leaned forward and the next

thing she knew he was kissing her, not violently or passionately, but tenderly, as though he meant it. She was shocked and hadn't seen it coming.

"What are you doing?" she said in a whisper, and he kissed her again, and this time she kissed him back. She hadn't expected anything like this from him.

"I'm kissing you." He answered and smiled at her, and did it one more time. "Every time I see you, something happens to me. You're everything I want in a woman, Annie. But I'm scared."

"Of what?"

"Of ruining what we have. Of you leaving me one day. Of the royal rules squeezing the life out of both of us. It terrifies me, but I know I want to be with you one day, and be married to you, and have babies with you, and I won't let it kill you, I promise." He sounded frighteningly serious about all of it.

"You don't know that it wouldn't kill me," she said, remembering her mother.

"I don't want anything bad to ever happen to you. I hate the idea of your being a jockey. You could break your neck and die, a lot easier than in childbirth. What I can never figure out is how we get from here to there. I've thought about it. How do we get from where we are now to a grown-up married life with children and dogs and all the good things that go with it?" He looked genuinely worried.

"Maybe we just wait till we're ready." He had opened new doors and windows to a vista she had never even considered, but she liked it. He put his arms around her and held her close as the fire crackled and she felt the warmth of him around her and on her lips when he kissed her. She had never felt anything like it for any man, until now.

"I don't want to wait," he whispered to her, and then pulled away slightly to look at her, "and this isn't just a clever plot to get you into bed on Christmas Eve and walk away the next day. I'm in love with you. I knew it the day I nearly killed you when we were racing. I just haven't figured out what to do about it. And you're too young to get married, maybe we both are. I still have some grow- ing up to do too, but I don't want to lose you while we wait. And I sure don't want to lose you to some stupid horse race."

"You won't." But he knew he could if she got her wish and was able to become a jockey. "So what do we do?" she asked softly.

"I don't know. Let's spend time together when we can. I can come to the stables when I have free time, and you can come to London to see me."

"Should we tell people?"

"Eventually. Not yet. They'll figure it out. And

there will be lots of people telling you I'm a player and not to take me seriously." She laughed at that.

"Victoria already has, after she saw the photo of us in the newspaper at your party for the Texan."

"She should talk." He rolled his eyes. "She's slept with half of Europe. I'm an amateur compared to her. And in the past she would have been right about me. I feel differently about you, Annie. You're different, and I'm different when I'm with you."

"And when you're not?" She wasn't entirely oblivious to his reputation.

"Leave that to me." He kissed her again then, with mounting passion, their champagne forgotten, all he wanted were her lips and to feel her in his arms. He derived strength from her, and he trusted her, and knew he could. She was a good woman. "Would you go away with me?" he asked her when he pulled away to catch his breath. And she was out of breath too, as she thought about it.

"Maybe. Not yet. It's too soon." He nodded and didn't argue with her. "I don't want to get pregnant. My mother did that. I don't want to start out that way, in a panic, and doing the wrong thing."

"There's a pill you can take now, not to get pregnant. They have it in the States."

"Oh." She didn't know about it, and had no reason to. She was entirely innocent. "I would do that. I don't want us to make any mistakes." He nodded, neither did he. He wanted this to be right, for both of them. It was a first for him, but he'd been thinking of her that way for a while, since the party.

"I'd love to go to Venice with you," he said, "or somewhere in France." She nodded, carried away with the images he was sharing with her, and eventually he carried her to the bed and lay down next to her and just held her. "I love you, Annie," he said peacefully, and she had never felt so safe in her life. He didn't try to do anything he shouldn't. Eventually when the fire died down and the room got chilly, he got up regretfully, and stood and smiled down at her. "My beautiful angel. I don't know why you dropped into my life. I don't deserve you, but I'll try. I promise you that." She smiled up at him, got off the bed, and followed him to the door of her room. He peeked out to make sure there was no one in the hall, and he didn't have far to go to his own room. He kissed her one last time. It had been an important night for both of them. Life-changing, if they stuck to it and all went well.

"I love you," she whispered to him. "Happy Christmas."

"Happy Christmas," he whispered back and then sped down the hall to his room and disappeared. She softly closed the door, wondering what would happen and if he really meant it. If he did, she had never been happier in her life. She was still smiling when she went to bed and burrowed under the covers. In his room, Anthony was standing at the window, looking at the snow on the ground, and thinking of his mother, hoping he would be luckier than his father had been. But with Annie, for the first time in his life, he thought he had a chance. He had opened his heart to her, and all he could do now was pray that he was right. She was the first woman he had trusted in his entire life. It was even more important than loving her.

Chapter 16

Everything about Christmas changed from the moment Anthony told Annie he loved her. It was the most beautiful Christmas of her life. They met at breakfast the next day, and all appeared to be normal. They sat next to each other and held conversations with the other people at the table as though nothing had changed. But their entire universe had altered overnight. Annie felt as though she was floating.

She called Jonathan and the twins to wish them a Happy Christmas.

Anthony snuck into her room that afternoon to kiss her, and again when she was changing for dinner. He could hardly keep his hands off her. She didn't want to do anything foolish, and he wanted to be responsible. After dinner on Christmas night, he stayed with her for hours and they talked about the future. It sounded magical to her. He lay on her bed and held her and they kissed endlessly, but they didn't make love. That was new for him. Any woman who hadn't slept with him before, he had lost interest in immediately. With Annie, it was all different, and he didn't want to do anything to hurt her or put her at risk.

They managed to avoid the scrutiny of the entire group by being discreet and appearing casual with each other. And no one suspected anything by the time they all disbanded on Boxing Day, the day after Christmas. The queen had to get back to Buckingham Palace, Victoria was going skiing with friends in Saint Moritz, and Cortina after that. Anthony's father had business to attend to. The young princes had to go back to school, and the prince consort was going hunting in Spain with the king. They all had their roles to play and their lives to pursue. He hated to let Annie go back alone on the train for the long trip back to Newmarket, but it was how she had come, and he had to drive his car back from Sandringham. He couldn't leave it there. His father had come in his own car, so he couldn't drive Anthony's back for him. And he was stopping to see people on the way back so couldn't offer Annie a ride.

The head steward put Annie on the train, and she felt as though she were in a dream all the way back to Newmarket, and in a cab back to the stables. It had been the most magical Christmas of her life. Anthony couldn't even call her at the stables, without everyone knowing. Instead he showed up three days later for the weekend. His father was away, and he had dinner at the pub with Annie, and the next day they rode out together on a trail that was muddy but not icy, and they were cautious so the horses didn't fall. He smiled at her as the horses walked along side by side.

"When are you coming to London?" he asked her.

"I have three days off in two weeks. I could come then."

"It's going to be so hard having you here," he said, impatient to spend time with her. "I'll get you a room at the Ritz," he said and she nodded. He came to her room that night, when the other trainers were out for dinner, and they lay on her bed for a while.

"How would I get that pill you mentioned?" she asked him shyly and he smiled. He didn't think she was ready and he was surprised. "I don't think I trust us," she said wisely.

"I'll take care of it," he promised. "I have an American friend who can mail them to me. They're easier to get there." He didn't want to make any mistakes either and spoil everything. She was too important to him.

He left the trainers' quarters before the others got back, and stayed in his father's house. She visited him there the next day, but they were circumspect, with a great deal of kissing and touching and fondling, but nothing more dangerous than that.

He hated to leave her on Sunday night, but she promised to come to London in two weeks on her time off. He wrote her short funny letters which made her laugh, and told her how much he loved her. She got a steady stream of mail from him, and had to force herself to concentrate on her work. And at the end of two weeks, she took the train to London, he met her at the station, and drove her to the Ritz. He hadn't intended to stay with her, or he would have taken her to his apartment. But in the end, he couldn't leave her, and she didn't want him to. He had come prepared just in case. He didn't want to risk an accident the first time.

He was as gentle as he could be with her, and made it as painless as possible, knowing she was a virgin. But she was a willing, exuberant lover and surprised him. They hardly got out of bed all weekend. It was raining and cold, and they were cozy in the suite. He had brought the birth control pills as promised, and warned her that they would take a week or so to be effective, so they were careful.

They slept and talked and ordered meals, and went for a few walks around the neighborhood of the hotel, and by the end of the weekend, they belonged to each other, and Annie felt like a woman of the world.

She felt as though everyone would notice how changed she was when she went back to the stables, and she could hardly pull herself away when he took her to the station and put her on the train.

"I love you, remember that," he whispered to her and they waved to each other, until the train pulled away and entered a tunnel, and then she sat dreaming of the weekend all the way back to Newmarket. He threw caution to the winds and called her that night. There was an open phone in the trainers' quarters, so she couldn't say much, but he told her again and again how much he loved her and she said she did too.

She almost wanted to tell Jonathan about Anthony, but she didn't dare. And remarkably, they managed to keep their affair a secret for the next several months. She stayed at his apartment in Knightsbridge the next time, and thereafter, and they cooked breakfast together, and at night he took her to dinner at his favorite restaurants.

Miraculously, they never ran into anyone they knew, and never got caught on their weekends together. She got two weekends off a month.

All she had done since Christmas was work and see Anthony. It was like living in a bubble, and in March, the queen's secretary called her to invite her to attend the Cheltenham Festival in Gloucestershire. It was a three-day event for chasers and hurdlers, with the Champion Hurdle, the Champion Chase, the World Hurdle, and the highlight of the jump season, the Cheltenham Gold Cup. She was thrilled to be asked. They had a horse running in the Champion Chase, and the secretary said she was welcome to invite her father as well if she liked. She didn't dare ask if she could bring Anthony too, but she knew he could ask to go with his father, since he would be in the royal box too.

Annie had seen the queen several times at the stables, but she hadn't seen her socially since Christmas at Sandringham. Lord Hatton and the trainers kept her running at work. She was familiar with the horse they'd have in the race and had exercised him several times. He was young and considered a long shot in the race, but the queen had a great deal of faith in him, and the jockey who would be riding him. He had won some impressive victories for them before.

Annie told Anthony about the race as soon as she accepted, and he said he'd arrange with his father to be there, and no one would find it unusual. They both wanted to remain discreet for now, or the queen and cabinet might start to interfere, and then the press and public opinion. Neither of them wanted to face that yet.

She invited her father and he was delighted. When the day of the race came, the queen and Lord Hatton invited her to the paddock before the race. The horse seemed tense, as though he sensed what was coming, and the jockey was calm. He was the same size as Annie, but powerfully built, with strong shoulders and arms, and a rider's legs. If they won, the odds were twenty to one.

When she went back to the royal box, Anthony had arrived. Victoria was there in a glamorous outfit with a dashing looking new man. She kissed Annie's cheek and was happy to see her. They kept promising to lunch with each other, but they hadn't yet. They all watched intensely as the horse took off, slowly and steadily at first and then stronger and stronger, as none of them dared to breathe or speak. Then with a powerful surge, driven forward by the jockey, their horse shot ahead gathering incredible speed, and finished four lengths ahead of the horse behind him. Everyone in the royal box gave a scream. Victoria and Annie were jumping up and down. The queen hugged Lord Hatton, Jonathan pumped his hand to congratulate him, and Anthony grabbed Annie and held her and they smiled at each other. The horse had won, at twenty-to-one odds. They all went to congratulate the jockey, who was covered in mud and wreathed in smiles. The queen hugged him and had mud on her face afterward and they all laughed. Her sons had come down from school for it, and there was jubilation in the royal box. The purse was a good one, and they had all bet on him.

Annie's eyes were alight afterward and Lord Hatton laughed at her. "You can taste it, can't you?" He could see how badly she wanted to be a jockey and win a race. "One day. It will happen," he assured her.

"I'll be an old woman by then," she said, looking discouraged.

"You're still a baby, you have time," Anthony's father said. She saw Anthony look unhappy and he said something afterward, when he gave her a ride to the restaurant. The queen had invited them all to dinner to celebrate.

"You still want to race as badly as that?" Anthony asked her, worried. He had heard the exchange with her father and saw the look on her face.

"Yes, if I could. But I don't think they'll ever let women race here in my lifetime."

"And if they do?"

"I'd like to try it," she said softly. It wasn't worth arguing about, since it wasn't a possibility.

"What if we're married and have children by then?" he asked pointedly.

"I suppose it would be too late then. Please don't worry about it. It's not happening."

"But it could, and you could break your neck out there." He looked anxious and upset. He was willing to think about settling down now. She wasn't. Racing was in her blood. She wanted that more than any man. He could see it in her eyes every time the subject came up.

"Thompson didn't break his neck today," she said quietly.

"He's been doing it for years, and one day he might. I don't want my wife and the mother of my children dead on a racetrack," he said, looking angry. But more than angry, he was afraid for her.

"It's been my dream all my life," she said quietly. "If I had the chance I'd do it." She was always honest with him. "But I don't have the chance."

"I hope it stays that way." He didn't speak again until they got to the restaurant and then he relaxed, and she noticed the queen watching them once or twice, and wondered if she suspected anything. But she had no reason to object. She'd known Anthony all his life, and there was nothing she could object to. His father was a lord, he was well educated, well brought up, and a gentleman. She might object to their having an affair, but they were both single, and it was 1967, not 1910. And thanks to Anthony and his friend in New York, she was on the pill, so she wasn't going to get pregnant and cause a scandal with a child out of wedlock. And they intended to get married. Someday. Although neither of them was in a rush. They had everything they wanted now. The queen didn't ask any questions, or comment, nor did Victoria, who was there that night too.

In May, on Annie's birthday, Anthony took her to dinner at Harry's Bar, and dancing at Annabel's afterward, since he was a member of both clubs. They ran into Victoria, who arrived at Annabel's shortly after they did, with a married American she'd been dating less than discreetly, which the queen wasn't pleased about. Victoria took one look at them, and could see what had happened. She sent over a bottle of champagne after wishing Annie a happy birthday, and in return, they toasted her and her handsome friend. He was a well-known actor, married to a movie star, and wanted to divorce his wife for Victoria. It had been all over the tabloids.

By coincidence, they left the club at the same time, and the paparazzi were waiting for Victoria and her movie star. They got photographs of Annie and Anthony too, and recognized both of them. It was a bonus for the paparazzi, and the tabloids were full of both couples the next day, with the headline over Annie and Anthony's photograph, ROYAL WEDDING BELLS? GOOD JOB, ANTHONY!

The queen called Annie that morning from Buckingham Palace and discreetly asked if the rumor was true. Were she and Anthony planning to get married?

"We're seeing each other," Annie admitted with nothing to hide, "but we have no plans to marry at the moment. It still seems too soon, to both of us." It was the truth.

"I have no objection, as long as he's sown the last of his wild oats. He was a bit of a playboy for a few years, I believe. But he's the right age to settle down, **if** he has." He had just turned thirty-one, and she was twenty-three now. "He's a lovely young man. I've known his family all my life. Just don't wait too long, if that's what you want to do. You don't want to become fodder for the tabloids, and have the paparazzi following you around all the time. Once you're married, they'll lose interest." Annie didn't want to marry just to get rid of the paparazzi, but the queen had made herself clear. She had conservative values and she preferred marriage to dating. "You're old enough now, dear." But Annie didn't feel old enough at twenty-three, and she was still getting used to the royal life. It was her first taste of what Anthony disliked so much, pressure from the Crown.

She reported the conversation to Anthony when he called her, and he was annoyed.

"That was my point earlier. I don't want the House of Windsor telling us what to do. We should get married when we want to. We're just getting started. What's the hurry?"

"I'd rather wait awhile too. Twenty-three seems so young to get married. I kind of thought twenty-five or -six," Annie said thoughtfully.

"Thirty-one seems young to me too. I used to think thirty-five was the right age for a man. We'll know when it's right. But it should be up to us. She's going to put the heat on now. And can you imagine what she must have said to Victoria today? She must be having a fit over that." She was, and had told her sister to break it off immediately before she disgraced herself again. Victoria was used to it by now. She'd been battling with her family over who she dated for twenty years, and seemed to take pleasure in shocking them, the public, and the press. Annie and Anthony didn't want to be part of that.

Lord Hatton called Anthony for confirmation too, and said he was delighted about Annie. He couldn't have made a better choice, and when were they getting married. He hoped it would be soon. Like the queen, he thought they should get out of the public eye and the press quickly, and marriage was the fastest way to do that. It seemed like the wrong reason to marry, to both of them.

Jonathan called to tell her he was thrilled, he liked Anthony immensely, and to do whatever she wanted. But the palace and even Anthony's father were pushing for a fast marriage, which felt rushed to them. They refused to be pushed, much to the queen's chagrin, but she had bigger problems with her sister.

Annie went to Saint Tropez with Anthony that summer for her holiday, and they were beleaguered by the paparazzi and followed everywhere and had to take refuge on a friend's yacht, and sailed for Sardinia, where it happened all over again. It was endless. Whenever they went out, in London or any other city, even if they went to the grocery store, they wound up all over the tabloids, kissing, not kissing, holding hands, having an argument in the park once. Anthony was seriously annoyed about it.

"I don't want them rushing us into marriage. And even if we get married, they'll follow us around now. If we have a baby, have kids, get pregnant, go skiing. Whatever we do, they're going to pursue us. I hate this." He looked furious, and she didn't like it either. "Do you want to get married now?" he asked her bluntly. "I'll do whatever you want." But it took the fun out of it, getting married because they were being pressured into it, by the queen or the tabloids.

"Not really," she said honestly. "Why don't we just call a moratorium on it, and make the decision in two years when I turn twenty-five. I'll be ready then. You'll be thirty-three. And screw what the tabloids think, or anyone else."

"Sounds perfect to me," he agreed. "Two years, and then we'll jump in. Done." He kissed her to seal the deal. It seemed like an unromantic decision, but the right one for them.

The press continued to follow them around after that. But not as avidly. They got bored with it without an engagement or a wedding date. And the queen continued to drop hints whenever she saw them, but she was much more upset about her sister, who seemed to enjoy creating scandals. She always had.

Annie and Anthony were happy as they were. She stayed with him when she was in London, and he stayed in her room at the stables now, since everyone knew about them anyway. His father lent him his house frequently. So everything calmed down, and their relationship continued. In their minds, they figured they'd get married, or at least engaged, in two years when Annie turned twenty-five. It seemed the right age to both of them. And to satisfy her longing to race, Anthony's father convinced her to enter the Newmarket Town Plate that fall. It was the only women's race under jockey club rules. She placed second and was jubilant. But it only made her hunger to race against men more acute. She entered again the following year and placed first. Shortly before her twenty-fifth birthday, before they could revisit their marriage plans, Annie got a call from a famous trainer in Lexington, Kentucky. He invited her to race for the stable he worked for, in the Blue Grass Stakes Thoroughbred race at Keeneland racecourse in Lexington. She would be competing against male jockeys for a million-dollar purse. It was a pari-mutuel race, the opportunity she'd longed for all her life. They had heard of her, and seen her race at the Newmarket Town Plate. She would be the first female jockey registered for the race in Kentucky, and her heart was pounding when she hung up after the call. She was so excited she could taste it. She had waited for this moment for years, and she knew she was ready. She had accepted on the phone, and now she had to tell Anthony. She hoped he'd be reasonable about it. She knew Lord Hatton would be excited for her, and Jonathan would too.

She waited until Anthony came up for the weekend, and didn't say anything to him about it before that. They were paying her a fortune to do it. But she wasn't doing it for the money, although that was nice too. She was doing it because it was her dream, and she knew she had to do it. And she expected Anthony to know that too.

There was no avoiding the subject. He could tell that she was hiding something, and she didn't want to conceal it from him. She told him about the call an hour after he got there.

"You turned them down, I hope?" he said, looking tense, his eyes never leaving hers.

"I couldn't. I've waited all my life for this, and you know it. I have to do it."

"And risk your life as a jockey? Competing against men?" He looked horrified.

"I'm not going to die, Anthony. This is my dream," she said quietly.

"I thought we were your dream, you and I. If I ask you not to do it, will you turn it down?" He was turning it into a proving ground, and a test, which wasn't fair. She didn't answer for a moment, and then shook her head. It was a crucial moment in their relationship, and she knew it. But she couldn't give up the race for him.

"I can't. Don't ask me to do that. It's not right. I've wanted to be a jockey as long as I've been riding."

"What about us?"

"Why can't we do both? I'm not going to race forever. But give me a year. There's talk that they'll allow women to race in the Kentucky Derby next year. It would be the high point of my life."

"I don't want to be married to a jockey. What do you want, Annie? Me? Us? Or to be a jockey? You can't have both." His eyes were like steel as he looked at her. He had dug his heels in. He had never said it as clearly before. She was twenty-five and didn't want to give up her dreams or lose them.

"Why not? Why do I have to give up my dreams to marry you?"

"Because I don't want to be married to a woman who could die any day of the week, or break her neck and be paralyzed, just because she wants the thrill of winning and can't give it up. It's not com-patible with marriage and having babies, and you know it."

"So we wait a year. Let me race for a year, and then I'll quit. I promise." After the Kentucky Derby if the runors were true and she could compete in it in a year.

"I don't believe you. You won't quit. It's in your blood. You have a decision to make," he said in a voice that was pure ice. "If you go to Kentucky and ride in this race, it's over with us. I'm finished. If you want to be married to me, turn the race down. Once you start riding as a jockey in legitimate races against men, you'll never give it up. I know you." She knew he was right, and she was willing to make the sacrifice for him, but not just yet. She wanted to live her dreams first. This was her chance. He gave her a hard look that left no room for argument. "Let me know what you decide," he said, and slammed out of his father's house, where they'd been discussing it. His father was in his office and had left them the house. She heard Anthony's car drive away.

She was heartbroken over his decision, but she thought he was being unreasonable, and there was no way she was going to give up this race for him. It was a huge deal and the beginning of a whole new chapter of her life. She had waited all her life to be a jockey, legally, in the big leagues, not some second-rate amateur race. She had waited two and a half years to get engaged and become his wife. There was no choice in her mind. She was going to the States, and if he couldn't live with it, then he wasn't the right man for her. She was **not** going to give up her dreams for him. And if he loved her, he wouldn't ask her to.

She didn't call Anthony and he didn't call her. Three weeks later, she was on the plane to Kentucky. Her dreams with Anthony were over. Her dreams of being a jockey just meant too much to her to give up, even for him, and she truly loved him. She expected him to understand how much the race meant to her. He did, which was why he had left her and hadn't called. The race meant more to her than he did.

Chapter 17

The race in Kentucky in June was the most exciting event of her life. It lived up to all her expectations. The horse she was hired to ride was spectacular. She had heard about the breeder for years but never met him. Lord Hatton knew him, and had guessed that they would give her a fabulous horse to ride and he'd been right. The queen had called to wish her luck. Victoria had sent a telegram, and Jonathan had called and told her she could do it, to focus and think of nothing else.

Anthony was heavy on her mind, and her heart, but she couldn't allow herself that now. She couldn't think of anything except the race. She would talk to him afterward, and try to make peace with him. But for now there was only the track she'd be running, the race, and the horse she'd be riding. Nothing else in the world mattered. She spoke to no one in the last week except the breeder, the trainer, and the owner. And she trained on the horse all week, getting to know him.

She slept two hours the night before the race, and woke up at four in the morning. She took a long hot shower and went for a run to try to relax, and was in the horse's stall and had a long conversation with him. She knew he could carry her to victory. The odds were thirty to one against her. No one thought a woman could do it in a race like this. It was a historic moment. There was one other woman registered to ride. She was riding a horse that had won numerous races in the States. He was a sure thing, and an easier ride than the horse Annie would be riding. Hers was named Ginger Boy, and no one was sure what he could do. Except Annie, who believed in him, and knew he could win.

She stood quietly stroking him, and talking to him. "We can do it, you know. I know I can, and so can you. Don't let them spook you, Boy. Just take it nice and easy at first." They weighed her, and she put on the colors of the owner she was riding for. Her helmet was secure, and the owner and trainer watched her as she mounted Ginger Boy. Her small white face was serious and her blue eyes looked huge.

"Good luck, Your Royal Highness," the owner said, hoping he had done the right thing hiring her. She looked so delicate, and her hands looked so small compared to the huge horse she was riding. He was a powerful beast.

"Annie will do," she said to the owner, and went to line up, as they watched her, and then the owner went to his box to watch the race. It was being televised around the world on sports channels everywhere. There were news crews all around the racetrack. Annie saw nothing as she lined up, except the track and the horse she was riding. She thought of nothing except what they had to do.

They got a slow start as she intended, and ran steadily, gathering momentum and speed as they went, passing horses, flying like the wind, pressing harder, going faster, and in the final stretch she pushed him as hard as she could, knowing what she needed from him, and Ginger Boy knew it too. "Give it to me now, come on, Boy, you can do it. We can do it!" He ran faster and harder than any other horse she'd ever been on. He flew over the ground, and she felt as though they were running above the ground in slow motion. She heard nothing except his breathing and her own, faster and faster. She heard people screaming and the roar of the crowd. She flew through the finish line with no sense of who or what was around her, or where the other horses were. All she knew and felt was Ginger Boy. She galloped him for a few minutes after the finish line to slow him down, and patted his neck with all her strength. "Good Boy, you did it! I'm proud of you," she said and finally looked up. She had no idea how they had finished, and she saw the trainer running toward them, he was crying and waving his hands as she slowed Ginger Boy, and the trainer reached up and hugged her.

"You did it! Oh my God, you did it!"

"How did we do?" she asked him, as Ginger Boy danced and she gently led him in a walk off the track. She could still hear the crowd screaming and see people waving.

"Are you serious?" The trainer looked at her as though she had just landed from outer space. "You came in first, by five lengths. You made history." She jumped down and he hugged her, and she led Ginger Boy off the track toward the winner's circle. Her legs were shaking and she was in a daze, as the grooms took his lead away from her, and people hugged her and lifted her off the ground. Camera crews were in her face, and then the owner was hugging her and his wife was crying. The other female jockey had come in eighth.

"You were the most beautiful sight I've ever seen," the owner said to her with tears running down his cheeks. At that moment, she wished she

could share it with Anthony and Jonathan and all
the people she loved. She couldn't wait to see the
footage of the race. But for that one moment in
time, it had been just her and Ginger Boy, and
nothing else in the world mattered. She was a born
jockey and she knew it. She knew she had done the
right thing coming to Kentucky. She couldn't have
given this up, and was glad she hadn't. This was her
moment. She wanted Anthony to be part of it, but
he wasn't.

She gave two TV interviews and one to the BBC
before she left the racetrack in the owner's Rolls.
Her legs felt like rubber and her head was pounding. She had gone to see Ginger Boy and thanked
him before she left.

She went back to the hotel and watched it all
on TV on the replays. Jonathan called her, and
the queen, and Anthony's father, and told her how
incredible she had been. Anthony didn't call, and
she realized now that it probably was over, but she
wasn't sorry, even though she loved him. She hadn't
given up her dream.

She flew back to England the next day, and had
a hero's welcome at the stables when she got back
to Newmarket.

The queen had sent a car and driver for her to
take her back to the stables, and she came to see her
the next day. She hugged Annie when she saw her,

and told her how proud she was of her. She was as excited as Annie, and knew how proud Charlotte would have been of her.

"How's Anthony?" the queen asked with a worried look.

"He's not," Annie said quietly. "He said that if I went, it was over with us. So I guess it is." She looked sad about it, but she didn't regret it, and her aunt nodded.

"He might get over it," she said gently.

"Maybe not," Annie said. "But I couldn't give it up for him. I waited too long for this."

"I'm glad you didn't," Alexandra said quietly. "You'd have regretted it all your life, and resented him for it." The owner had accepted the trophy for her. No one could take away the records she'd broken, or the victory she'd had with Ginger Boy. Winning first place had been incredible.

After the queen left, Annie got a call from the owner of a horse farm in Virginia. He wanted her to ride his horse in the Kentucky Derby next year if female jockeys were admitted, and it looked as though they would be. She accepted on the spot.

She called Jonathan and told him that night and asked him to go with her, if she rode in the Derby next year. She was on a high now, and Anthony was still lodged in her heart like a glass splinter, but she didn't have to give any of it up now, and she couldn't. He was right.

She called Anthony the day after she got back from Kentucky, but he didn't pick up, and he didn't call her. She called him at his office, and they said he was in a meeting. And he didn't return that call either. So she had her answer. She had won a major female racing victory in horseracing history, but lost her man. He had said it would be that way, and he was sticking to it. He knew what he wanted and so did she. But she couldn't let him control her or force her to give up her dreams. It would have been so wrong. In the end, her being a princess hadn't done them in, but her being a jockey had.

She saw him in the paper the next day, at a party with a famous model. She was wrapped around him like a snake. So he had gone back to his old life. And she had too. The life where the only thing that mattered was the horses, and now the victories. It hurt seeing him in the papers, but not as much as giving up the race would have. She couldn't let him cheat her of this, and she hadn't.

She saw him in the papers again a week later with a different girl. The owner who had asked her to ride for him next year in the Kentucky Derby flew to London to meet her. She saw Anthony in the papers again with a Hollywood starlet in London to promote her new movie. They'd gone dancing at Annabel's. Somehow the thrill of the women he was presumably sleeping with didn't seem equal to the race she had won, or racing in the Kentucky Derby, whether she won or lost next year. She hoped he was happy, but doubted that he was. His were hollow victories. She still loved him, and she missed him. She had wanted to share this with him, but not in a million years would she give this up for him. She couldn't.

She had dinner with Anthony's father at his house two weeks after she got home. He congratulated her and they talked about the race for half an hour, and then he told her how sorry he was about her and Anthony.

"So am I," she said sadly. "I just couldn't give it up for him, and he wouldn't settle for anything less. It was all or nothing."

"That's how life is sometimes," he said. "You did the right thing. There are some things you can't compromise and shouldn't. This was one of them. My son is a stubborn man, and a fool sometimes. We all are, I suppose. You're worth a million of these idiots he runs around with, or used to. I'm sorry to see him go back to that." Not as sorry as she was. But not sorry enough to back down and give it up.

"So am I," she said softly.

"He'll regret it," his father said. It was small consolation.

"Maybe not. Maybe we just weren't meant to be."

"What would you rather be? One of the most famous jockeys in history, the first woman to win a race like that, or his wife after you gave all that up?"

"I wanted both," she said honestly.

"It doesn't always work that way."

"I guess not."

A month later, in July, she flew to Virginia to meet the horse she hoped to ride the following year in the Derby. It wasn't sure yet. She and the owner had dinner, and discussed the race and his horse's history. He was an interesting choice for the Derby, and had won some big races before, but he had an irregular record at others.

"My boy will like the Derby," the owner said and smiled at her.

"So will I, Mr. MacPherson." She smiled back at him.

She rode him before flying back to England, and he was incredible. He responded to the lightest touch, voice commands, and almost to her thought processes as though he was psychic. The competition in the Derby would be stiff, and she would train with him before the race and study the other horses' histories too. She spoke to Lord Hatton about it, and he gave her some advice without ever having seen Aswan, the horse she'd be riding. He knew his bloodline, the trainer, and the owner.

She went to spend two weeks in Kent with Jonathan and the boys then, and spent August at Balmoral with her royal family. It was peaceful and relaxing, with barbecues and picnics and family dinners. George, Albert, and William had grown up even more, and she felt at home with all of them.

She had heard that Anthony was in Saint Tropez for the month and tried not to think about it. Her heart still ached when someone said his name.

The queen brought up her spectacular win in Kentucky again.

"Your mother would have been proud of you, and green with envy," she said, and Annie laughed. "She would have given anything to do what you just did. We're all proud of you, Annie."

"Thank you, ma'am," her niece said respectfully.

"Lord Hatton and I have a question to ask you. Will you ride for us in the Gold Cup Race at the Royal Ascot Meeting next June? We'd be honored to have you race for us. We'd like you to ride Starlight." He was a beautiful white horse, but he was young, and hadn't been in many races. "Not an obvious choice, but we think he's ready for his first big race, and a strong showing, and if anyone can make it happen, you've proven that you can. Will you do it?" she asked, as Annie looked at her in amazement.

"Are you serious, ma'am? I'd be honored. I'd like to start working with him soon. I haven't ridden him much." She loved the idea of riding on home turf, in England, on one of their horses, for her queen and aunt. It didn't get better than that. She thought the horse was ready too. He was at Lord Hatton's stables in Newmarket, so she could work with him anytime. And Royal Ascot was in June, and the Kentucky Derby in May, so she could ride in both races.

The Gold Cup was the highlight of the four-day Royal Ascot Meeting. At two miles and four furlongs, it was one of the longest races of the flat season, and a real test of stamina for horse and rider. Annie couldn't think of a greater thrill than riding in that race for the queen. The Ascot racecourse was in Berkshire, six miles from Windsor Castle, so Annie assumed the whole family would stay there. She was so excited she could hardly speak, she just beamed. And the queen was equally pleased she'd accepted.

Her aunt Victoria called her that night from the South of France. She was due at Balmoral any day.

"Well, you're certainly giving us some dignity, dear girl. I'm so proud of you, I could burst. George called me at midnight the night you won the race in Kentucky. He stayed up to watch you. Actually, half of England did. I won a thousand pounds on a wager, so thank you for that. I'll take you to lunch with my winnings when you come to London."

"Aunt Alexandra just asked me to ride for her in the Ascot Gold Cup next year."

"Fantastic!" Victoria said enthusiastically.

She hesitated for an instant then, and decided to tell her. "I saw Anthony the other night, at a party down here." She knew it was a delicate subject.

"How is he?" Annie tried to sound neutral about it, but she wasn't. It still hurt terribly, and Victoria could hear it. But she didn't want to keep it secret that she'd seen him, in case Annie heard it from someone else.

"Actually, he's a mess. He looks terrible. He looks like he's been drunk since you left for Kentucky. I saw him before that. I think he got sacked from his job, but I'm not sure of it. He didn't tell me, someone else did. You know how London is, a hotbed of gossip. He didn't mention you, but I suspect he misses you terribly. He's a fool if he doesn't. But he's probably too proud to admit it."

"I called him a few times, but he didn't pick up or call me back. It's just as well. There's nothing much to say now. I did exactly what he forbade me to."

"'Sorry I was an idiot' is always refreshing, but they never say that, do they? They paint themselves into a corner, and then go up in smoke. He had some dreadful woman with him. He looked like he was ready to kill her. Maybe he will, and go to prison. Suitable punishment for leaving you. He should at least apologize for that."

"It was a point of pride for both of us," Annie said in a subdued voice. They had been apart for three months by then instead of getting engaged. And she was booked for two major races next year, which he would never tolerate.

"It always is with men, darling girl. It always is. Well, I'll see you at the races, as they say. I'm glad Alexandra asked you to ride for us. You might as well instead of winning for the Americans. Give us some of that magic dust." Annie was happy talking to her, and she liked hearing about Anthony, even if he was unhappy and hated her for putting her dreams ahead of everything else, for a while anyway. She doubted that she'd do it forever, but for a while. She could pick and choose which races she'd do now, which was a nice position to be in. She hadn't expected it to happen this quickly. No one had. And she least of all. Anthony had predicted it.

She lay in bed and thought about him after she and Victoria hung up. She wondered if he was as unhappy as Victoria thought he was, or if he also felt he had done the right thing. He probably wouldn't admit it to anybody, and she'd never know. She doubted that he'd ever speak to her again, or not for a long time. Their paths would cross inevitably at some point. They had gone out for almost three years, but that meant nothing in the end, and certainly not now. Whatever they had shared was dead and buried. He wanted nothing to do with her. He hadn't even congratulated her for her victory in Kentucky. He was history in her life now.

She went back to Newmarket at the end of August, and began training with Starlight for the Gold Cup race at Ascot, which was still nine months away. She had gotten confirmation that she could ride in the Kentucky Derby in May, and planned to spend March and April in Virginia, training with Aswan for the Derby.

She spent the next six months working hard for Anthony's father, training new horses and working with Starlight. She worked diligently with Starlight for Ascot and was pleased to find that the horse was both high-strung and receptive and easy to work with. Within a month, Annie felt in harmony with him, and was able to direct him with the slightest touch, and when she gave him his head, he flew over the terrain and was steady and sure-footed. His size and strength were in his favor, and even though he lacked age and experience, she could sense that he would be a great racehorse one day. What she needed to do was move him ahead quickly to a level of training he hadn't achieved yet when they started.

"How's he doing?" Lord Hatton asked her when he came out to the field where she was working with him, and watched him for a while. She had a remarkable, almost psychic sense of the horses she worked with, and he was impressed by the results she had gotten. Starlight was unpredictable and sometimes uneven in his progress, but she was able to get from him what no one else had yet, and she could see that the giant animal trusted her completely. He was a different horse than when she'd started working with him.

She spent Christmas at Sandringham with the royal family and New Year's with Jonathan and the boys in Kent.

Jonathan accompanied her to Virginia in March and stayed with her while she trained with Aswan. It had been an arduous year, nothing but work, and her skills were stronger than ever.

Jonathan was there when she came in second

at the Kentucky Derby. It was an extraordinary win and made headlines worldwide. She returned to a hero's welcome in London, and celebrated her birthday with the family at Windsor Castle two weeks after she returned. She had just turned twenty-six.

It had been exactly a year since her breakup with Anthony. She was surprised when he sent her a note congratulating her for her heroic win at the Derby, and wishing her a happy birthday. She hadn't heard from him in a year. She thanked him, and was completely focused on training for Ascot. She was staying at Windsor Castle until the race in June. Their paths hadn't crossed in a year.

The day before the race, she let Starlight rest, so he'd be fresh and anxious to perform on the day of the big event. He was nervous and excited when they got him into his stall at the racetrack, and she took him out to exercise him briefly. They had brought two grooms and one of the trainers with them. That night, Annie went out to check on him and spoke to him soothingly.

The morning of the race, she could see he was aching to run. It was what he wanted to do with her now.

The royal party arrived in horse-drawn landaus and paraded along the track in front of the crowd.

The entire family entered the royal box. Everyone

had come. The queen and Prince Edward were there, Victoria, and Alexandra's three boys had come from school. Jonathan and the Markhams were there, he'd brought the twins, and Penny, the woman Jonathan had been dating for some time now. Lord Hatton was seated next to the queen, and when Annie checked the box with binoculars, she gave a start when she saw Anthony standing just outside the box. She assumed he had come for his father, but she felt odd seeing him and wondered if their paths would cross after the race. She hoped not, and was sorry she'd seen him now. She watched him take a seat between Victoria and William, who was nearly hopping up and down he was so excited. She smiled when she watched him. They had brought him home from Eton. He had just turned sixteen, and the other boys nineteen and twenty. It was a major event, and one of the most important races in England. She never thought she'd see the day when she'd be racing in it. She was the first female jockey, and the only woman racing that day. There were very few who were ready for the transition, but the queen was setting the example in England after the Kentucky Derby. Annie had been one of two women at the Blue Grass Stakes and the Kentucky Derby. And in future, she knew that eventually there would be others, but not many yet.

She let Starlight walk a little, but he was too

anxious to leave him out for long. She spoke to him soothingly, and then it was time to take their places. Annie was wearing the queen's royal colors of purple with gold braid, scarlet sleeves, and black velvet helmet with gold fringe. It was the greatest honor of her life. She was satisfied with the order for the race, and avoided looking for familiar faces as they rode to the start. She kept her mind and her eyes on Starlight, and nothing else. She praised him as they waited and then they were off. She gave him his head quickly because she knew him well now, and it was how he liked to run. He began strong and then settled into his pace, as she edged him forward and kept him steady on course, and then she urged him to increase his speed, pushing him harder and harder to his limits, using his strength and his size to gain momentum, and then she forced him on past what he wanted, but using his trust in her to push him beyond anything reasonable. He pounded and pounded and pounded the ground, faster and faster until his hooves barely seemed to touch the earth. If someone had asked, they would have thought she was flying, and then she pushed him for the final furlong, and she could see the others slip away as she and Starlight moved ahead, and with a final burst of agony and insanity, she asked his utmost from him, and drove him even harder, and they crossed the finish line alone. They kept going until she could slow him down without his getting injured, and came back, and looked toward the royal box with a broad grin. They had done it. Starlight had come through for his owners, his queen, and his jockey.

She had no doubt this time. They had finished in first place. And the announcer declared the winner, Her Majesty Queen Alexandra's horse Starlight, ridden by the queen's niece, Her Royal Highness Princess Anne Louise Windsor. It was the proudest moment of Annie's life, and one of the queen's best too. Annie could see them jumping up and down in the box, and could almost hear them screaming. The roar of the crowd had been tremendous, and Starlight looked startled by the noise, but Annie kept him in control. The queen and Lord Hatton came down from the royal box to accept the trophy with her, and the queen reached up and patted Annie's arm and thanked her. They were both crying and didn't even know it.

"What a wonderful race you ran, Annie," she said happily.

"It was all Starlight," she said modestly, and Lord Hatton was grinning broadly, as he thanked her, and she rode Starlight back to his stall. She stayed with Starlight for a few minutes until he started to calm down, and then she left him to the grooms and trainer, and walked toward the royal box to find her family. She was still feeling dazed herself and unsteady on her feet. She didn't even bother to clean up. She was covered with mud, and had splashes of it on her face and all over her helmet, when she walked straight into Anthony coming toward her. She stopped when she saw him and didn't know what to say.

"You were fantastic!" he said, and then folded her into his arms without caring about the mud all over her, still wet from the race.

"I'm filthy, don't . . ." He kissed her before she could stop him and it reminded her of the first time in Sandringham when he had surprised her and told her he loved her. When he finally stopped, she was even more breathless than she'd been from the race. And just as surprised as she'd been the first time he kissed her.

"I'm sorry I was such a fool. I wanted to tell you before the race, but I didn't want to throw you off. My God, you were incredible. You were a blur on the racetrack." Anthony was smiling at her as she looked up at him in amazement.

"Why did you come?" she asked him, rubber-legged from the ride. She imagined that he was there for his father.

"Why do you think? To tell you I love you and that I'm sorry. I was wrong, and you were right. This is what you were born to do. I was wrong to try and stop you. Thank God you didn't listen. It's a damn fine dream, and if we wait ten years to have children, then so be it." She was only twenty-six.

"I just wanted one year, not ten," she said softly. "I've already done what I wanted. This race was my dream, to do it here, for England, and for Alexandra. I won't do it forever, I promise," she said, and he stopped her and kissed her again.

"Don't make promises you can't keep. You're the best jockey I've ever seen. My father thinks so too. And to think I damn near killed you racing to a tree. Lucky I didn't," he said, and she laughed as she fell into step with him and he tucked her hand into his arm. She wanted to see the others now too.

"Why didn't you call me back?" she asked as they walked around the racetrack to the royal box.

"Because I wanted to be right, and I knew I wasn't. I got sacked, by the way. I was drunk for three weeks and screwed up all their events. I want to work with my father, and help him manage the farm. I belong there, and so do you," he said softly, and then stopped her for a minute before they reached the others. "Will you marry me, Annie, even though I was a fool?"

"Yes," she said in a voice so soft that only he could hear it.

"Do I have to ask your aunt?"

"Probably. And the prime minister, and the

cabinet, and the lord chamberlain, and a million other people, and my father." They were both laughing as he followed her up the stairs to where they were all milling around and congratulating each other. The queen smiled when she saw them. Things had improved immeasurably in the last few minutes, and she wasn't sure if Annie was smiling because she'd won, or because Anthony had just kissed her. The queen had seen it through her binoculars and was pleased.

"I have a question to ask you later, ma'am," he said softly, and her smile widened.

"The answer is yes," she said, and he hugged her.

"Thank you, ma'am." They all stayed in the box for another half hour, and then left. They were having dinner at Windsor Castle that night, and there was much to celebrate. Annie left the box with them, with an arm around each of her brothers, and her three young cousins right behind them. Her face was still splattered with mud, and she'd never looked happier. And before they got into the van the queen had brought for them, Anthony stopped Annie and kissed her again. "You are one hell of an amazing rider," he said with a look of awe on his face. "Thank God you didn't let me bully you. I'm sorry I did," he said after the others were in the van.

"It doesn't matter. I didn't listen to you. I couldn't. But I love you and always will. I never stopped loving you all this year." But it had been a long, lonely year without him.

"I hope our children ride like you do. You made history today, Annie." And they both knew she would again. Possibly many times, and then one day she'd retire, but she would always have the memory of what she'd accomplished. No one could ever take that from her now. Anthony knew better than anyone that no one ever should. This moment, and this day, and this achievement belonged to her, and rightfully so.

"Are you two coming, or are we going to die of old age waiting?" Victoria shouted out of the van at them.

"Sorry," Anthony said, helped Annie into the van, and hopped in behind her. They took off for the castle with everyone laughing and talking about what a great and utterly unforgettable day it had been.

Chapter 18

Jonathan and Annie were waiting in a small room at St. Margaret's Church on the grounds of Westminster Abbey, the Anglican parish church near the Palace of Westminster. It had been built in the eleventh century. She had chosen a simple white lace gown with long sleeves and a tiny waist, and she looked more than ever like a fairy or a very young girl. She was wearing a veil, and the gown had a train which stretched behind her as she stood nervously with her stepfather, waiting for their cue to start down the aisle.

Sir Malcolm Harding, the queen's secretary, came in holding a leather box and handed it to Annie as she looked at him in surprise. Her grandmother, the Queen Mother, had given her a double strand of her own pearls that morning as a wedding gift, and said they had been a gift from her grandmother, Queen Alexandra, on her wedding day. The queen had given Annie a heart-shaped brooch by Carl Fabergé encrusted with diamonds and pearls on pale pink enamel, which she had worn at her wedding, and she had no daughters to pass it on to, so she was giving it to her sister's child. And even more meaningful to her, Annie was wearing the gold bracelet with the gold heart charm that had been her mother's and Alexandra had given her.

"Who's this from?" Annie asked Sir Malcolm about the antique leather box she took from him, and he smiled.

"Your husband, ma'am. He wanted you to have it immediately." She opened it in haste and smiled when she saw it. It was the tiara he had borrowed from Garrard's for her, that had been given to Queen Victoria by her husband, Prince Albert. Theirs was one of the great love stories of the British monarchy. "He was hoping you could wear it with your veil. It's your wedding gift, ma'am." It fit perfectly over it, and was just the right proportion, as though it had been made for her. Annie had loved it when she'd seen it, when Anthony borrowed it for her for the party. She had remembered it, and apparently so had Anthony. It was back in the right hands, with Queen Victoria's great-great-great-granddaughter.

Sir Malcolm took the box and disappeared with it. Annie looked up at the man who had been her father for most of her life.

"You look like a queen, not just a princess," Jonathan said, in awe of the moment. She had chosen to have no attendants, only him walking her to her husband in the small chapel.

"I love you, Papa," she whispered.

"I love you too, Annie," he said as the music started, the door opened, and they headed toward the aisle. When they reached it, she saw Anthony waiting for her at the altar. It was meant to be, just as everything that had happened was. Being brought back to the Windsors, where she belonged, learning about her mother, meeting Anthony, winning the races, and now this moment when nothing else mattered. She had lost him for a year and found him again, or he had found her. She knew she would love him forever, like Victoria and Albert.

They walked slowly down the aisle, and she stopped next to Anthony, who was beaming at her. They had already been through so much, and knew each other so well, their fears and their dreams, their hopes for the future. Her dreams had already come true, and now she had him, and hopefully one day their children.

Jonathan took his place in the pew next to Penny and the twins, and across the aisle, the prince consort sat next to the queen, as Alexandra and her sister Victoria held hands, watching Annie, and remembering when there were three of them so long ago. The Queen Mother sat next to them, with tears in her eyes, remembering Charlotte too, and all three of them were struck by how much Annie looked like her. She was the image of the mother she had never known.

"She looks just like her, doesn't she?" Victoria whispered to Alexandra, and the Queen Mother took Victoria's other hand and held it. They were all there now, with their history and their stories, their loves and their losses, and George the future king sat right behind his mother, with his brothers beside him. Just as the past stood behind them, the future lay ahead with George and his brothers, and Annie wore the tiara their great-great-great-grandmother Queen Victoria had been given by her husband. It was all woven together like a never-ending chain of love stories and people and monarchs, as Annie looked into the eyes of the man she loved and was about to marry.

"Thank you," she whispered to him, and pointed to the tiara.

"I love you," Anthony whispered back, as Jonathan watched the little girl he had loved and taught to ride and had become a princess. They all stood together, as Alexandra and Victoria thought of Charlotte, and seeing their niece standing there in her image, it was almost as if Charlotte had come home at last.

As Anthony and Annie exchanged their vows, the past and the present, and the future, blended into one shining moment which united them all in memory forever.

About the Author

DANIELLE STEEL has been hailed as one of the world's bestselling authors, with almost a billion copies of her novels sold. Her many international bestsellers include **Daddy's Girls**, **The Wedding Dress**, **The Numbers Game**, **Moral Compass**, **Spy**, **Child's Play**, **The Dark Side**, and other highly acclaimed novels. She is also the author of **His Bright Light**, the story of her son Nick Traina's life and death; **A Gift of Hope**, a memoir of her work with the homeless; **Pure Joy**, about the dogs she and her family have loved; and the children's books **Pretty Minnie in Paris** and **Pretty Minnie in Hollywood**.

daniellesteel.com
Facebook.com/DanielleSteelOfficial
Twitter: @daniellesteel
Instagram: @officialdaniellesteel

LIKE WHAT YOU'VE READ?

Try these titles by Danielle Steel,
also available in large print:

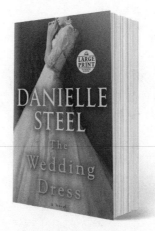

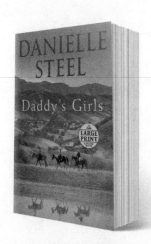

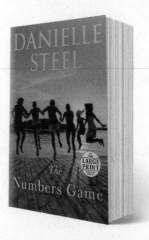

The Wedding Dress
ISBN 978-0-593-17194-3

Daddy's Girls
ISBN 978-0-593-21351-3

The Numbers Game
ISBN 978-0-593-17193-6